MW01681618

Behind Bars

An Ian Bragg Adventure Series

Craig Martelle and Larry Hoy

Craig Martelle, Inc

This book is a work of fiction.

The characters, organizations, and events portrayed in this novel are either products of the author's imagination or are used fictitiously. Sometimes both.

Version 1.0

Cover by Juan Padron

Editing by Mia with LKJ Books (lkjbooks.com)

Formatting in Word and in Atticus

Socials

Craig Martelle Social

Website & Newsletter: https://craigmartelle.com

Amazon: https://www.amazon.com/author/craigmartelle

Facebook: https://www.facebook.com/martelle2

Larry Hoy Social

Website & Newsletter: https://LarryHoy.net

Facebook: https://www.facebook.com/LarryHoyAuthor/

Broken Badge (Broken Badge #1) – https://geni.us/BrokenBadge1

Behind Bars (Broken Badge #2) – https://geni.us/BrokenBadge2

Deadhand's Vengeance (Broken Badge #3) – https://geni.us/BrokenBadge3

Contents

DEDICATION

Always to my wife, who loves me even though I work every day writing stories and prefer to stay in over going out.

The Ian Bragg team includes:

Beta Readers and Proofreaders – with my deepest gratitude!

James Caplan

Kelly O'Donnell

John Ashmore

Get ***The Veracity of Failure*** for free when you join my newsletter. The billionaire's race to Mars.

https://craigmartelle.com

Foreword

PEOPLE OFTEN ASK WHY there aren't more motorcycles in my books. Fair question for a guy whose tagline is "Biker – Writer – Legend."

So this time, Shepard got a bike.

Back in 2023, my wife and daughters handed me the perfect gift: a motorcycle trip across historic U.S. Route 66. More than two thousand miles of deserts, roadside diners, forgotten towns, neon signs, and enough strange characters to fill a dozen novels.

Somewhere along that highway, this story found its voice.

And yes, before anyone asks, I've spent time around motorcycle clubs. The respectable kind...and the other kind. Years ago, I even wore a full patch myself.

Thankfully, that was a different lifetime.

Chapter 1

I GRABBED THE STEERING wheel and hauled myself into the driver's seat of my truck, Bigger. It was a bright-red Ram 1500 with a supercharged HEMI under the hood.

I shut and locked the door behind me, then closed my eyes for a moment. My hands clutched the steering wheel and waited for the voices of the ghosts to quiet.

It was over.

I killed him.

The last of the adrenaline ebbed away as I mentally pushed through the memories of the last few hours. I'd saved my old partner's life. Caught the man who killed my wife and daughter. Stared into his eyes as I sent him straight to hell.

The sight of the blood on the wall, as his body slid down to collapse at my feet, was something I'll never forget. The top of his skull open to form some mockery of a crown. The king of the streets lay dead at my feet. The chaos around me seemed to stop in time as I reveled in my short-lived satisfaction.

I fought back a sob as tears pooled at the corners of my eyes.

I'd been arrested—only to be released by the very man who kicked me off the force, what, six months ago?

I wiped the tears away with the back of my arm and turned the key in the ignition.

The man who killed my wife and daughter was in hell, and somehow, I was still alive.

Blood leaked from a dozen places, the worst of it a gunshot wound in my leg. My vision swirled. The street seemed to sway as I drove. With Memphis shrinking in the rearview mirror, I knew I only had so much time before blood loss stopped me cold.

The risky part was I wasn't more than a few miles outside the city.

I turned south off the main road. It was a gamble, but I was out of options.

The truck slid across the dirt road. Up ahead, a rusty chain stretched across the path. A corroded metal sign dangled from it, the words TRAINING GROUND barely recognizable beneath rust and grime.

I pushed harder on the throttle. The truck responded with a deep growl and leaped forward.

Bigger ripped the chain from its mounts and dragged it into the dirt behind me.

Black stars swam across my vision. I forced them away with a few deep breaths. The gunshot wound throbbed somewhere in the background, distant and dull. I barely felt it anymore.

That scared me.

I slapped the wound.

White-hot pain detonated up my leg, burning the fog out of my brain in a heartbeat.

The road curved left. The truck drifted right, gravel spraying as I slid toward the ditch. The right side dipped off the road, tearing up grass, and I eased Bigger back under control.

"Sorry, buddy." I patted the dashboard. "We're almost there."

My truck settled into the ruts of the road, and I relaxed behind the wheel, knowing the truck would get me safely there.

Ahead, the outline of a shack appeared, a single naked bulb hanging beside the door. On one side of the door, an American flag was nailed to the wall; on the other side of the door was an old Revolutionary War flag, yellow with a rattlesnake above the words 'DON'T TREAD ON ME.'

I blinked sweat from my eyes and rolled the truck to a stop beside the building, then leaned on the horn.

A light snapped on inside.

A minute later, the door flew open, and a grizzled man with a long black beard stepped out, a black-framed 1911 leading the way as he approached my truck.

"Who the hell are you, and why are you here?" he demanded from behind the pistol.

I opened the door and raised my hands where he could see them.

"Hello, Jason. How are things?"

He lowered the hand cannon and squinted at me.

"Shepard? That you?"

"Yeah, buddy. Any chance you could give me a hand?"

I reached for his shoulder and promptly fell out of the truck.

I'll say this for Jason, he's fast.

He stepped in, caught me across his shoulder, and somehow didn't collapse under my weight, though he staggered back a step.

"Damn," he muttered. "Looks like you went toe-to-toe with a bear...and lost."

He hooked an arm around my side and hauled me into the shed. With his help, I staggered toward the couch, but he spun me toward the kitchen table instead.

"Ain't no way in hell you're bleeding all over my couch," he said. "Table. Stretch out."

I collapsed with a grunt. Jason had to help lift my bad leg.

Partly because we were friends, and partly because he was a good Christian, he opened a cabinet full of medical supplies and went to work. Without a single smartass comment, he grabbed a pair of trauma shears and cut away my jeans.

"There's your problem," he said after poking around the wound. "You've got a hole in your ass. Well...a new hole."

I slid an arm beneath my head, searching for something that resembled comfort.

"If you dig around in there," I said, "you might find something special."

"I hope it's just a bullet," he replied. "Otherwise, there're gonna be a whole lot more questions."

He shoved something into the wound.

My head shot off the table as a roar tore out of me.

"Damn it! Easy down there."

I grabbed the edge of the table and ground my teeth as my leg lit up with fire.

"Quit being a baby," he said. "You don't see me whining."

He turned back to the cabinet and pulled out something that looked suspiciously like a pair of long needle-nose pliers.

"Now," he said, "hold still."

He leaned over the wound and dug in with the pliers.

I gripped the edge of the table hard enough to leave marks in the wood and sucked air through gritted teeth.

"Are those things sterile?" I asked between breaths.

"If you live, I'll give you a shot," he said. "Now, shut up and let me work."

I met Jason a few years back when MPD sent some of us to the Training Ground for advanced security drills. Jason and his team ran urban warfare scenarios for military units, government contractors, and civilian mercenary groups, but most of his business came from local militias.

Regular people called them preppers.

I'd been out here at least a couple of times a month. Sometimes teaching. Sometimes training. Sometimes just background noise while they ran large-scale simulations.

Outside of Andre, my old partner back on the force, Jason was probably my closest friend.

That's the only reason I finally let myself pass out.

Everything hurt.

I took a deep breath and opened my eyes.

The plain wooden walls of the shed were strangely comforting. The IV line disappearing beneath a bandage at my elbow was expected.

The silver handcuff securing me to the bedframe was...less expected.

I tugged at it.

Real.

Locked tight.

It wasn't the first time I'd woken up handcuffed to furniture. I relaxed and decided I had to trust that Jason wasn't the kind of man to turn me in before hearing my side of the story.

I lay there taking in the rustic simplicity of the shack. Outside of the bed, there were only a few rough pieces of furniture in the single room. A cabinet and sink sat in one corner, but there was nothing on the counter.

Not even a coffeemaker.

I'd have killed for a cup of coffee.

After spending far too long thinking about little else besides a steaming mug of black coffee, Jason stepped into the room, quickly shutting the door behind him.

"How you feelin'?"

"I'm still looking down at the grass instead of up at it," I said. "Thanks for that."

He nodded, opened a cabinet, and pulled out a small propane burner and a black stainless-steel coffeepot.

I breathed a sigh of relief.

It only took him a few seconds to get the burner going. Eventually, he leaned against the counter and crossed his arms while the coffee heated.

"I never got a chance to see you after your family," he said quietly. "I'm sorry they're gone."

I nodded.

From where he stood, I noticed how much gray had crept into his beard.

"When I heard what the city did to you afterward..." He shook his head. "It just wasn't right."

I took a slow breath. "It doesn't matter anymore."

Jason turned back to the cabinet and pulled out two stainless-steel camping mugs—the old oval military kind that clipped to the bottom of a canteen. The wire handles folded out as he filled them and handed me one.

I worked myself into a sitting position and accepted it with my free hand. Then I twisted my cuffed wrist to get his attention.

He ignored it.

"Some of my buddies were listening to the scanners last night," he said. "They heard about a shootout at a bar in the city. Nasty place. Belonged to a drug dealer. Word is a rival gang tore it apart."

He paused.

"The guy who died? Turns out, same one who killed your family."

I didn't look at him. I focused on the coffee and took a careful sip.

Hot. Black. Strong. Perfect. It reminded me of my days on the force. Many nights, this was the only thing that kept us functioning after a sixteen-hour shift.

"Is there a question?" I asked.

Jason stayed quiet while he considered it. I waited.

"No," he finally said. "Guess there isn't."

"Then I've got one," I replied, rattling the handcuff chain.

He nodded, reached into his pocket, and tossed me a key.

I unlocked myself and took another sip of coffee.

"I do a lot of business with the city," he said. "You can stay here for a few days. That's all I can offer." He paused, looking guilty. "Don't make me regret this."

I gently touched the thick pad of gauze wrapped around my hip.

"You already did more than enough. I appreciate the patch job. Sorry. I nearly kicked your door in."

"Oh yeah," he said. "You owe me fifty bucks for the gate."

"What gate? All I saw was a piece of chain across the driveway."

"So you did see it," he said. "You ripped it clean out of the mounting bracket. I've gotta sink a new pole. Honestly, I'm surprised it didn't peel the side of your truck open."

I raised a hand in surrender.

"All right. Fifty for the gate. What about the doctoring?"

"No charge. Yours wasn't the first bullet I've pulled." He took another sip while watching me over the cup.

"You probably saved my life, in more ways than one. Thank you."

"Ain't no 'probably' about it," he said. "You'd have bled out in a couple hours. I don't have time to attend your funeral."

We drank our coffee in silence for a few minutes.

"What about the training grounds?" I asked. "You working today?"

"There's a group of government rent-a-troopers down on Field Three," he said. "They asked for privacy, so I'm not needed. That's fine by me. They play hunt-the-infidel, run their little practice scenarios, I cash the check and stay the hell out of the way."

I stared into the steam rising from my mug.

"I don't want to impose," I said. "And I won't stay a minute longer than absolutely necessary, but—"

"Your truck's in the barn. I've got a duffel with your stuff in the closet." He nodded toward a wardrobe against the wall. "I tossed in some clothes for you. I'll stay out of your way. As far as the world knows, you were never here."

I saluted him with my mug and drained the last of the magic elixir.

No sooner had I set it down than someone started hammering on the door.

"Jason! Jason, we need help!"

Jason moved fast, planting a foot behind the door so it only cracked open enough to talk—not enough to expose me. I leaned back against the wall, mostly hidden by the doorframe.

"What the hell's got you busting into my home?" he demanded.

"It's the mercs," the man said. "They were running an exercise, but one of the dipshits brought live ammo."

Jason didn't hesitate. "I'll grab my gear. Anybody call an ambulance?"

He slammed the door shut and crossed the room in two long strides, yanking a massive green canvas bag with a red cross off the top shelf.

"I might have to bring them back here," he said quietly. "It was good seeing you. Now get the fuck out."

Then he was gone, exploding out the front door before anyone could glimpse inside.

"It's a chest wound," the voice outside said. "Hospital's sending a helicopter."

"Get me there," Jason replied.

Gravel sprayed as a vehicle tore off.

That put me on a timetable.

I swung my legs over the side of the bed and pushed myself upright.

The room instantly went black.

I woke up on the floor, pain blooming from a fresh lump on the side of my head. My ears buzzed, and my eyes couldn't focus.

As some invisible bastard took the opportunity to pound out the *1812 Overture* on my skull with a hammer, I gritted my teeth and—slowly this time—worked my way back to my feet. How long had I been out?

The room swam.

With both hands locked onto the table, I waited for the spinning to settle.

Shuffling across the room, I made it to the wardrobe and pulled out the duffel. I dumped the contents onto the table. I'd already lost too much time.

From the pile, I grabbed a pair of overalls and a sweatshirt.

Looked like I was going commando.

It took longer than I liked to get dressed. I found my sneakers beneath the bed and wrestled them onto my sockless feet.

Finally dressed, I grabbed my wallet, phone, and keys—the last things left in the bag—and pushed myself upright again, gripping the edge of the table until the room stopped moving.

I eased the front door open.

The barn sat across an open gravel lot Jason used for parking. I stared at the distance and decided this was not the time for another fall.

One careful step at a time, I made my way across.

Sweat soaked through the armpits of my shirt. By the time I reached the barn, I was breathing hard like I'd just sprinted two miles.

I slid the door open, silently thanking whoever invented sliding doors. The little things matter when you're running on fumes.

I climbed into the driver's seat and turned the key.

The engine roared to life.

Another win.

Backing out into the field, I spotted the med-flight helicopter cutting across the treetops toward the training grounds. With everyone's attention pulled toward the back field, I dropped the truck into drive and headed for the road.

Fifteen minutes later, I was back on the highway.

I'd headed north without realizing it. I didn't know where I was until I stopped at a dusty old gas station. Something scratched at the back of my brain—like I should recognize the place—but nothing clicked.

I handed the cashier three twenties for fuel, an aging hamburger rescued from beneath a heat lamp, and a Coca-Cola-flavored ICEE.

As I turned away from the counter, I glanced up and froze.

A pair of teenagers stared back at me from a police booking photo taped to the wall.

Half a year ago, those two had stolen my truck from this exact gas station—the last time I fled Memphis.

My hand drifted toward my pocket, to find the keys were still there.

"Those two still on the run?" I asked, nodding toward the photo.

"Yeah," the cashier said. "Skipped bail a while back. Five-thousand-dollar reward if you know where they are."

I took a long pull from the ICEE, savoring the cold relief—until a spike of pain stabbed straight through my skull.

I sucked air through clenched teeth as I headed back toward the truck.

When the brain freeze eased, I took another deep drink.

Pain slammed into the center of my forehead again.

I grinned anyway.

"Totally worth it," I muttered before taking a massive bite of the burger.

Grease ran down my fingers.

The burger tasted like lukewarm heaven.

By the time I finished eating, I felt mostly human again.

Mostly.

I pulled my phone from my pocket.

I'd put this off as long as possible.

It was time to check in.

I'd come to Memphis to put an end to the man who killed my family. He was evil incarnate. He kidnapped my old partner and planned to murder him. He was the biggest drug dealer in the city—and somehow untouchable.

I ended all that with a bullet through his skull.

But part of my job was being invisible.

That part, I failed at.

The only reason I was still free was because one hard-line politician had a brief moment of conscience and let me walk.

Now I was on the run.

Again.

I pressed the only number on my speed dial.

Gunny was retired—though there's no such thing as retired in his world—from the USMC. He was also my trainer.

I was an assassin.

And still a rookie.

Memphis had been my second contract. The first one I'd completed on my own.

The phone chirped through a series of beeps and rang once before he answered.

"Rookie."

At that one word, I was sitting at attention.

"You have four hours to get here. Do not be late."

The line went dead.

A cold wave rolled through my stomach. Maybe dread. Maybe the ICEE.

I pressed harder on the accelerator. Bigger responded, and the speedometer climbed. There was a rumble in my truck, laughing at me?

As much as I dreaded that meeting, being late wasn't an option.

I licked a line of grease from my wrist.

If this was going to be my last meal, I wanted every drop.

Chapter 2

The irony wasn't lost on me that the Training Ground outside Memphis was made up of large fields hidden in a nearly dead stretch of Arkansas. The secret militia had wisely tucked themselves away from the rest of civilization.

Secrecy being the better part of valor.

The Peace Archive had a different opinion.

I turned off the highway and followed my GPS to a private neighborhood. A very accusatory speed limit sign announced that the top speed for the neighborhood was strictly enforced at twenty miles-per-hour. I passed a family on bicycles, each wearing matching helmets. Even the baby riding on the back of Mom's bike was sporting the same designer hardware. Dad rode at the back of the line and motioned for me to slow down.

My foot wasn't even near the accelerator. I pressed the brake, deciding it was better to ride the brakes than to get in trouble with the HOA.

A bit farther up the road, a man stood at his grill and clicked his tongs as meat smoked over the fire. He looked up and waved at the stranger in the big red pick-up. I waved back.

The super-secret organization of assassins operated its primary training facility out of a plain suburban house on the outskirts of Chicago. The neighbors were completely oblivious to the fact that some of the most active killers in the country were being trained in a cul-de-sac where kids played basketball in the street.

As I turned into the driveway, the garage door began creeping upward.

Standing just inside was Gunny.

Combat boots. Khaki military fatigues. A black T-shirt stretched across his chest with a stylized USMC logo faded from too many wash cycles.

As the garage door lifted past his face, it revealed his permanent expression of disappointment with the human race.

He stepped aside and I pulled the truck in.

At least he had the patience to wait until the garage door closed before he started chewing my ass.

Bigger rattled as I shut him down. My leg screamed when I climbed out, but I ignored it. Gunny noticed weakness the way sharks noticed blood.

Limping would only make things worse.

He stood in the middle of the garage with his arms crossed, campaign hat pulled low over his eyes—like he'd been carved out of old wars and bad intentions.

The years hadn't softened him.

They'd just stripped away anything that didn't matter.

"You're late," he said.

"I'm not." I pulled out my phone. "I made it with two minutes and thirty seconds to spare."

His eyes flicked toward his watch.

Then back to me.

"You're bleeding."

"Minor."

"You're limping."

"Temporary."

"You stink of gasoline, sweat, and bad decisions."

I raised a finger to argue, then lowered it.

"Yeah. All right. You got me on that one."

Gunny stepped forward and drove a finger into my chest hard enough to rock me backward against the side of the truck like an insect pinned to a display board.

"You don't get to be cute anymore, Rookie."

I clenched my jaw and held my ground.

There was a blur.

His fist cracked into the side of my jaw before I even saw it move. My head snapped sideways, and the rest of me followed. My arm caught the tailgate and—more from luck than skill—I managed not to collapse.

Pain flared hot and bright.

Copper flooded my mouth.

"Lesson one," he said calmly. "We do not exist. We do not leave trails. We are not seen, and we sure as hell do not get arrested."

He grabbed my collar and hauled me upright.

We stood nose-to-nose, close enough for me to see the tiny blood vessels threaded through his eyes.

Not anger.

Disappointment.

That was worse.

"You went loud in Memphis," he said. "You went emotional. You got arrested."

"I got away."

"You got lucky," he snapped. "Somebody blinked. And blinking gets people killed."

I pushed back instinctively, only to stop short against the truck.

"He had my partner," I said. "The only family I've got left."

Gunny leaned closer. I could smell burnt coffee on his breath.

"And now you've got a bullet hole in your leg and every set of eyes in Memphis pointed in your direction."

Silence stretched between us.

Somewhere outside, a basketball slammed against a backboard. Kids shouted. Somebody got dunked on hard enough to trigger laughter from half the neighborhood.

Normal life.

Ten feet above a murder school.

Gunny finally stepped back.

"Stand up."

I pushed off the truck and forced myself into something resembling attention. The world tilted gently beneath my boots.

He looked me over slowly. The bandages. The stiffness. The exhaustion.

Then he nodded once, like he'd just completed an inventory of damaged equipment.

"You should be dead," he said.

"Working on it."

"Not today," he replied. "Today, you learn."

He turned and started toward the interior door.

"If you puke, bleed, or pass out," he said over his shoulder, "you clean it up yourself."

"Fair."

"Stow your gear upstairs. There's food in the fridge. Then report to the basement." He opened the door and paused. "I expect this debrief is going to take a while."

I hauled my gear upstairs, which took far longer than it should have, and found a plate waiting for me in the refrigerator. A thick lunch-meat sandwich and a side of potato salad.

Beside the coffeepot sat a heavy ceramic mug with ROOKIE printed across it in bold black letters.

Of course it did.

I took the plate and coffee, and I headed for the basement door.

A retinal scan later, access was granted to the training headquarters.

The stairs descended into a single large, open room divided into sections. One corner was decked out with gym equipment and enough free weights to make the local YMCA green with envy. Another contained an embarrassing amount of guns and ammunition stacked on military-grade shelving. A Remington sniper rifle lay in pieces across a long wooden table that served as the cleaning-and-maintenance station.

Most of the real work happened in the computer section.

A corner desk, kept immaculately clean, had three monitors positioned in the corner, along with a large-screen television mounted higher on the wall.

That's where I found Gunny.

He sat in a leather-covered executive chair, slowly turning to face me while a wall of glowing monitors cast pale light across the room behind him.

The basement smelled like concrete, old gun oil, and coffee burned one too many times.

Gunny liked it that way.

The stairs creaked beneath my weight as I descended. Each step sent a dull pulse through my leg, but I kept my face neutral.

Limping was weakness.

Weakness invited correction.

"Have a seat."

He pointed toward a stiff wooden chair positioned at the corner of his desk.

Gunny didn't like visitors getting comfortable.

Comfortable people lied.

I sat carefully.

"I see you found the food."

"Thank you," I said, setting the plate down.

"Before we get started," Gunny said, "what's the extent of your injuries?"

I rolled up my sleeves so he could see the cuts along my arms.

"Looks worse than it is. Everything's superficial. Only serious injury was the bullet in the back of my thigh. Slow bleeder. Took a while to find a medic. Lost some blood, but I'm better now."

I took a bite of the sandwich and washed it down with coffee.

"Are you stable," he asked, "or do I need to drag you to a nurse?"

I raised a hand. "No. I'm good. If I take a turn, I'll let you know."

"Good enough."

He lifted his own mug—dark green with six chevrons, three up and three down, crossed rifles in the center. He took a long sip before setting it back on the desk.

"Go."

I took a breath.

"Mission objective was the elimination of Tyrone Jackson."

"You don't get to use his name yet," Gunny interrupted. "Tell me the contract. Not your feelings."

I nodded.

"Primary target. Confirmed identity. Termination with prejudice. No collateral."

"And?"

I walked him through setting up a hotel room across the Mississippi. Acquiring transportation. Picking up a police scanner. Weapons. Surveillance equipment.

Gunny mostly responded with low grunts, pushing me forward whenever I slowed down.

I explained how I tagged the target's vehicle. After a week of live surveillance, I caught wind of a major drug shipment coming in. I was fairly certain the target would be on-site.

"Hold up," Gunny said sharply. "You thought the delivery was the right time for the hit? Do you know what was actually happening there?"

"Yeah," I replied. "Drugs."

Gunny slowly lowered his coffee mug.

"No," he said. "You were thinking like a cop. He wasn't bringing in product. He was bringing in muscle. How many people were there?"

"Twenty or thirty," I admitted.

"Thirty witnesses," Gunny corrected. "All armed."

I nodded quietly.

"You planned a hit at thirty-to-one odds." He leaned back in his chair. "Did you have an exit strategy?"

I lifted my mug to my mouth but didn't drink.

"You stupid bastard," he said quietly. "I'm wasting my time with you."

The words hit harder than the punch.

"I thought we were past this." He leaned forward. "You're still living in the shadow of their deaths. Why are you even here? Why didn't you eat a bullet after you killed him?" His eyes narrowed. "That was the plan, wasn't it?"

I shook my head and set the mug down.

"I was hurting," I admitted. "This whole thing damn near broke me. Yeah, at first, I figured I'd go out in a blaze of glory." I paused. "But not anymore." I met his eyes. "I'm better. It's like the weight of their deaths finally came off my shoulders. I'll have bad days. I'll always miss them. But I'm not checking out. I promise."

Gunny studied me for several long seconds.

"Fine," he finally said. "Do I need to set you up with a shrink?"

A laugh slipped out before I could stop it.

"No. I'm good."

"Good," he replied. "Then let's continue. You charged in thirty-to-one."

I walked him through it again. Saving my partner. Getting shot in the ass. Building a nest on the warehouse roof. My partner returning at the worst possible moment and ruining the shot.

Gunny shook his head.

"That is exactly what I mean. You were still thinking like a cop." He leaned forward in his chair. "Your job wasn't to protect your partner. Your job was to complete the contract. If you had, the rats would've scattered. Your partner probably walks away just fine." He shook his head again. "Cops don't have the stones to end things. Every contract we take is researched and approved at multiple levels before it ever goes out for bid. The people we remove are bad people."

He held my gaze. "The world is better without them."

The monitors behind him cast cold light across his face.

"Don't lose sleep over it," he continued. "The company doesn't make mistakes." He pointed at me. "Now continue."

I walked him through the rest of it—how I was captured, dragged back to Tyrone's club, and how I finally planted a pistol beneath his jaw.

That stopped him.

We both went upstairs for a coffee refill.

Upstairs was civilian territory. Even though the house was probably the most secure building in Illinois, we never discussed business aboveground.

Gunny started a fresh pot while I leaned against the counter. A moment later, he shoved a tall glass of orange juice into my hand.

"Drink," he said. "You look like hell. You could probably use an IV, but this will have to do."

"Yes, Gunny." I had to remove the IV myself and leave the half-full bag in my truck, but he probably already knew that.

Once the coffee finished brewing, we headed back downstairs and resumed the interrogation.

"I want to revisit the part where you got arrested," Gunny said.

"All right." I sat back down carefully. "You've got a question?"

"You got released," he said flatly. "Explain."

"One of the city politicians intervened; he worked as lead counsel for the Memphis PD. He shoved me into his personal vehicle. On the way to the jail, he pulled over and let me go." I paused. "I punched him and stole his car afterward. Figured it gave him some deniability."

Gunny's jaw tightened. "Same guy who got you kicked off the police force?"

"Yeah. But he also told me he was the one who introduced me to the man running this outfit."

Gunny's eyes sharpened immediately.

"Name."

"James Smith."

"That's a problem."

"It shouldn't be hard to track him," I said. "He's the Memphis mayor's right hand. The department calls him Roll-Over Rover. Any time there's a lawsuit, he throws money at it, then guts police funding to pay the bill."

I shifted in the chair.

"I don't like it, but he's my problem. There's another issue too. Maybe a bigger one."

Gunny leaned forward slowly, making sure he had my full attention.

"You burned a city," he said. "You burned your anonymity. You burned goodwill. And the only reason you're still breathing is because somebody with power decided you were more useful alive than dead."

I swallowed. "I didn't ask for that."

"No," he said. "But you benefited from it. And debts like that always get collected." He stood. "You're not suspended. You're not benched. You're not fired."

Despite myself, my chest tightened.

"You're downgraded," he continued. "Probationary status. Remedial training. No independent operations."

"What about—"

He cut me off with a raised hand.

"You don't ask for another contract," he said. "I assign one. And if you screw it up, I put you in the ground myself before someone else gets the chance and before you give up any details on the Archive."

I nodded once. "Understood."

Gunny turned and headed toward the stairs.

"One more thing," he said without looking back.

"Yes, sir."

He paused at the bottom step.

"You don't get to die yet," he said. "You haven't earned it."

He climbed the stairs and shut off the light.

Gunny waited until the basement lights were out and the house settled back into its quiet civilian rhythm.

Then he locked the basement door.

The Rookie could spend the night downstairs. Maybe sleeping on concrete would teach him something.

Gunny moved into the small utility room off the garage—the one without windows, decorations, or anything else that might encourage comfort.

He removed a burner phone from the metal lockbox bolted to the wall, thumbed it awake, and dialed a number that wasn't stored anywhere.

The call connected on the second ring.

"Sir," Gunny said.

There was a pause on the other end. Paper shuffling. Keyboard clicks.

Someone who never stopped working.

"You don't call this late unless something's on fire," Ian Bragg said. "So, talk."

Gunny leaned back against the concrete wall.

"We've got a problem out of Memphis."

Another pause.

Longer this time.

"Define 'problem'," Ian said.

"City politician," Gunny replied. "Not the mayor. His fixer. Name's James Smith."

The line went silent.

When Ian spoke again, his voice had changed.

Flatter.

Colder.

"Say that again."

"James Smith. Mayor's right hand. He personally intervened after Shepard's arrest. Pulled him out. Cut him loose."

Ian exhaled slowly.

"That name's been circling, despite the fact that it sounds like it's a cover. Did Shepard give you anything else?"

"He admitted it clean," Gunny said. "Said Smith also claimed responsibility for introducing him to us."

That earned a sharp breath on the other end.

"That's not an introduction," Ian said. "That's a fishhook."

Gunny nodded, even though Ian couldn't see him.

"Exactly my concern."

Ian's tone shifted from analysis to calculation.

"If Smith knows Shepard is still alive—and more importantly, that we exist—then he's either fishing or already compromised."

"Or arrogant enough to think he can control it," Gunny said.

"Which is worse," Ian replied.

Gunny crossed his arms.

"Shepard went loud. Killed his target in public. Got arrested. Survived because Smith blinked." He paused. "Or because he wanted Shepard followed back to us."

"And now?" Ian asked.

"And now he's sitting in my basement with a hole in his leg and too much attention attached to his name."

Silence stretched across the line.

Then, "Do you think Shepard's compromised?"

Gunny didn't answer immediately.

"No," he finally said. "He's angry. Injured. Reckless. But not compromised."

"That's not exactly a ringing endorsement." Ian sucked his teeth audibly.

"It's an honest one," Gunny replied. "He followed the contract. He just followed his conscience too."

Ian gave a dry chuckle.

"Those two things don't coexist very well in our profession, while being critical in the very best that we have to offer. Our operators have to have consciences; it's the final line of defense against making a fatal error."

"True," Gunny agreed. "But he's still salvageable."

"And Smith?" Ian asked.

Gunny's jaw tightened.

"A man like that doesn't make accidental moves. If he stepped in to save Shepard, it wasn't mercy."

"It was investment," Ian said. "He's the one who put out the contract on the druggie."

"Or insurance," Gunny replied.

Ian went quiet again. Somewhere in the background, Gunny heard the faint hum of computer fans spin louder.

"If Smith is touching our operators," Ian said, "then we have a structural problem beyond a ubiquitous contract with nothing linking back to us besides a money trail that also leads to Smith, but the people contracting with us usually avoid getting personally involved."

"Which is why I'm calling you," Gunny replied. "Not asking permission. Flagging a threat."

"You want Shepard benched."

"No," Gunny said. "I want him controlled."

Ian smiled faintly on the other end. Gunny could hear it in his voice.

"Probation," Ian said. "Remedial status. Tight leash."

"And no independent contracts," Gunny added. "I decide where he goes and when."

"And if Smith reaches out?"

Gunny answered immediately. "Then Shepard becomes bait."

Ian considered that.

"That's dangerous."

"So is pretending this goes away," Gunny replied.

Another pause.

"Keep him," Ian finally said. "But if he drags our name into the light again—"

"I'll handle it," Gunny said.

"I know you will," Ian replied. "That's why he's still breathing. We absolutely cannot have any rogue operators."

The line went dead.

Gunny stared at the phone for another moment before powering it down and returning it to the lockbox.

Outside, the neighborhood sat quiet and peaceful.

Suburban.

Innocent.

Downstairs, a man who should have died was being rebuilt into something sharper.

Gunny turned off the utility-room light and finally went upstairs to steal a few hours of sleep.

Chapter 3

I WOKE UP TO pain again.

Not the sharp, screaming kind.

This was worse.

Deep. Everywhere. The kind of pain that settles into your bones and reminds you that yesterday's decisions were terrible.

I lay still and took inventory.

Head: pounding but intact.

Ribs: sore, wrapped tight, every breath a negotiation.

Leg: stiff, hot, and angry. The gunshot wound throbbed like it had developed its own heartbeat.

I opened one eye.

The only light came from the monitors. An amorphous blob crawled across the screensaver, its colors shifting as tendrils stretched through the darkness for something to grab.

I knew exactly how the thing felt.

There wasn't a light switch on my side of the locked basement door. I checked my cellphone.

4:45 a.m.

My body had officially decided we were done sleeping.

Using the flashlight on my phone, I returned the plate weights I'd used as an improvised pillow to the rack and folded the towels I'd stolen from the gym corner of the basement.

I had briefly considered sleeping in Gunny's oversized executive chair, but I was already on thin ice with him.

And like I admitted yesterday, I no longer had a death wish, which was a revelation to me, too.

I found an open patch of concrete and slowly stretched the stiffness out of my muscles. Then I crouched there with my elbows resting on my knees, breathing through my nose the way Jason had taught me years ago.

Don't rush the pain.

Let it introduce itself.

Eventually, the stiffness receded enough for me to stand.

My right leg immediately buckled, just enough to remind me it was in charge today. I caught myself against the weight rack before gravity finished the job.

I straightened carefully and tested my weight again.

Slow.

Controlled.

The limp was still there, but subtle. Manageable if I stayed disciplined and moved slowly.

I checked myself in the mirror.

Even in the weak glow from my phone, I looked like hell.

Bruising crept up my neck and along my jaw where Gunny had tagged me. My eyes looked sunken and bloodshot. A fresh red bloom stained the bandage on my leg where blood had seeped through overnight.

Honestly, I'd expected worse.

I made a mental note to thank Jason if I ever saw him again.

The overhead lights exploded on without warning.

I hissed and threw a hand over my eyes.

"Rookie, you awake?" Gunny called from the top of the stairs.

I limped toward the staircase. Every step sent a dull ache through my leg, but I kept my pace even.

Weakness invited correction.

Gunny stood in the doorway, backlit by the kitchen behind him. A steaming mug of coffee rested in one hand, a glass of orange juice in the other.

"How's the leg?"

"Attached."

"That wasn't the question."

I exhaled slowly and limped my way up the stairs.

"It hurts."

"Good. Pain means you're paying attention."

He handed me the orange juice. Cold condensation slicked against my palm.

"Drink."

I did.

The sugar hit my system hard. My stomach twisted once but decided to cooperate.

"You sleep?"

"Some."

Gunny crossed his arms and studied me like a mechanic inspecting a damaged engine.

"You're not training today," he said.

I opened my mouth.

"Not because you're injured," he continued. "Because you're sloppy."

"You ran hot in Memphis. Emotional. Predictable. You let the mission steer you instead of you steering the mission."

"He had my partner—"

"I know." His voice never changed volume. "And you still don't get to lose control."

Silence stretched between us.

"You're going to rest this morning," Gunny said. "Eat. Hydrate. This afternoon, we start over."

"Remedial," I said.

"Yes."

I nodded once. "Understood."

He took a slow sip of coffee.

"You're alive," he said. "That means you still have value. Don't waste it trying to atone all at once."

My recovery started with a hot shower and a fresh bandage on my leg.

I offered a silent prayer of thanks for Jason as I examined what remained of my ass in the mirror. The wound had been stitched clean and tight. The bleeding had nearly stopped.

I pulled on a fresh pair of sweats and a T-shirt from my bag.

The shower worked miracles.

By the time I made my way downstairs again, my limp was barely noticeable.

Barely.

I wandered into the basement gym and found Gunny pushing iron like it had personally insulted him.

No music.

No timer.

Just raw effort.

His workout clothes were soaked dark with sweat.

"You're looking better," he said, racking the weight before turning toward me. "I started without you, like I promised. You've got the morning off." He turned back to the barbell and curled it again. "If you're not in too much pain, you can push the mower around the yard. Best way to keep that leg from stiffening up is to keep moving."

"I'm on it, Gunny."

I made a quick U-turn. The mower was in the garage.

I already knew about the man's obsession with detail, but mowing the lawn turned into an all-day affair. By the time I finished, I was drenched in sweat and sore in places I didn't know existed.

I couldn't help wondering if this was Gunny going easy on me.

Hours later, I shuffled back inside. Grass clippings clung to my legs like I'd lost a fight with a salad bar.

Gunny wasn't around, but a thick sandwich waited on the counter beside a tall glass of iced tea.

That alone convinced me the old man was getting soft.

After lunch—and my second shower of the day—I returned downstairs.

Gunny sat at the computer station. The stiff wooden chair sat at the corner of his desk exactly where it always did.

I took my seat and waited.

"Do you know what I'm doing, Rookie?" he asked without turning around.

I glanced at the monitor over his shoulder.

I recognized the interface immediately.

Memphis Police Department.

"You're reviewing the incident report for Tyrone's hit."

"What?" Gunny didn't turn around. "I don't recall giving you permission to use his name."

I corrected myself immediately.

"You're reviewing the incident report for the execution of my contract."

"Exactly," he said. "And do you know what I don't see?"

I shrugged before remembering he couldn't see it.

"No idea."

"I don't see your name."

I frowned.

"Okay," I said slowly. "I don't understand."

Gunny clicked through windows filled with reports, bodycam logs, dispatch records, and evidence reports.

"We know at least two officers on-scene recognized you," he said. "Even with turnover, there should've been more. But nobody reported you."

Another click.

"Not a whisper." He opened another report. "James Smith's vehicle isn't listed either. No mention of his involvement. It's like you were never there."

"That sounds..." I hesitated. "Good?"

"No," Gunny said flatly. "That's bad." He leaned back slowly in the chair. "Someone's going to assume you owe them. By extension, they'll assume the Archive owes them." He looked over at me. "I don't like debts I didn't agree to." He turned back to the monitor. "Worse, I have to assume they ran your blood, fingerprints, or DNA through the system."

My stomach tightened.

"And when they did," he continued, "they found you erased."

Click.

"Deleted."

Click.

"No employment history. No active law-enforcement records. No usable digital footprint."

The monitor light reflected in his eyes.

"They now know somebody can do that."

A cold knot formed in my chest.

"Erase cops," Gunny said quietly. "Rewrite databases. Remove people from official systems." He finally turned toward me fully. "That makes us a threat." The fury behind his expression barely stayed contained. "And threats get answered."

The room suddenly felt much smaller.

"Do you understand now," he asked, "how your sloppiness put this entire organization at risk?"

I didn't answer because I didn't have one.

Gunny stared at me another second before turning back toward the monitors.

"Fuck off for the rest of the day," he said. "I need to figure out exactly how bad this is." His fingers started moving across the keyboard again. "Training starts tomorrow morning."

Another click.

"Now get out of my basement."

I stood and left without another word.

Somewhere between the basement stairs and the kitchen, the lesson finally broke through my thick skull.

Invisible didn't just mean unseen.

It meant nobody could ever prove you existed in the first place.

At 0430, the lights snapped on, and my bedroom door slammed open hard enough to rattle the frame.

"Up."

That was it.

No greeting. No explanation.

I rolled out of the bunk and nearly kissed the floor when my bad leg protested. White-hot pain lanced up my thigh and settled somewhere behind my eyes.

I caught myself against the wall and forced the limp under control.

Weakness still invited correction.

Gunny stood in the hallway, already dressed.

Combat boots.

Faded utilities.

Campaign hat pulled low like it had grown there.

"You sleep?"

"Some."

"Good enough."

It was still dark when we stepped outside. The cold morning air bit through my sweatshirt, and our breath rolled out in pale clouds beneath the streetlights.

"You have five minutes to stretch," Gunny said as he pressed a button on his watch.

An electronic chirp announced the timer had started.

Then Gunny dropped into a yoga pose and closed his eyes.

The suburban street looked painfully normal.

Perfect lawns.

Sprinklers ticking softly.

A newspaper sitting untouched at the edge of somebody's driveway like the world still made sense.

I started working the stiffness out of my leg while Gunny flowed from one position to another with impossible precision. Every movement looked effortless. Balanced. Controlled.

At one point, his arms were held perfectly parallel to the ground in complete defiance of gravity.

I moved to a tree and stretched my hamstrings against the trunk.

It felt like only seconds had passed before Gunny's watch beeped again.

Without a word, he started down the sidewalk at a brisk walk that became a jog without warning.

I stayed with him.

By the third block, sweat soaked through my shirt.

By the fifth, my leg burned.

By the seventh, my lungs felt lined with broken glass.

Gunny never changed pace.

We cut through an alley and crossed into a small park. Dew soaked my sneakers as we moved across the grass.

Gunny finally stopped beside a set of pull-up bars and turned toward me.

"Drop."

I dropped.

Push-ups.

Slow. Controlled.

He counted every single one out loud.

"Back straight."

"Core tight."

"That one didn't count."

My arms trembled. My vision tunneled. Copper filled my mouth again.

"Up."

Sit-ups.

Planks.

More push-ups.

Gunny watched everything.

My breathing.

My posture.

The subtle way my injured leg compensated when fatigue set in.

"You're protecting it," he said.

"It's injured."

"It's alive. That's not the same thing."

We moved on.

Sprints.

Short. Brutal. Endless.

Back and forth across the wet grass until every pivot sent fire through my leg.

I learned quickly that slowing down was worse than pain.

Slowing down earned commentary.

Pushing through earned silence.

I preferred silence.

After the sprints came balance drills.

Eyes closed.

One foot.

Then the other.

"You don't get stable when things go quiet," Gunny said. "You get stable when everything's wrong."

He shoved me hard.

I stumbled, recovered, almost lost it again.

"Again."

By the time we finished, my hands shook uncontrollably, and my shirt clung to me like a second skin.

Gunny gave a single nod.

"Baseline."

That was all.

Back at the house, he tossed me a towel and pointed toward the kitchen table.

"Eat."

I sat down heavily. My hands shook badly enough that I had to brace my fork against the plate just to stab the eggs.

The food tasted like victory.

Gunny watched me chew.

"You think this was punishment," he said.

I looked up.

"It wasn't."

He took a sip of coffee.

"It was a diagnosis."

He leaned back against the counter with his arms crossed. "You're fast. You're stubborn. You don't quit." A pause. "You're sloppy."

That one also hit harder than the punch.

"You move like a cop," he continued. "You plan like a cop. You react like a cop." He pointed at me with his mug. "And that's a problem."

I shoveled more food into my mouth instead of answering.

"You compromised your objective. You still think your job is saving people." His expression hardened. "It isn't."

Silence settled between us. The only sounds were my chewing and the hum of the refrigerator.

"You're not here to be comforted," Gunny said finally. "You're here to be corrected." He pushed off the counter and headed toward the basement door. "Finish eating. Gear up."

"For what?"

He didn't look back.

"Everything you think you already know."

The basement door shut behind him.

I finished my breakfast in silence.

Gunny never told me where we were going.

That should've been my first warning.

We drove for nearly an hour through suburbs that slowly dissolved into scrub brush and thin woods.

No signs.

No gates.

Just a dirt road that looked intentionally forgotten.

Eventually, Gunny pulled into a rutted parking area filled with beat-up trucks, rusted vans, and a school bus that had absolutely no business still running.

People geared up around us.

Helmets.

Chest rigs.

Masks.

Fake rifles.

Airsoft.

I stared through the windshield.

"You're kidding."

Gunny shut off the engine.

"Get out."

I climbed out slowly. My leg complained, but it held.

Around us, maybe thirty people moved between picnic tables and tree lines, checking magazines, adjusting masks, and talking too loudly.

Weekend warriors.

Teenagers barely old enough to shave.

A few grown men taking the whole thing way too seriously.

Nobody looked at us twice.

"That's the lesson already, isn't it?" I asked.

Gunny opened the trunk.

"You exist too loudly," he said. "Today, you don't exist at all."

He tossed me a plain gray hoodie and a mesh face mask.

No vest.

No fake rifle.

No protection.

"What exactly am I supposed to do with this?" I asked.

"Survive."

He pointed toward the woods.

"Game starts in five minutes. Blue team versus red team." He looked directly at me. "You are neither."

I followed his finger toward the field.

Trees.

Plywood shacks.

Abandoned cars.

Stacked pallets.

Visibility maybe thirty yards at best.

Plenty of cover.

Plenty of angles.

Gunny leaned closer.

"Rules are simple," he said. "You don't touch anyone. You don't talk. You don't interfere." A faint grin tugged at the corner of his mouth. "Your job is to cross that field, touch the red flag, and come back without anybody realizing you were ever there."

"And if I get hit?"

"You already failed."

A whistle shrieked through the trees.

People shouted.

Boots pounded against dirt and leaves.

Plastic BBs snapped through the woods like angry hornets.

Gunny gave me one final look.

"You go loud, Rookie, and I'll make you run this again tomorrow," he said. "And the day after that. Until you learn."

Then he stepped away.

I moved into the woods.

At first, instinct took over.

I moved too fast.

I hugged cover, tracked sightlines, watched muzzle direction, and mentally cleared angles like I was back on a warrant service.

I thought I was doing well.

Then a kid no older than sixteen sprinted past me close enough that I could've touched his shoulder.

He never saw me.

I smiled.

Three BBs exploded against the tree inches from my face.

I froze.

"CONTACT LEFT!"

Boots thundered through the brush nearby.

I hadn't been seen.

But I had been felt.

My movement disturbed the pattern.

Broken branches.

Shifting shadows.

Movement where there shouldn't have been movement.

The woods noticed me even if the players hadn't.

Gunny's voice echoed in my head.

You exist too loudly.

I slowed down.

Matched my breathing to the wind.

Stepped only when others moved.

Let noise cover noise.

Let chaos hide intent.

Time stretched strangely after that.

At one point, two players crouched behind the same fallen log I was using for cover. They were close enough that I could smell cheap cologne and sweat beneath their tactical gear.

One scratched at his nose.

"Dude, I swear half these campers haven't moved all game."

I didn't blink.

Didn't breathe deeper.

Didn't shift my weight.

Eventually, they moved on.

The red flag finally came into view.

It hung from a length of rebar near an abandoned plywood shack.

Three defenders guarded it.

One pacing.

One kneeling behind a pallet wall.

One staring in completely the wrong direction.

I waited.

Not because I was afraid.

Because patience was the lesson.

When the moment came, I didn't rush.

I simply walked forward.

Calm.

Relaxed.

Like I belonged there.

I touched the flag.

Nobody noticed.

Then I waited again.

The return trip proved harder.

The field had changed.

Players were alert now. Movement patterns shifted constantly. People watched longer and reacted faster.

A BB clipped my arm at one point. I felt the sting through the hoodie.

But nobody called the hit.

Nobody pointed.

Nobody noticed me.

When I finally stepped out of the woods and back into the parking area, Gunny leaned against the truck with his arms crossed.

He checked his watch.

"You took your time."

"No one saw me."

He nodded once.

"You learned."

I peeled off the mask. Sweat ran down my neck in cold streams. My leg throbbed. Exhaustion settled into me in a way that had nothing to do with muscle.

Gunny opened the driver-side door.

"Tomorrow," he said, "you do it again."

"With a weapon?" I asked.

He looked at me like I'd completely missed the point.

"No," he said. A faint grin touched the corner of his mouth. "Tomorrow, they'll be hunting you."

He climbed into the truck and shut the door.

I stood there for another moment listening to the distant laughter, shouting, and constant popping of BB guns deeper in the woods.

That was when I finally understood what invisibility really meant.

It wasn't hiding.

It was not mattering.

For the rest of the day, Gunny walked me through tactical surveillance methods and a brutal breakdown of everything I'd done wrong in Memphis.

Which turned out to be almost everything.

By the time he finally ended the briefing, it was pushing midnight.

I lurched to my feet with a groan.

"I won't pretend that wasn't informative," I said, "but your presentation style could use some work. Maybe next time, we cover this over beer and wings."

I was halfway up the stairs when Gunny called after me like the thought had just occurred to him.

"Get your go bag. Meet me at the car."

I stopped halfway up the staircase.

"Seriously?"

His only response was pulling a canvas duffel from beneath his desk and heading toward the stairs.

"You'd better not leave me waiting, Rookie."

I muttered several deeply respectful things under my breath and limp-sprinted upstairs.

I grabbed my bag from beside the front door and bounded back down just as the garage door finished crawling open.

Gunny climbed into his baby-blue Prius.

The physical embodiment of urban camouflage.

An hour later, we turned onto a dirt road cutting through a thick wall of trees. Gunny parked among a row of battered vehicles.

Beyond them stretched several acres of open ground broken up by squat concrete buildings, telephone poles, rusted fencing, and stacked junk.

It reminded me of the Training Ground outside Memphis.

Only cheaper.

And meaner.

All around us, people unloaded gear while laughing and talking like they were heading into a backyard cookout instead of mock combat.

Helmets.

Rifles.

Plate carriers.

Masks.

"What's this?" I asked.

"Let's call it an urban familiarization exercise," Gunny said, killing the engine. "From this point forward, you do not speak unless I ask you a direct question."

I nodded once.

The night air hit cold as I stepped from the car. Everyone else looked geared for combat.

I looked like a man who'd lost a bar fight and wandered into the wrong parking lot.

Gunny opened the trunk and tossed me a dark hoodie and a battered mesh mask.

"No gun?" I asked.

"No." He shut the trunk. "You're going into the field. One of the people out there has a red bandana in their back pocket. Your job is to identify them and return here with a description." He looked directly at me. "Without being noticed."

I glanced toward the players loading magazines, checking optics, and slapping each other on the shoulder.

"They're shooting."

"Yes."

"With airsoft rifles."

"Yes."

I looked down briefly at my leg.

Still stiff.

Still tender.

"And if I get hit?"

Gunny finally turned fully toward me.

"You fail."

I pulled on the hoodie and settled the mask over my face just as a whistle shrieked through the darkness.

The field erupted into chaos.

I moved into the shadow of a dumpster and started scanning.

The place looked like the remains of an abandoned rail depot.

Dead security lights.

Graffiti layered thick enough to read history through it.

A bonfire burned inside a rusted steel drum, throwing flickering orange light across chrome, leather, and broken concrete.

Chain-link fences patched together with scrap wire and duct tape carved the field into narrow alleys.

"You see weapons?" Gunny asked quietly beside me.

I barely stopped myself from jumping.

I hadn't heard him move.

"Knives on belts," I whispered. "Shoulder holsters. Shotgun leaning against a crate near the fire."

"Good." His voice stayed calm. "You're authorized to use anything you find that helps complete the mission."

I glanced back.

Gunny was already gone.

I stepped away from the dumpster.

Hands loose.

Shoulders relaxed.

Head slightly lowered.

Pace steady.

Not rushed.

I passed two men arguing beside the stripped frame of an old motorcycle. Its seat had been torn open, foam hanging out like exposed organs.

Neither of them looked at me.

Good.

Plastic BBs snapped through the air, smacking into wood and metal with sharp cracks. Players shouted callouts while flashlights swept through the alleys like prison search beams.

Everyone moved aggressively.

Everyone moved loudly.

A man clipped my shoulder as he passed.

"Watch it."

"Sorry," I muttered without making eye contact.

Already moving again.

I drifted closer to one of the barrel fires. Heat rolled across my face.

Somebody laughed behind me.

A woman leaned against a rusted bike frame nearby, eyes sharp enough to cut wire. She cataloged everything around her without appearing to look at anything directly.

So I didn't look at her.

I followed a line of stacked crates and stepped around scattered concrete chunks like I'd walked the route a hundred times before.

Halfway between two buildings, something prickled at the back of my skull.

That instinct.

The one that never really shut off anymore.

Eyes.

I felt them before I saw them.

I crossed the street and slowed, pretending to check my phone. In the reflection of a dark storefront window, a shape peeled itself out of a doorway behind me.

Male. Mid-thirties. Beard. Black leather vest over a hoodie.

He wasn't following me. He was tracking me. I turned the corner without looking back. Mistake. The alley narrowed fast. Dead end. Trash piles. Wood pallets. A burned-out sedan with no tires. His footsteps never sped up. They didn't need to.

"Hey."

I kept walking.

"Hey."

I stuffed my hands in my pockets and lowered my head. My only thought was to keep going.

"Don't do that," the man said. "Makes you interesting."

I stopped and turned slowly.

He stood about ten feet back with his hands open and empty. No visible weapon.

His eyes looked sharp.

Amused.

"You ain't drunk," he said. "You ain't lost. And you sure as hell don't belong here."

I shrugged lightly.

"Just passing through."

He smiled.

"That's the problem."

Two more figures peeled out of the darkness.

One blocked the mouth of the alley.

The other leaned casually against a dumpster with his arms crossed.

I'd been made.

Not because I moved wrong.

Because I didn't move wrong enough.

"You military?" the first man asked.

"No."

"Cop?"

I shook my head.

He nodded like he already knew the answer.

"Cop or soldier, you all got the same problem," he said. "You think not acting is invisible."

He took another slow step closer.

"It ain't."

The guy by the dumpster chuckled.

"Dude ghosted us."

The leader pointed at me. "Invisible people still affect a place," he said. "You didn't affect shit."

That landed harder than I expected.

Engaging would end the exercise.

Running would confirm everything.

Talking was the only move left.

"I'm just here to observe," I said carefully.

The leader's grin widened. He tapped two fingers lightly against my chest.

"Problem is," he said, "this ain't a place for observers." He leaned closer. "Everybody here wants something."

"What do you want?" I asked.

He smiled wider at that.

Then he leaned in close enough for me to smell smoke, oil, and stale beer on his clothes.

"I want to know," he said softly, "how a man with blood in his eyes walks into our field and thinks nobody notices."

A blinding spotlight snapped on and locked onto me.

"That's enough."

Gunny's voice rolled across the field.

The three men backed off immediately.

The leader laughed and lifted his hands.

"Training exercise, right?"

Gunny approached without even glancing at them. His eyes stayed fixed on me.

"You failed."

"Yes, sir."

Gunny finally looked toward the others.

"Good work." He handed the leader a folded bill. "First round's on me."

The man grinned.

"Your boy might be dangerous," he said, "but he ain't subtle."

Then the three of them disappeared into the darkness like they'd never been there.

Gunny waited until we were alone.

"Tell me where you screwed up."

I exhaled slowly.

"I tried to be invisible."

Gunny shook his head once.

"No." He stepped closer. "You tried to be nothing. In their world, nothing doesn't exist."

The spotlight clicked off behind us, plunging the alley back into darkness.

Gunny's face became a silhouette beneath the brim of his campaign hat.

"Next time, Rookie," he said quietly, "you don't hide."

He turned and started walking away.

"You belong in a way that doesn't matter."

Chapter 4

GUNNY DIDN'T GIVE ME time to stew in the failure.

He grabbed my shoulder and steered me back toward the Prius without a word. Behind us, the sounds of the field faded into the night—plastic rounds snapping through the dark, engines revving, music pounding near the bonfire.

I expected a lecture.

Instead, Gunny popped the trunk.

"Strip."

I blinked.

"Sir?"

"Everything that says you don't belong," he snapped. "Hoodie. Mask. Shoes."

I peeled off the borrowed gear, my leg protesting as I bent over. Gunny dug into the trunk and tossed me another bundle of clothes.

Leather vest.

Faded band T-shirt.

Oil-stained jeans.

Heavy boots with cracked soles.

I stared down at the pile.

"You want me to cosplay?"

Gunny stepped close enough that his shadow swallowed me whole.

"I want you to stop acting like you're better than the room."

That shut me up.

I changed quickly. The boots were half a size too big. The jeans smelled like gasoline, sweat, and stale cigarettes, just like my three tormenters. The leather vest hung heavy across my shoulders in a way that felt earned instead of worn.

When I looked into the Prius window, I barely recognized myself.

"Don't stand like you're waiting for orders," Gunny said. "And for the love of God, stop looking like you're counting exits."

"I always count exits."

"Not like that," he replied. "You count them like they belong to you." He stepped back and looked me over again. "Same mission. Find the bandana. Bring me a description." A pause. "This time—"

"No ghosting," I said.

The corner of Gunny's mouth twitched.

Almost a smile.

"You learn fast when you bleed," he said.

Then he jerked his chin toward the field.

"Go."

The whistle shrieked through the darkness again.

This time, I didn't head for cover.

I walked straight into the light.

The bonfire crackled as I passed. Heat rolled across my face. Somebody laughed and slapped me on the shoulder like we'd known each other for years.

I nodded once and kept moving.

Slow.

Loose.

Like I had nowhere else to be.

Belonging wasn't silence.

Belonging was friction.

I stopped beside a group loading magazines and crouched down like my knee was bothering me.

Which wasn't much of an act.

One of the players glanced at me briefly before going back to his gear.

No challenge.

No suspicion.

I drifted through the field.

Not skulking.

Drifting.

I leaned against a stack of pallets and watched two guys argue over firing lanes. I borrowed their posture. Their rhythm.

When somebody bumped into me, I didn't apologize.

I muttered, "Watch it."

And they did.

That was when I spotted the bandana.

Just a flash of red cloth hanging from the back pocket of a man near the fence line.

Mid-forties.

Gray threaded through his beard.

Cigar clenched between his teeth.

1911 resting casually in one hand.

Calm eyes.

He wasn't playing aggressively.

He was observing.

Without looking directly at him, I grabbed the shoulder of the guy beside me. He was trying to light a cigarette.

"Pass me a smoke," I said. "Left mine back at the bike."

He shook a Marlboro loose from a soft pack and handed it over.

I took it with a nod and drifted after the man with the bandana.

I didn't stare.

I let my eyes slide naturally across the field with practiced disinterest.

When I stepped beside him, I nudged his arm lightly with my elbow.

"Got a light?"

He pulled a brass Zippo from his pocket and handed it over without hesitation.

I turned slightly away and cupped the flame against the wind.

Then I 'fumbled' the lighter.

"Shit."

The Zippo hit the dirt with a dull clink.

I bent to retrieve it.

My left hand scooped up the lighter.

My right hand lifted the red bandana from his back pocket.

One smooth motion.

I brushed the Zippo against my jeans like I was cleaning it off and pressed it back into his hand.

He glanced at me.

I met his eyes.

Then we both nodded once like two strangers sharing a cigarette break.

That was it.

Ten minutes later, I peeled away from the field completely unchallenged.

Unremarkable.

Unnoticed in the way that mattered.

When I reached the Prius, Gunny waited beside the trunk with his arms crossed.

"Well?"

"Male," I said. "Mid-forties. Gray beard. Carries a 1911. Smokes cigars. Red bandana in the right rear pocket."

Gunny didn't respond immediately.

He opened the trunk and handed me a bottle of water.

"Better," he finally said. "Not good. But better."

I cracked the bottle open and drained half of it in one pull.

"Anything else to report?" he asked.

"When I was a kid," I said, "I thought about becoming a magician. Learned a little sleight of hand."

I pulled the red bandana from my pocket and dropped it into his palm.

Gunny stared at it for a second before tossing it into the back of the Prius.

"Why'd you quit magic?" he asked.

"Stephanie Farmer."

Gunny snorted.

"If you wanted to meet girls, you should've joined the Corps. Women love a man in uniform."

We stood there quietly for a moment, watching the lights and movement across the field.

"What changed?" he finally asked.

"I stopped trying to disappear," I said. "I gave them something they could place."

Gunny nodded once.

"Invisibility isn't absence," he said. "It's context."

He pointed back toward the field.

"Give people a way to categorize you and you vanish into the group. They'll forget your face the second you're gone." He shut the trunk. "Get in. We're done for tonight."

We didn't talk during the drive home.

To be fair, I was one step short of complete exhaustion and may have dozed off once or twice before we reached the house.

The next morning, my eyes snapped open and I bolted upright in bed.

Light streamed around the edges of the window shade.

Crap.

Gunny was going to kill me for oversleeping.

I yanked on workout clothes and hurried downstairs. The ROOKIE mug sat beside half a pot of coffee next to a one-word note.

'Downstairs.'

I poured coffee into the mug and headed for the basement.

I could smell sweat halfway down the stairs. Gunny must've cranked the heat. It had to be pushing a hundred degrees in the room. The clank of heavy iron hitting a rack echoed through the basement.

Gunny rose from the bench press, wiped sweat from his face with a towel, then moved to the preacher curl station. He planted his elbows and started curling a crooked bar loaded with enough weight to injure normal people.

Veins stood out along his forearms as the bar rose and fell.

"Did you get a good night's sleep?" he asked.

"Yes, s—"

"I don't care," he cut in.

The bar rose again.

Fell again.

"Your skills behind a gun were never the problem," he said. "What you showed me last night tells me you're capable of moving without blowing your cover to pieces."

Another curl.

"That means what happened in Memphis was emotional failure."

Which I already knew.

Gunny finished the set and locked the bar back into place.

"I think it's time you stop sitting on your ass in my basement," he said. "You need to get back into the field."

Gunny re-racked the weights and sat upright.

I straightened slowly, the coffee mug suddenly feeling heavier in my hand.

"Your next assignment is on the computer," he said, nodding toward the desk while moving back to the bench press. "Strictly information gathering. You are recon. No action. No freelance heroics. You report regularly."

I moved over to the computer and carefully set the coffee away from the electronics.

A file already waited on-screen.

The photograph looked grainy. Head and shoulders only. The man sat astride a motorcycle wearing a black do-rag, sunglasses, a black leather vest, and sporting a thick beard.

"That's Silas Pike," Gunny said. "Road name: Preacher. President of a Deadhand Dominion chapter."

"Not much of a picture."

"Nope," Gunny replied. "That's one of the reasons you're going. Research is thin. He lives mostly off-grid. I want identity confirmation, contact, and whatever intelligence you can gather."

A heavy hand landed on my shoulder.

"You're sitting in my chair."

I'd gotten locked onto the screen and never heard him approach.

Again.

I stood and moved back to the stiff wooden chair near the desk.

"You can ride a motorcycle, can't you?" he asked.

I smiled faintly.

"Yeah. I had a dirt bike as a kid."

Gunny snorted.

"Sure, that's the same thing," he said dryly. "Except heavier, faster, and far more interested in killing you." He nodded toward the screen. "I suggest you buy an old bike somewhere out west and ride your way into the assignment."

I squinted at the last confirmed sighting.

"Arizona?"

"Good," Gunny said. "We've established you can read. Yes. Arizona. Roughly two thousand miles for you to relearn how not to die on a motorcycle."

"What brought him to our attention?"

"Deadhand Dominion handles the usual business model. Drugs. Weapons. Protection. Prostitution."

He took a hand towel from around his shoulders and used it to clear the sweat from his face.

"They used to be small-time in Arizona. Now they're expanding into Southern California."

"That's new money."

"And new attention," Gunny replied.

"Who's paying for the contract?"

Gunny slowly turned his head toward me.

"That's not normally something we discuss, but this request originated out of Los Angeles, the President of Los Angeles City Council, Caroline Mendoza. Think of her as second in command to the Mayor of L.A."

"So we're working for the government now?"

"No," Gunny said flatly. "You work for me. I work for somebody else. He works for somebody else. That's all you need to know. The city's struggling because the club operates across state lines. That makes prosecution messy."

I nodded slowly.

"Then why not let the Feds handle it?"

Gunny's mouth twitched slightly.

Not amusement.

Disgust.

"They want the problem solved," he said. "Federal solutions take time. Politicians hate waiting."

He clicked through several news feeds.

Burning buildings.

Looting.

Street riots.

Smoke rolling over L.A.

"Watch yourself around these people," Gunny said. "They're getting bolder. Instigating riots. Looting operations. Wildfires."

Another click.

A jewelry store burned on-screen while masked people ran through smoke.

"Somebody's turning up the temperature," Gunny said quietly. "And it's making the club dangerous."

"And I'm still recon only."

"For now," Gunny confirmed. "You keep me informed. I decide if we escalate or walk away."

"And by escalate, you mean—"

"Cut the head off the snake."

The room felt quieter after that.

Gunny fixed me with a hard stare.

"You good with that?" he asked. "Your previous contracts were personal. This one isn't."

I looked back at the burning city across the monitors.

"I'm good."

"Then prove it." He stepped closer. "No mistakes. You make the plan. You observe. You embed if necessary. You do not rush. You do not improvise unless improvisation is the only option left."

"And if I abort?"

"Then you abort," he said. "And you explain why."

I nodded once.

"Timeline?"

"Open-ended," Gunny replied. "Which means the pressure belongs to you, not the clock."

I looked back at the photograph of Silas Pike.

Something about him bothered me. Not fear. Not respect. Recognition.

"He looks..."

Gunny's eyes narrowed. "Careful."

"...comfortable," I finished.

Gunny nodded slowly. "Good instinct." He stood and grabbed his towel. "Don't make me regret this, Rookie."

"Yes, sir."

Gunny turned away, already mentally moving on.

"One more thing."

I waited.

"Pack light," he said. "Arizona's hot."

I didn't go to a dealership.

That was rule one.

Dealerships asked questions. They wanted names, addresses, financing, and service plans. They smiled too much and remembered faces.

I needed something quieter.

Something that already had dust on it.

I took an Uber into town and stopped at a junk yard. I found the bike behind a corrugated metal shop on the edge of town—the kind of place that sold used tires, lawnmower blades, and whatever happened to fall off a truck last week.

There wasn't even a proper sign.

Just a crooked piece of plywood with OPEN painted across it in fading red letters.

The Victory sat out back beneath a sagging awning, blacked out so completely it looked like light slid off it instead of sticking.

An old 8-Ball.

No chrome worth mentioning.

Dark pipes scarred from heat.

Low handlebars.

A cracked solo seat that looked like it had suffered too much time under the desert sun.

Perfect.

The owner came out, wiping his hands on a rag that had probably never been clean.

Mid-fifties.

Sunburned.

Permanent squint.

He didn't introduce himself.

Neither did I.

"You ride?" he asked.

"Yes."

He nodded toward the bike.

"Ride that?"

I looked at the Victory.

"If it starts."

The man grunted and tossed me the key.

I thumbed the starter.

The engine caught after half a turn and settled into a low, uneven idle like it was clearing its throat after a long night.

The vibration rolled up through the frame and into my bones.

Heavy.

Honest.

No apology in it.

I swung a leg over and settled into the saddle.

The fit wasn't perfect.

That was fine.

Perfect was for people planning to keep things.

I eased the bike onto the service road and rolled the throttle just enough to feel how it carried itself.

Torque came on early and stayed with me.

Brakes felt solid.

No wobble.

No twitch.

The bike didn't want to dance.

It wanted to go.

I brought it back and killed the engine.

"What's wrong with it?" I asked.

The owner shrugged.

"Nothing that'll kill you quick."

Comforting.

"Buddy of mine dumped it six months ago," he continued. "Still in the hospital. After that, I kinda lost the taste for riding." He patted the seat. "Bike's solid, though. Won't let you down."

"I've never heard of Victory," I said. "Some kind of rice burner?"

That earned a short laugh.

"No. All-American. Polaris made 'em. Killed the brand so they could push Indian again." He shrugged. "Nobody builds bikes like this anymore."

"So Victory's dead."

"Yep."

"They still make parts?"

"You won't need 'em," he said. "Already fixed everything important. Just feed it gas and hold on."

I asked the price.

It came in lower than I expected.

"Why so generous?"

"I misplaced the title."

I nodded like that explained everything.

Which, honestly, it did.

I pulled a short stack of hundreds from my wallet and handed it over.

"You got any gear?" I asked. "Helmet, jacket, whatever."

I added two more bills to the pile.

"What size boots?"

A minute later, he returned with a battered leather jacket, gloves, a half-helmet, and a pair of riding glasses with foam around the lenses.

He handed me a scrap of paper with the VIN scribbled across it.

"There's your bill of sale. You should be able to get a replacement title."

I slipped the paper into my pocket and pulled on the gear.

Then we shook hands.

This time, when I settled into the saddle, the bike felt like it belonged under me.

I thumbed the starter.

The engine came alive with a low growl that felt almost conversational.

Hell yeah.

Let's go find a highway.

The owner stepped beside me holding the riding glasses.

"These'll keep the dust and bugs outta your eyes."

"I appreciate it."

I rolled into the street and kept things slow at first, letting the engine warm before asking anything from it.

By the time I reached the highway, the sun was dropping and the evening air had cooled enough to feel clean.

I rolled the throttle back hard.

The Victory surged forward.

I leaned and slipped past the rear bumper of the car ahead of me by inches. Wind clawed at my jacket as the engine roared beneath me. Seconds later, the car vanished into my mirrors like it had been parked.

"Hell yeah!" I yelled.

The wind stole the words before they finished leaving my mouth.

Somewhere in the back of my mind, a quiet voice suggested I should probably head back and let Gunny know I was leaving town.

That voice drowned beneath the roar of the pipes.

I blew past another car like it was tied to a post.

Wind tore at my beard.

An insect exploded against the lens of my riding glasses.

Then I spotted flashing blue lights in the mirror.

"Shit!"

The word barely carried over the wind.

Nabbed before I even escaped Chicago.

Gunny was going to kill me.

A cold finger crawled up my spine as I briefly wondered whether that was still just a figure of speech.

I'd been warned to stay invisible.

Running from the cops on a blacked-out motorcycle was pretty much the opposite of invisible.

The irony hit me a second later.

Had it really been that long since I was the one wearing the badge, chasing motorcycles across the Memphis bypass?

Up ahead, a highway sign flashed past.

Exit ramp.

Two miles.

I twisted the throttle harder.

The tail of my jacket snapped behind me like a cape.

Hero.

Villain.

Hard to say anymore.

I leaned hard into the exit ramp, slipping past a gray minivan as I bled speed.

Too much rear brake.

The back tire slid left.

I eased off instantly and pressed the right handlebar down harder.

The bike bit into the turn.

My heel scraped sparks off the pavement.

Then I snapped through the apex and came out clean.

Green light ahead.

I pumped the brakes once and whipped another hard right into a sleepy little town that looked like it locked its doors by nine o'clock.

I ducked behind the first building I saw and killed the engine.

Seconds later, the police cruiser blasted through the intersection with its siren screaming.

I grinned.

I dropped the kickstand and rested the helmet over the headlight.

I had successfully evaded the police by hiding behind an ice cream shop.

That deserved a reward.

Hot fudge.

Peanuts.

Possibly whipped cream if I was feeling reckless.

It hadn't even occurred to me till much later that I was truly happy on the bike. Something I hadn't felt in a very long time.

Inside the shop, a faded highway map covered one wall.

A thick orange line stretched all the way from Chicago to Los Angeles.

Route 66.

The Mother Road.

It called to something deep inside me.

My mission had officially begun, and Arizona was still a long way off.

That was all right.

The bike didn't seem to mind.

Chapter 5

Route 66 didn't care who I was or where I was going.

It offered me a respite from the rigors of life.

Chicago fell away in pieces, glass and brick thinning into grain silos, rusted water towers, and stretches of farmland that rolled toward the horizon forever. The road straightened, then bent again, like it was testing whether I was paying attention.

I learned its rhythm quickly.

Long empty runs.

Short forgotten towns.

Gas station coffee, ranging from exquisite gourmet blends to tepid water that could have gotten its color from a soggy crayon.

The Mother Road felt separate from the world around it, like its own living thing flowing beside modern America instead of through it.

Illinois was packed with traffic. Cars seemed personally offended by the sight of a motorcycle sharing the road with them. Drivers tailgated me within inches. Others drifted into my lane like I was invisible.

Eventually, self-preservation won out.

I abandoned the interstate and hunted down the old historic route instead, hiding there until I crossed the state line.

Missouri spotted me and shoved me right back into traffic near St. Louis.

Apparently, Illinois had taught the city how to treat bikers.

Cars pushed me toward semis. Semis pushed me toward guardrails. I split lanes through traffic and took the first exit I could find, disappearing into a maze of tangled side streets and one-way roads.

I circled the same block three times before I finally found my way west again.

Once I escaped the city, the landscape opened into endless green fields, and I settled back into the ride.

Technically, Route 66 clipped through Kansas.

It was a blink-and-you-miss-it kind of crossing.

I blinked.

Oklahoma was where the trip started changing.

The pressure of cities faded into long stretches of open country and dying towns left behind when the interstate moved a mile north and forgot they existed. Restaurants looked genuinely surprised when someone walked through the front door.

Service was enthusiastic.

The food usually involved hot dogs.

Texas announced itself loudly.

Everything got bigger.

The towns swelled wider, the skies stretched farther, and the restaurants competed to see who could serve the thickest steak. By the end of the state, I wouldn't have been surprised if a waitress led an entire cow to the table with a knife and fork strapped to its back.

Outside the cities, giant windmills covered the desert in every direction, their blades turning slow and steady against the horizon.

New Mexico felt abandoned.

Calling some of the places "towns" seemed generous. A few houses beside an ancient gas station didn't exactly qualify as civilization. Most of the buildings looked like they'd already accepted defeat and were simply waiting for the desert to reclaim them.

But the emptiness became beautiful after a while.

Massive plateaus rose from the earth like the graves of fallen titans. Sunlight painted the stone blood red during the day and deep purple at dusk.

Arizona felt different the second I crossed into it.

Older.

Wilder.

Hotter.

The historic road carried me through the Painted Desert, where the endless browns and grays suddenly exploded into streaks of red, blue, purple, and orange. Route 66 twisted through towering stone formations and empty wilderness so vast it felt untouched by time.

Wild burros wandered near the roadside—descendants of animals abandoned during the silver rush more than a century ago.

The desert had inherited them.

I rode until my hands buzzed long after the engine shut down.

I slept in shoebox motels with flickering neon signs outside the windows. I showered when I could and washed clothes in sinks when I couldn't.

The Victory took all of it without complaint.

Oil stayed where it belonged.

Bolts stayed tight.

Nothing rattled loose.

The bike felt less like a machine and more like a promise that had been satisfied.

At night, the desert cooled fast, and the stars came out sharp enough to cut you. I rode beneath them until my eyes burned and my leg reminded me it still wasn't healed.

I stopped when pain told me to stop.

Not before.

Every mile west stripped something off me.

The road had a way of sanding people down.

That nagging voice in the back of my mind had gone silent; the only noise was the wind in my ears.

Whatever I'd been when I started the ride was scattered somewhere behind me across gas stations, diners, and cheap motel rooms.

The moon hung high overhead when my headlight caught a weathered wooden sign beside the road.

WELCOME TO KINGMAN, ARIZONA

I'd arrived.

Every bone in my back ached as I rolled the bike into the gravel parking lot of a motel on the edge of town.

The building was simple beige stucco with faded trim and cracked sidewalks. The motel sign had been bleached almost white by decades of desert sun, but the red neon VACANCY still flickered stubbornly in the night.

That was good enough for me.

When I'd started the trip, there hadn't been many motorcycles on the road.

The farther west I rode, the more appeared.

By the time I rolled into the motel parking lot, there was only one car—a faded Honda old enough to qualify for social security—but more than a dozen bikes.

Something told me I was in the right place.

My neck popped as I swung off Beyoncé.

Yeah. I named the bike Beyoncé.

If you'd seen her ass, you'd understand.

I twisted side to side, enjoying the snap and crackle as my spine slowly came back to life, then headed toward the motel office.

A short Hispanic woman sat at a tiny table watching television near the counter. The bell above the door clanged when I entered.

She glanced up.

Then she met me at the desk.

"Hola. ¿Cómo estás?" she asked.

Her face looked carved from old leather, weathered by sun and hard years. Thick black hair hung in a braid that reached past her waist.

I couldn't tell if she was thirty or a hundred.

"Muy bueno," I replied, using up nearly my entire Spanish vocabulary.

Truthfully, I usually spoke better Spanish after a couple cervezas.

"I need a room."

She smiled politely.

"Cash or credit?"

I pulled my wallet free, the chain rattling against my belt loop.

"Cash," I said. "Be the resistance."

She tilted her head slowly.

I sighed.

"Sorry. My dad used to say that all the time."

"How much for one night?"

"Fifty dollars," she said. "You leave by noon."

"Fair enough."

I counted the bills onto the counter.

She climbed onto a small stool behind the desk and pulled down the last key hanging on the wall.

A cracked plastic tag dangled from it.

13 written in faded Sharpie.

"Room thirteen," she said. "Around the side."

"Thanks, Grandma."

Her eyes narrowed instantly.

"Grandma? I'm only thirty-five."

I turned back with a grin.

"Sorry. Your beauty dazzled me."

She snorted.

"Good recovery. Has that line ever worked before?"

I stepped back to the counter, gently took her hand, and lowered my head enough to kiss her knuckles.

"Not that line."

A slow smile spread across her face.

Dangerous smile.

The kind that suggested she'd stabbed at least one man in self-defense.

"All right," she said. "I forgive you this time. But don't let it happen again." She pointed at me. "Next time, it'll cost more than a kiss."

Then she flipped a switch behind the counter.

Outside, the red VACANCY sign buzzed once and went dark.

I glanced down at the key.

"If you need to discuss things further," I said, "I'll be in room thirteen."

She pointed toward the door without missing a beat.

"Go to sleep, cowboy."

I laughed and headed outside.

Beyoncé rumbled to life, and I idled around to the front of my room. My backpack came off the sissy bar and over my shoulder before I unlocked the door and stepped inside.

The light flicked on.

Three cockroaches immediately sprinted toward the bathroom like I'd interrupted a meeting.

Honestly, not the worst motel I'd stayed in.

I shut the door and dropped my bag onto the bed.

The shower knob squealed when I cranked the water hot. While it warmed up, I sat on the toilet and unlaced my boots, briefly appreciating the efficiency of accomplishing both tasks at once.

Even if it felt morally questionable.

Once the desert dust was finally washed off me, I started feeling human again.

Wrapped in a towel, I stepped back into the room and reached for the light switch.

Then I looked toward the bathroom.

I slowly withdrew my hand.

The lights stayed on.

I pulled back the covers, shoved a pillow over my face, and tried not to imagine cockroaches crawling across me in the middle of the night.

Eventually, exhaustion won.

I slept.

I woke late.

Not because I'd slept well but because my body had finally shut itself down.

The Arizona heat was already pressing against the motel room. I could feel it radiating through the door. Desert heat didn't rise. It waited. I peeked through the window; the motorcycles in the lot were still there. Different positions. Same count.

I cleaned up as best I could, pulled on dusty jeans and a fresh T-shirt, then rolled Beyoncé out of the lot.

First stop was gas.

Both the bike and I needed food.

I pulled into a mom-and-pop station with two ancient pumps sitting out front like museum pieces. Before I could even drop the kickstand, a tiny old man appeared from the doorway.

He was so short and thin I wondered if I'd wandered into some forgotten Lilliputian kingdom.

"Morning, young fella," he said, a toothpick hanging from the corner of his mouth. "Can I top off your tank?"

I nodded.

"Thanks, Pops. Fill her up."

I popped the gas cap, and he slipped the nozzle in. The pump rattled alive, honest-to-God spinning-number dials clicking as fuel flowed into the tank.

When it finished, he carefully pulled the nozzle free.

One drop of gasoline slipped toward the paint.

A wrinkled old hand darted out and caught it with a rag before it landed.

"Final total's eighteen fifty-two."

I handed him a twenty and waved off the change.

"You know anywhere around here I can get breakfast?"

His face split into a black, toothless grin.

"Miss Tilly runs the grill. Mile up the road on the right. Can't miss it."

He wasn't kidding.

The place looked like two old trailers welded together and wrapped in stainless steel. Like somebody had tried to build a diner out of a baked potato.

A line of dusty motorcycles sat along the side.

I eased Beyoncé in beside them.

Inside, the air smelled like bacon grease, coffee, and sugar.

My stomach immediately came back to life.

Country music drifted quietly from speakers mounted near the ceiling. Loud enough to cover chewing. Quiet enough for conversations.

A long bar stretched the length of the room.

About half the stools were occupied.

Every man wore a black leather vest with a skeletal hand flipping the world off.

Deadhand Dominion.

As I walked past them, conversations slowed.

Eyes followed me.

I stopped beside an open stool.

"Mind if I sit?"

The man nearest me looked carved from sunburnt leather. His white beard reached nearly to his belt buckle, and old tattoos crawled up both arms like faded roadmaps.

He glanced at the stool.

Then at me.

"Looks empty."

I sat.

A middle-aged waitress barely four feet tall appeared beside me like she'd teleported.

She dropped a mug in front of me and filled it with coffee.

"What can I get ya, sweetie?"

"What's good?"

"Billy makes a hell of a breakfast burrito. Put some meat on your bones."

"Sold."

I lifted the coffee and took a sip.

The brew hit my tongue like industrial solvent.

"Damn," I muttered. "You oughta issue a knife and fork with this stuff."

The old biker beside me barked out a laugh.

"Miss Tilly makes it that way on purpose," he said, sliding cream toward me. "Keeps people from camping on stools all day." He stuck out a hand. "I'm Bash. What brings you to our little slice of hell?"

I mixed cream into the mug and tried again.

Much better.

"Benji," I said, shaking his hand. "Just traveling. Needed a change of scenery."

"Benji, like the dog?"

"Yeah. Mom loved the movie. Swore I was named after her father Michael, but I've got my doubts."

Bash laughed again. "Where you coming from?"

"Chicago."

"Well, you're about as far from there as a man can get without swimming." He nodded toward the window. "What're you riding?"

"Old Victory 8-Ball."

His eyebrows lifted slightly.

"Nice bike."

"Had a Road Glide once," I said. "Lost damn near everything in a divorce. Figured I'd grab the first thing with two wheels and disappear for a while."

Bash nodded slowly. "Half the guys in this town got that same story. What about work? You carrying enough cash to survive California?"

"Enough to get there," I said. "Figure I'll sort the rest out later."

"Bad plan," Bash said immediately. "California'll bleed you dry, if the gangs don't get there first."

I raised an eyebrow.

"You offering career counseling?"

He smirked.

"I'm suggesting you stop by the clubhouse tonight. Have a beer. Meet some people. Somebody might need a hand."

The smile stayed on his face.

But his eyes stayed sharp.

"Arizona's not a bad place," he added. "If you can survive the heat."

Miss Tilly returned carrying two massive breakfast burritos, a bowl of salsa, and enough sour cream to patch a hole punched through drywall.

Bash rose from the stool and tossed a twenty onto the counter.

"His breakfast is on me." He clapped a hand onto my shoulder. "Take a look around town. Stop by the clubhouse around nine. I'll introduce you to the guys."

Then he headed for the door.

Two other club members followed after dropping cash beside their plates. Outside, they paused long enough to admire Beyoncé before mounting up and rolling out.

I cut into the burrito, dipped it in salsa, and took a bite.

Absolutely phenomenal.

After breakfast, I headed back to the motel and paid for the rest of the week.

The woman behind the counter smiled when she saw me.

"And if I stop by your room tonight?" she asked.

"I'd be a lucky man," I said, "but I might be out late. The motorcycle club invited me over."

Her smile faded slightly.

"Well," she said, "your loss."

She reached under the counter and slid a roach trap toward me.

"Some folks mentioned your room has a bug problem."

I picked up the trap.

"Appreciate it."

"And be careful around those Deadhand boys," she added. "Some of them can be dangerous."

I smiled. "You don't think I'm dangerous?"

"Honey," she said, leaning against the counter, "if you ever kiss my lips the way you kissed my hand, I know you're dangerous." Her smile widened. "And I can't wait to find out exactly how dangerous."

I gave her a wink and headed back toward my room.

Once my gear was secured, I spent the afternoon making a slow lap around Kingman.

Grocery store.

Discount department store.

Mechanic shops.

Bars.

Restaurants.

And, eventually, the clubhouse.

Kingman had everything a man needed to survive.

Nothing more.

By the time the temperature pushed into triple digits, I retreated back to the motel to wait out the worst of the heat.

Inside the room, I locked the door, sat on the edge of the bed, and pulled out my phone.

I sent Gunny a single text.

'In Kingman. First contact made.'

Chapter 6

I ROLLED OUT JUST before nine.

The heat had eased enough to breathe. The Arizona sky burned purple and orange as the sun finally surrendered to the horizon.

Beyoncé rumbled steadily beneath me, patient, like she already knew where we were headed.

The clubhouse sat outside town against a low rise of rock and scrub desert. No sign visible from the road. No lights beyond what they actually needed.

Just a long, low building made from corrugated steel and patched concrete, surrounded by chain-link fencing reinforced with scrap metal.

Motorcycles filled the gravel lot in loose rows.

Not neat.

Not sloppy.

Intentional chaos.

I parked where there was space and killed the engine. I stayed seated for a second, letting the sound settle naturally into the background.

Let the place notice me without feeling challenged by me.

A kid barely pushing twenty approached, swinging his arms too hard like he was trying to act relaxed and failing spectacularly at it. Acne crawled across his cheeks, and the hand not holding a beer rested carefully on the grip of a hunting knife strapped to his leg.

"Can I help you?" he asked.

His voice hadn't squeaked in a while, but it still hadn't fully committed to adulthood either.

"Evening," I said. "I'm Benji. Bash told me to stop by."

The kid visibly relaxed.

"Oh, yeah. Glad to have you." He pointed around the building. "You don't gotta worry about your bike. Me and Pizzaface are on watch tonight. We'll clean her up while you're inside."

I smiled. "You don't need to."

He glanced nervously over his shoulder.

"The brothers asked us to."

I waved a hand. "All right then. Have at it. Just don't get any ideas about another man's motorcycle."

The kid jumped backward half a step and raised his free hand.

"No, sir. We're just cleaning. I wouldn't touch another man's bike unless I was told."

"Fair enough."

Another teenager shuffled toward us carrying two buckets—one full of soapy water, the other packed with beer bottles buried in ice.

He looked even younger than the first one.

I nodded toward him.

"That Pizzaface?"

The first prospect grinned and stuck out his hand.

"Nah. I'm Zits."

I shook it, barely managing not to laugh.

"You boys have a good night."

As I walked away, I caught sight of the backs of their cuts.

No three-piece patch.

Just a single rocker stitched across the bottom.

PROSPECT.

The side door stood propped open. Rock music spilled into the night loud enough to vibrate the gravel under my boots.

Painted on both sides of the building was the club logo—a skeletal hand with its middle finger raised toward the world.

Classy.

Inside smelled like sweat, motor oil, stale beer, and questionable food.

The clubhouse was gloriously disorganized, while everything was properly in its place.

Pool tables crowded one side of the room. Old biker posters and photos of naked women draped across motorcycles covered the walls. Tables were scattered everywhere, packed with leather-clad men and women wearing considerably less.

"Hey, friend. Have we met?"

A mountain of a man blocked the doorway.

His beard and hair merged into one enormous red mane, and his shoulders looked wide enough to bench-press motorcycles. The patch on his vest read:

SERGEANT AT ARMS

I'd never seen anyone more physically qualified for a job title.

"Yeah," I said. "Bash invited me over."

"One second." He turned toward the crowd and barked, "Billy! Go find Bash. Tell him his guest made it."

Billy disappeared instantly into the sea of bodies.

The giant turned back toward me.

"Shouldn't take long. Saw him a minute ago." He stuck out a hand. "Name's Bear."

"Benji."

"Benji?" He frowned. "Sounds like that little dog from the movies."

I shook his hand.

My entire arm disappeared into his grip.

"Yeah," I said. "I've heard that once or twice."

Before Bear could respond, Bash appeared beside us carrying a grin and a fresh beer.

"There he is," Bash said. "Thanks, Bear. Met him over at Miss Tilly's this morning. Figured I'd show him around."

Bear released my hand without permanently damaging it.

"Well," he said, "if you stick around long enough, we'll probably find you a better road name."

Bash slapped my shoulder.

"Come on. Let's get you a drink."

He guided me toward the bar.

Behind it stood a younger guy wearing a black vest with a PROSPECT patch stitched onto the front. Bash held up two fingers.

Two beers appeared.

I looked around the room.

"How many prospects do you guys have?" I asked. "There were two outside trying to detail my bike when I rolled in."

Bear leaned against the bar beside me.

"Those were the Acne Brothers," he said. "Bartender's Scotch. Got a few more running around too. We're recruiting heavy right now." He glanced around proudly. "Good timing on your part."

Over the next couple hours, I met more of the club.

Switchblade.

Clubfoot.

Roadrunner.

Dusty.

Chip.

Half a dozen others whose names immediately collided in my skull and died there.

Faces came easy.

Names took time.

The beers never stopped.

Every time my bottle got low, another magically appeared in my hand.

Dangerous system.

A stunt like that nearly got me killed once in Mexico.

This time, I kept my beer half full whenever possible. I mimed drinking when people watched and only finished bottles when it mattered socially.

Nobody noticed.

Which meant I was finally learning.

At one point, one of the brothers ordered a round of shots.

A glass got shoved into my hand before I could object.

I tossed the whiskey into my mouth, then quietly spat it into my beer while everyone else drank. A second later, the overloaded bottle made its way to a nearby table and 'accidentally' got knocked over.

Nobody noticed.

A little after midnight, one of the patched members leaned close and murmured something into Bash's ear.

Bash nodded and stood.

"Benji," he said, "you good to ride?"

"Yeah," I replied. "I can ride."

I set my beer aside and followed him outside.

The cold desert air hit me like a wet towel. Sweat still clung to my back beneath the leather, and the sudden chill sent a shiver crawling up my spine.

I took a few slow breaths while crossing the lot toward Beyoncé.

The cold helped clear my head.

Bash swung onto his bike and brought the engine roaring to life. I followed suit, easing the throttle just enough to wake the pipes without making a scene.

The third member of our little convoy—Switchblade, I was pretty sure—climbed onto the back of Bash's bike with a beer still clutched in one hand.

Bash rolled out first.

I followed him into the darkness.

We left town behind quickly and turned onto a narrow road twisting through scrub desert and low hills. Up ahead, Bash suddenly killed his engine and coasted.

I matched him immediately, thumbing the kill-switch and rolling silently alongside him.

We tucked the bikes behind a patch of scrub brush overlooking a small trailer park.

Maybe a dozen trailers sat in two uneven rows. One weak yellow light hung from a telephone pole in the center, barely illuminating the middle units while the outer edges disappeared into darkness.

Switchblade moved first.

He crossed the desert in a crouched sprint.

"What's going on?" I asked quietly.

"You watch left," Bash said, pulling a pistol from inside his vest. "I watch right. If something moves that shouldn't, tap my shoulder."

"What's the job?"

"Switchblade is borrowing a car," Bash replied. "Owner won't miss it till morning."

That told me everything I needed to know.

I nodded and settled beside him.

Switchblade slipped along the far edge of the nearest trailer and dropped beside a sedan parked in the shadows.

I scanned the area. Windows. Doorways. Movement. A television flickered behind cheap curtains. Somewhere farther back in the park, a dog barked once before deciding life wasn't worth the effort.

Switchblade eased the driver-side door open.

The interior light flashed on.

He leaned inside, jammed a screwdriver beneath the steering column, and cracked it once with a hammer. Too easy. He slid behind the wheel. The engine turned over.

Then everything exploded at once.

A trailer door slammed open.

A heavyset man stumbled outside, wearing only shorts and carrying a pistol.

"Shit," I whispered, slapping Bash's shoulder and pointing.

"Hey!" the man shouted as the sedan jerked backward. "Get out of—"

Bash moved before the sentence finished.

His pistol barked three times.

The rounds slammed into the dirt beside the trailer, spraying gravel and sparks into the air.

The man froze instantly, trying to find the shooter in the dark.

Bash never yelled.

Never threatened.

He calmly fired one more round into the dirt.

Message received.

The man scrambled backward so fast he tripped over his own feet before vanishing inside his trailer. The door slammed hard enough to rattle the windows.

The stolen sedan dropped into drive and tore onto the road in a spray of gravel.

"Let's move," Bash said.

We mounted up and rolled out clean behind Switchblade.

No sirens.

No screaming neighbors.

No gunfight.

Back at the clubhouse, the bikes slid into their original spots like nothing had happened.

Switchblade drove the sedan into an open garage bay. As the headlights swept past me, I caught sight of a sticker stretched across the trunk.

Two giant marijuana leaves beside three smaller ones.

Apparently, someone was using weed plants to count family members.

I could only imagine how well that worked at elementary school pickup.

Why do they have trees on their car?

Billy says those mean they smoke weed.

Why was Jenny's dad smoking from a soda can?

The garage door rolled shut behind the sedan.

Whatever guilt I might've felt about stealing the car evaporated instantly.

Bash turned toward me and pressed two folded hundred-dollar bills into my hand.

"Good job," he said. "We appreciate the help."

I glanced at the cash.

"Easy money," I said. "Nobody got hurt."

"That's usually the goal," Bash replied. "Most nights."

Inside, the party had never slowed down.

Music blasted from the speakers.

Beer bottles clinked together.

Women laughed somewhere near the pool tables.

I grabbed another beer and leaned against the wall, quietly watching the room.

After a while, Bash wandered over carrying two fresh bottles and handed me one.

I drained the beer I already had and set the empty bottle onto a nearby table.

Bash studied me for a second.

"So," he said, "now that you've had time to think about it... What'd you think?"

I shook my head slightly, clearing the fog while Gunny's lessons replayed themselves in the back of my mind.

Everyone needs a reason for what they do.

Give them one they can believe.

So I gave Bash my story.

Not the truth.

But something close enough to wear its skin.

It wasn't even a year ago that everything looked different.

I had a family.

A steady job.

A future that didn't look like it was circling the drain.

I worked construction.

There were maybe twenty-five of us renovating the inside of an old three-story factory. The exterior was finished, but inside, we were still framing walls, running conduit, plumbing, and HVAC.

I was on the third floor pulling electrical conduit when the foreman called everybody together.

That alone told us something was wrong.

Then he walked in with a dozen cops.

That's when the room went quiet.

The owner of the company was dying. His wife had sold everything—contracts, trucks, tools, inventory, all of it—to another construction company.

We stood there stunned, waiting for the next shoe to drop.

When it finally did, it crushed us.

The new company already had crews.

They didn't need us.

I still remember the feeling.

Like getting hit in the chest with a sledgehammer.

I bent over with one hand on my knee, trying to process it. Nobody had savings anymore. Hell, most of us were one missed paycheck away from drowning.

Then came the rest.

They were withholding our final checks "to ensure a peaceful transition."

That was why the cops were there.

Before I realized it, my hand had already drifted toward the hammer hanging off my toolbelt.

I shouted something.

Honestly, I don't even remember what.

One of the officers hit me with a taser before I got another word out.

My whole body locked up.

It felt like somebody plugged my spine directly into a wall outlet. I hit the concrete hard enough to crack my teeth together and lay there twitching while black spots swam across my vision.

When the electricity finally stopped, I could breathe again, but my legs wouldn't work.

One of the other guys helped drag me upright.

Half a dozen more workers were already on the ground.

Somebody grabbed my arm and marched me toward the stairs before I'd even gotten my balance back. I was halfway outside before I realized I'd dropped my hammer upstairs.

The foreman told me there was no way in hell I was going back in to get it.

I climbed into my truck and drove home.

I didn't really have anywhere else to go.

The drive usually took about three hours.

My wife's car was already sitting in the driveway when I pulled up.

She worked in corporate real estate. No regular schedule. No guaranteed hours. I sat behind the steering wheel, staring at the house and trying to figure out how to tell her we were about to survive on her paycheck alone.

The only good part was that it was Thursday.

The kids stayed late at school for tutoring on Thursdays.

Eventually, I forced myself out of the truck and went inside.

Three steps through the front door, I knew.

Her dress hung over the back of the couch.

A man's jacket lay beside it.

Her panties were tangled in the hallway.

A pair of men's jeans sat kicked against the wall.

I opened the bedroom door.

She was on top of him in our bed.

That's when something inside me snapped.

Neither of them even heard me come in. The bedroom door was at the foot of the bed.

I grabbed her by the hair and yanked her off him.

She screamed when she hit the floor.

My hand reached automatically for my hammer.

It wasn't there.

Honestly, that's probably the only reason I'm not still sitting in prison.

The guy scrambled backward across the mattress, trying to get away. I caught him by the ankle and dragged him off the bed hard enough to shake the floor.

I hit him once.

Then again.

Then I just kept going.

He was talking.

Begging, maybe.

Didn't matter.

Blood sprayed across the wall. His nose collapsed. Teeth scattered across the floor.

I would've killed him.

I know that now.

The only reason I stopped was because the lights went out.

Next thing I remember, I woke up face-down on the carpet with a cop's knee grinding into my spine.

My wrists were cuffed so tight my hands went numb.

It took two officers to drag me out to the cruiser because I kept fighting the entire way.

They left me in a holding cell overnight.

The next morning, I got stitched up.

Cuts.

Bruises.

Minor concussion.

Apparently, my wife managed to convince everybody she was the victim in all of it. I didn't exactly help myself. I spent most of the morning screaming at anyone who got close enough to hear me.

The court gave me nine months for assault.

My final week inside, my wife showed up carrying divorce papers.

She wanted everything.

Custody.

The house.

The accounts.

Even my parental rights.

If I signed immediately, I walked away with ten thousand dollars cash.

Her lawyer assured me it was perfectly legal.

That was the carrot.

The stick was worse.

If I refused, she'd still divorce me, still take the kids, and bury me under enough child support and alimony that I'd never recover financially.

So I signed.

When I got released, her lawyer was waiting outside the gate with an envelope full of cash.

I spent six grand on the bike.

The rest I burned on the road.

I opened my wallet and thumbed through the cash inside.

"With the two hundred you gave me, I've got just under a grand left," I told Bash. "After the kind of year I've had, helping a brother borrow an old sedan doesn't exactly keep me up at night."

Bash barked out a laugh and slapped me on the shoulder hard enough to jolt me sideways.

"Yeah," he said. "Like I told you—half the men in this place could tell the same damn story."

He whistled and held up two fingers.

Scotch appeared at the table a moment later, carrying two fresh beers and a pair of whiskey shots balanced carefully in his hands. He set them down without interrupting whatever conversation he was half-listening to behind him.

I picked up my beer and drained half of it in one pull. Telling the story had left my throat raw.

Bash watched me for a second, his expression thoughtful now instead of amused.

"Unless you've got other plans," he said, "meet me at Miss Tilly's tomorrow. Around eleven. I wanna talk business."

I nodded slowly. "What kind of business?"

He tipped his bottle toward the bar.

"Till then, relax. Beer's on the club tonight. If you need a place to crash, shove a couple chairs together." He paused. "There're some people I need to talk to first, but I think we can find a use for you around here."

"A use?" I asked.

Bash grinned.

"Don't worry," he said. "We ain't putting you behind the bar or making you wash bikes."

"That's a relief."

His grin widened slightly.

"I've got something else in mind." He tossed back the rest of his beer and stood. "We'll talk tomorrow."

Then he disappeared into the chaos of the clubhouse, leaving me alone with my drink, the music, and the uncomfortable realization that the deeper I went undercover, the easier it was pretending I belonged there.

Chapter 7

For the first time in weeks, my leg wasn't the most pissed-off part of my body.

My head felt like it was trapped in a mechanic's vise—cold steel jaws squeezing from both sides, pressure building behind my eyes threatening to launch them out of my face, like my skull might split open at any second. My mouth tasted like someone had stuffed it full of old cotton socks.

I cracked my eyes open and found myself slumped in the corner of a bar that looked like the official welcoming station for a one-way trip to hell.

Disco lights spun lazily overhead, washing skeletal hands—each flipping the world off—between grinning skulls with glowing red eyes. Thankfully, the only sound came from a handful of men snoring in different corners of the room. A couple of them sounded like motorcycles with bad mufflers.

I took a slow breath and instantly regretted it.

The air was thick with stale beer, piss, cigarette smoke, and old vomit. I braced a hand against the wall and forced myself upright.

Behind the bar, a glowing digital clock informed the world it was almost ten in the morning.

I leaned heavily on chairs as I worked my way toward it. Sitting in the center of the bar was a serving tray holding a giant bottle of aspirin, a half-empty bottle of whiskey, and several beers floating in a bucket of melted ice water.

Civilization.

I twisted the cap off the aspirin, dry-swallowed four of them, then chased the chalky mess with cold beer.

Fragments of the night drifted through my head in disconnected flashes. Loud music. Too many drinks. Someone cheering. A dangerous level of comfort.

That part bothered me.

If I stayed undercover with Deadhand Dominion, drinking was part of the act. But there was a fine line between pretending to fit in and forgetting why I was there.

I vaguely remembered kissing a woman.

That mystery got partially solved when I checked my back pocket and came up holding a lacy black bra.

I stared at it for a long moment.

No face came with it. No name. No memory beyond a flash of perfume and someone laughing near my ear.

"Outstanding work, Shepard," I muttered.

I stuffed the bra back into my pocket just as my brain reminded me I was supposed to meet Bash for breakfast.

I checked the clock again.

Three minutes later than the last time I looked.

The thing glared at me with judgmental red numbers. I glared back, waved it off, and staggered toward the exit.

The Arizona sun hit me like a shotgun blast.

I recoiled, one hand going to my forehead as heat and light drilled straight through my skull. I leaned against the front wall of the clubhouse and concentrated on breathing until my vision steadied.

The parking lot had thinned out overnight. Most of the bikes were gone.

Beyoncé sat alone near the edge of the lot, angled just right, glaring at me in silent disappointment.

"Don't start," I muttered.

I swung onto the bike and sank into the seat with a groan. My riding glasses were still hooked over the throttle where I always left them.

At least drunk-me had some standards.

I winced when I thumbed the starter, but Beyoncé's low growl didn't stab fresh nails into my skull, so I counted that as mercy.

I rode back to the motel, took the hottest shower the plumbing could manage, and sent Gunny a short text before heading back out.

'Inside clubhouse. No sign of Silas.'

Clean, shaved, and almost human again, I rolled into Miss Tilly's around quarter after eleven.

Bash was already there, one empty stool waiting beside him.

I slid into it and raised a hand toward the counter.

"Couple breakfast burritos," I said. "And whatever passes for coffee around here."

Miss Tilly poured from the same scorched pot of black sludge and slid the mug toward me.

"Morning," Bash said. "Have a good time last night?"

I took a sip and immediately regretted it.

"Yeah," I grunted. "Little fuzzy around the edges. Was I with a girl?"

Bash barked out a laugh and slapped me between the shoulders.

"That'd be Bucktooth Sally," he said. "But you better call her Sally Sweet Cheeks around the clubhouse unless you wanna hurt her feelings."

"I may need you to point her out next time."

"Don't worry," he said. "She'll find you."

I took another sip of coffee and felt something crunch between my teeth.

Grounds.

I paused mid-swallow.

"Damn," I said carefully, "that coffee is—"

I stopped when Miss Tilly glanced our way from behind the grill.

Bash leaned closer. "Secret is getting here early," he whispered. "She doesn't empty the filter between pots. Just keeps adding more coffee on top."

I stared at him.

"What?"

He grinned.

"She dumps it eventually. Like coffee roulette. Only five chambers loaded."

I picked a chunk of grounds out from between my teeth.

"Miss Tilly," I called, "could I get a water?"

"'Course, sweetheart."

The water arrived with my burritos.

While I ate, Bash chatted with another biker sitting on his far side—a guy I didn't recognize from the night before. I mostly kept quiet and concentrated on surviving breakfast.

When I finally finished, I dropped a ten on the counter and followed Bash outside.

Near the edge of the lot, away from the windows, he handed me a thick envelope.

"What's this?" I asked.

"A job," Bash said. "Address is inside. I want that place to go away. If you can make it look natural, even better. Cash and anything you find inside is yours."

I looked up from the envelope.

"Make sure nobody's home," he added. "Nobody gets hurt."

That mattered.

I weighed the envelope in my hand for a second, then folded it and slid it into my pocket.

"You sure about this?" Bash asked.

"I've got it," I said.

He nodded once. "When it's done, stop by the club."

Message received.

Getting back inside the clubhouse depended on burning down a house.

I stopped at a thrift store on the edge of town and bought a black hoodie and a pair of cheap work gloves. Nothing unusual about that. At least that's what I silently projected at the cashier while she took my money.

Come to think of it, she never rang anything into the register.

No receipt either.

That somehow made me feel worse.

I headed back to the motel and tossed the clothes onto the chair beside the bed. The job needed darkness, and darkness was still hours away.

That gave me time for the other problem.

Gunny.

His number wasn't saved in my phone. None of them were. Even the text chain disappeared after every message exchange. Part of the system. No loose ends. No records.

I dialed the number from memory.

The phone rang twice before a woman answered with a cheerful recorded voice.

"You have reached RCA Television Repair. Our business hours are Monday through Friday, nine a.m. to three p.m. If you would like a return call from one of our technicians, please leave your name and number after the tone."

I frowned at the phone.

Had I screwed up the number?

Or worse—had I remembered it wrong from the beginning?

I mentally retraced every text I'd sent since arriving in Kingman. Nothing too detailed. Nothing openly incriminating.

Still.

The beep sounded.

"Sorry," I muttered. "Wrong number."

I hung up and checked the call log.

Same number.

"Fantastic," I said to the empty room. "I'm stranded in Arizona with bikers, arson homework, and no backup."

The phone rang in my hand.

I answered immediately. "Hello?"

"This is RCA Television Repair."

This time, I recognized the voice beneath the act.

"Gunny?"

"Yes, Rookie," he said. "Everything all right? Give me a report."

For the next two hours, I walked him through everything.

Meeting Bash at Miss Tilly's.

The clubhouse.

The stolen car.

The prospects.

The test.

And finally, the envelope sitting on the motel nightstand waiting for me to decide whether or not I was willing to burn down a stranger's home for a motorcycle club.

When I finished, Gunny was quiet for a moment.

"It's a loyalty check," he said finally. "They need something with your fingerprints on it. Something they can hold over your head if they need leverage later."

"You think they'll be watching?"

"I'd bet money on it," he replied. "Wouldn't surprise me if they record the whole thing."

"Comforting."

"Wake up, Rookie," Gunny said. "We kill bad people for money. Compared to assassination, arson barely registers."

I leaned back against the motel wall and rubbed a hand across my face.

"Still feels different."

"That's because you can picture the family that lives there," he said. "You're emotionally attaching to a target you've never seen." He paused. "If you're conflicted, walk away now. I'll find another route into the club. But based on what you've told me, I don't see a problem."

I looked over at the envelope again.

"You think this gets me closer to Preacher?"

"Yes."

That answer came too fast to question.

I sighed.

"Haven't put eyes on him yet," I admitted. "There's a backroom at the clubhouse. Full-patch members only. If he's around, that's where he stays."

"Then you need inside that room," Gunny said. "And right now, this is the tollbooth."

I hated that he was probably right.

"Understood."

Gunny's voice softened slightly.

"You're doing fine, Rookie. Better than Memphis."

That surprised me enough I didn't answer immediately.

"Whatever you decide," he continued, "I'll be waiting for your next report."

"Thanks, Gunny."

I ended the call and tossed the phone onto the bed.

Outside, the Arizona sun hung high and merciless over Kingman.

I closed the curtains, darkening the room, then stretched out on top of the covers with one arm across my eyes.

The envelope sat on the nightstand beside me like a ticking bomb.

Waiting for sunset was harder than I expected.

When the first stars arrived in the darkened sky, it was almost a relief.

The waiting was nearly over.

That didn't mean I'd decided what I was going to do.

I'd mapped the drive to the address a dozen times while lying awake in the motel bed, staring at the ceiling and listening to the air conditioner struggle for its life. Every turn. Every mile marker. Every possible exit if things went bad.

I pulled on the black hoodie and gloves, then stepped outside and climbed onto Beyoncé.

Bash never called it arson.

He handed me the address like it was a favor and said, "Make the address go away."

No explanation.

No justification.

That was the justification.

I rode fifteen miles out of town before turning onto an unmarked dirt track I'd never have noticed if I hadn't been looking for it. The trail twisted another mile through scrub and rock before the trailer finally appeared at the end of it.

It squatted alone in the desert like something abandoned by the rest of the world.

Windblown trash had piled up against the base where the scrub pressed close, like the desert itself was trying to bury the place. I killed the engine and turned the bike around so it faced back toward the road.

Always leave facing the exit.

Beyoncé stood silent against the empty desert, black paint swallowing what little moonlight there was.

There wasn't a damn thing nearby tall enough to hide behind, so I approached on foot.

The trailer's aluminum skin was blistered and scarred from years of heat and neglect. Any paint it once had was long gone. One window glowed dim yellow through greasy plastic sheeting taped over the frame. Somewhere behind the building, a generator rattled and coughed.

The smell hit before I reached the door.

Chemical sweet mixed with rot.

Burned candy and cat piss.

Meth lab.

That answered enough questions for me.

I slowed my breathing and circled wide around the structure.

Behind the trailer sat a dumpster collapsing under the weight of garbage. Empty blister packs. Torn-open cold medicine boxes. Rotting fast-food bags. No vehicles nearby. No voices. No movement besides the generator shaking itself apart.

Still, I treated the place like a tiger's den.

The back door was chained shut, but one quick tug told me the chain was mostly decoration. I left it alone and moved to the side window instead, peeling back the plastic sheeting just enough to look inside.

The place was a disaster.

Plywood tables balanced on sawhorses. Buckets of chemicals. Glassware. Rubber tubing. A hotplate humming quietly near the center of the room. A filthy mattress shoved into the corner, stained dark from years of supporting unwashed bodies.

Beside it sat a revolver.

Then the feeling hit me.

That crawling itch between the shoulder blades.

The old instinct.

I'd felt it a handful of times back when I wore a badge. The kind of feeling that shows up right before somebody points a gun at your head.

Someone was watching me.

I moved slowly, easing one hand into my pocket and pulling out the folding knife. The blade snapped open with a metallic click that sounded deafening in the desert silence.

I turned inch by inch, scanning the darkness.

Nothing.

Then something shifted inside the dumpster.

I stepped toward it carefully. Left hand reaching for the lid. Right hand bringing the knife up.

The metal lid shrieked when I shoved it aside.

A blur exploded upward.

I jerked backward as a skinny raccoon launched itself out of the trash and tore past me into the darkness, ringed tail vanishing around the trailer.

I let out a slow breath.

"Fantastic," I muttered. "Now there's a meth raccoon out there somewhere plotting revenge."

So much for stealth.

If anyone had been nearby, they definitely heard that.

No point wasting more time.

I kicked the back door hard enough to rip the chain loose and stepped inside carefully, picking my way around the clutter.

Meth labs don't forgive mistakes.

The revolver beside the mattress turned out to be a massive .357 Magnum. Heavy enough to use as a hammer if you ran out of bullets.

I tucked the knife away and picked up the pistol instead.

Loaded.

Of course it was.

I slid it into my waistband while a dozen *Dirty Harry* quotes floated through my head. For half a second, I almost wished someone else was here just so I could use one.

The search didn't take long.

No money worth taking. No drugs I wanted touching my skin.

Just poison.

The fire needed to look accidental.

Electrical.

Chemical.

Something caused by stupid people doing stupid things.

Near the kitchenette, an extension cord ran beneath a filthy rug to power the hotplate. One section of insulation had already split open, exposing frayed copper wires.

Perfect.

I nudged the exposed strands together just enough to create heat without an immediate spark, then pulled the rug back over the cord and shoved a plastic chair leg down on top of it.

That was all it needed.

I didn't use accelerant.

Didn't have to.

Outside, I unplugged the generator and counted slowly to ten before plugging it back in.

Inside the trailer, the hotplate hummed back to life.

I walked away.

Halfway back to the bike, the trailer gave a low coughing sound, followed by the sharp crack of popping glass.

Then came a muffled whump.

Orange light bloomed through the filthy windows, brighter than fire had any right to be.

Chemistry.

I climbed onto Beyoncé and rolled back toward the highway just as flames punched through the roof seam.

By the time I reached the pavement, black smoke was clawing upward into the desert sky, thick enough to swallow the stars.

When I got back to the clubhouse, Bash didn't ask for details.

He studied me for a long moment instead, eyes searching my face for hesitation.

For guilt.

For weakness.

He didn't find any.

"That place was poison," he said.

"Not anymore," I replied.

Bash nodded once.

"Good," Bash said. "Preacher likes clean work."

It was the first time I'd heard the name spoken out loud.

Preacher.

Not a rumor. Not a patch in the background. Not a shadow behind a closed door.

Real.

And hearing it felt like crossing a finish line, even though the real work had not yet begun.

Bash grabbed a bottle from the table and poured whiskey into a glass already half-full.

Always the optimist.

"No beer tonight, Hammer," he said. "Tonight, we celebrate."

I frowned. "Hammer?"

Bash grinned, dark tobacco staining the edges of his gums.

"Your road name," he said. "I was listening to your story. That hammer back in Chicago?" He tapped the table with one thick finger. "It brought you to us."

He stepped back and reached behind his chair.

When he turned around, he was holding a black leather vest.

Simple. Broken in. Real.

On the back sat a bottom rocker.

PROSPECT.

"Your cut," Bash said. "Welcome to the brotherhood."

For half a second, nobody moved.

Then chairs scraped backward all around the room.

Men stood.

Hands crashed against my shoulders and back hard enough to rattle my teeth. Voices called out my new name from every direction.

"Hammer!"

"'Bout damn time!"

"Get this man a drink!"

Whiskey splashed into my hand. Someone shoved a bottle at me from another direction. Women pressed close, perfume mixing with sweat, smoke, leather, and beer.

The clubhouse tightened around me—not hostile.

Not soft either.

Accepting.

And that was the dangerous part.

I slipped the cut on slowly.

The leather settled across my shoulders with surprising weight. Not physically heavy.

Permanent heavy.

The room erupted again when the patch settled into place.

"Hammer!"

I raised the whiskey glass because it seemed expected.

Because Hammer would.

The burn hit hard on the way down, warm enough to blur the edges of the room for a second.

Across the clubhouse, Bear nodded once from beside the pool table.

Scotch lifted a beer in salute behind the bar.

Even the prospects looked at me differently now.

Not outside anymore.

Inside.

Bash leaned close enough that only I could hear him.

"Enjoy tonight," he said quietly. "Tomorrow, you start earning it."

Then he slapped my shoulder and disappeared into the chaos.

I stood there in the middle of the noise and smoke with the cut hanging from my shoulders and realized something that bothered me more than the fire ever had.

Being accepted felt good.

Way too good.

Chapter 8

I WOKE BACK IN my motel room as a thin sliver of sunlight forced its way between the curtains—just enough illumination to explain the damage from the night before.

I wasn't getting my security deposit back.

A lamp lay shattered in the corner. The small table had been overturned. One chair was missing a leg entirely. Blankets and sheets hung from furniture and light fixtures like flags of surrender. The mattress sat halfway off the frame, and one of those cheap landscape paintings motels buy in bulk had been ripped clean down the middle.

I was naked except for my leather cut.

And a black bra covered in glitter dangled from my wrist like some kind of war trophy.

I leaned over the mattress and spotted Bucktooth Sally sprawled beside it, asleep and gloriously unconscious. Mascara streaked down her face, mixing with smeared lipstick until she looked like a televangelist who'd lost a custody battle with a raccoon.

I slid down beside her and let my hand drift along her side.

That earned a sleepy giggle.

She caught my wrist and shoved my hand lower.

Apparently, chaos hadn't finished with us yet.

I leaned forward and kissed the back of her neck.

A knock hit the motel door.

I froze.

Sally groaned into the mattress.

"You're not leaving me here like this, are you?" she asked.

"I might have to." I rolled away from her warm body with a groan of my own. "It could be one of the brothers. Bash told me prospects stay available twenty-four/seven."

Crossing the room turned into an obstacle course.

I stepped over the dresser, narrowly missed crushing the television lying face-down on the floor, shoved a chair aside with my foot, and grabbed a pillow to preserve what little dignity I had left before cracking open the door.

Arizona heat rolled in immediately.

A woman in khaki housekeeping clothes stood beside a cleaning cart, digging through towels. A thick black braid streaked with gray hung down her back.

"Housekeeping," she said in a heavy accent.

Then she looked past me into the room.

"¿Santa Madre de Dios..." Her eyes widened.

"Uh," I said intelligently. "No housekeeping today."

"How about towels?" Sally called from somewhere behind me.

Her head popped up over the edge of the mattress like a prairie dog emerging from a very questionable burrow.

I nodded quickly.

"Yeah. Towels would be great."

The housekeeper grabbed a thick stack without looking away from the disaster behind me and shoved them into my arms.

The sparkly bra still dangled from my wrist.

"Thank you," I said. "Have a nice day."

I shut the door before she could answer.

"Good news," I announced. "Not the brothers. Just housekeeping."

"All right then," Sally purred. "Throw the towels down and come ravage me."

The towels hit the floor.

"Yes, ma'am."

I launched myself back toward the mattress.

Sally somehow rolled me mid-flight and ended up on top when we hit. We crashed through blankets and pillows, bounced off the mattress, and nearly took out the remains of the lamp all over again.

By the time the sun started leaning toward evening, Sally finally pushed herself upright and planted a hand against my chest.

Sweat plastered her hair to her cheeks. Whatever makeup she'd started with had long since surrendered.

"You know what we need?" she asked.

My brain was barely operational.

"Huh?"

"Chili cheeseburgers."

I nodded immediately. "Absolutely."

I started to stand, but she hopped onto my back and smacked my ass hard enough to echo.

I carried her through the wreckage of the motel room while she laughed loud enough to wake the dead.

The shower afterward felt holy.

We washed road dust, sweat, and bad decisions off each other while the motel plumbing fought for survival. When the hot water finally gave out, we climbed out dripping and started searching for clothes.

Most of mine were still piled safely on the dresser.

Sally's wardrobe situation was less successful.

The only thing we found was the sparkly black bra.

"It's fine," she said. "My room's on the way to the clubhouse."

Wrapped in a towel and carrying the bra like a flag of victory, she marched outside.

To be honest, that almost started the whole process over again.

Parked outside the room sat an old mud-covered Jeep.

Sally slid behind the wheel and patted the passenger seat.

"Get in, big boy. I'm starving."

"Hold up," I said, climbing in beside her. "I should probably stop by the office first. Make sure the manager's not planning to murder me over the room."

Wearing nothing but a towel, Sally pressed the clutch with one bare foot, slammed the Jeep into gear, and hit the gas.

The towel climbed steadily higher as we bounced across the parking lot until it wasn't really covering much of anything anymore.

By the time we stopped at the office, I was breathing harder than I cared to admit.

Inside sat the same tiny Hispanic woman who'd checked me in.

"Evening," I began.

She looked up—and instantly straightened.

"Oh. Good evening." Her eyes dropped to my cut. "I didn't realize you were with the club."

I glanced down at the leather vest.

"Oh. Yeah. Got patched in last night."

Her entire posture changed.

"Well...congratulations."

"Thanks," I said slowly. "Anyway, housekeeping stopped by earlier and—"

"It won't happen again," she interrupted immediately.

I blinked.

"When you leave the room, just let me know," she continued quickly. "We'll clean while you're gone. You won't be disturbed again."

"Right," I said. "Well...the room's pretty wrecked."

"There's no problem."

"No, seriously. I broke the television."

"We'll handle it."

I frowned.

"And the furniture."

"No problem."

"The wall art literally exploded."

She smiled nervously. "We'll take care of everything."

Something had definitely shifted.

"Would you like us to wash your clothes while you're out tonight?" she asked quickly.

"Huh?"

"We have to wash the sheets anyway."

"Uh...sure?"

"Of course," she said. "And again, I'm very sorry you were interrupted earlier."

"Yeah," I said slowly. "No problem."

I backed out of the office and climbed into the Jeep.

Sally pulled away from the curb before I had the door fully shut.

"That was weird," I said.

"What happened?"

"The manager treated me like I was famous or something. She offered to repair the room and do my laundry."

Sally reached over and tugged lightly on the edge of my cut.

"That's because you are famous now," she said. "Welcome to the club."

She pulled up outside a small brick apartment building and killed the engine.

"Be right back."

She kissed me hard enough to leave me dizzy, then disappeared inside.

A few minutes later, she came back out wearing skin-tight jeans and a bright red tube top.

Honestly?

I preferred the towel.

We went back to Miss Tilly's Grill for dinner, and the burger was phenomenal.

My stomach damn near growled loud enough to rattle the silverware when the plates hit the table.

A massive double cheeseburger sat in front of me—two thick, hand-pressed patties stacked high beneath melted cheddar. None of that frozen fast-food nonsense. Miss Tilly had ringed the plate with fries, then buried the whole thing under molten cheese sauce and a heavy helping of chili. The top bun looked decorative at best.

This was a knife-and-fork operation.

Sally stole a fry from my plate, dragged it through the cheese, and popped it into her mouth with a satisfied hum.

"Mmm," she said. "That's exactly what the doctor ordered."

I grabbed my fork and knife and went to war.

The burger fought back immediately.

Grease ran down my hands. Chili hit my beard. A blob of cheese made a desperate break for my shirt before Sally caught it with the side of her finger.

"What a shame," she said. "Looks like you're gonna need another shower."

A hand landed on my shoulder.

One of the prospects stood beside the table. Pizzaface. Or Zits. Hell if I knew which one was which.

"Hey," he said. "We've been looking all over for you. Club meeting tonight. Ten o'clock. Mandatory." He leaned slightly closer and glanced at Sally. "Members only."

"All right," I said. "Thanks. I'll be there."

We traded numbers while he stood there awkwardly shifting his weight.

"What should I put you in as?" I asked.

He stared at me like I'd forgotten my own name.

"Pizzaface," he said slowly. "We use road names."

"Right," I said. "Of course."

He wandered off toward another table.

I turned back to Sally.

"Looks like we left my bike at the clubhouse last night. I'm gonna need a ride."

I shoved another bite into my mouth too fast. Chili splashed onto the front of my shirt beside the cheese stain.

Sally sighed dramatically.

"You been feeding yourself long?"

She scooped a little chili onto her finger.

I caught her wrist before she could lick it off and cleaned it away myself.

"Mmm," I said. "Not bad."

Her eyes sparkled with trouble.

Then she casually dropped a fry down the front of her tube top.

"Oops."

My hand started moving on instinct.

Miss Tilly appeared beside the table before I could complete the mission.

"If you two need privacy," she said dryly, "I can box the food up to go."

I jerked my hand back immediately.

"Sorry, Miss Tilly," I said. "We'll behave."

Sally looked completely unrepentant.

"But," I added, "I am on a bit of a schedule. Could we get the check?"

Miss Tilly walked away, shaking her head.

The second she turned her back, I reached over, tugged lightly on the bottom edge of Sally's tube top, and caught the falling fry before it hit the table.

I popped it into my mouth triumphantly.

Sally grinned.

We called a temporary truce long enough to finish dinner. Both of us stared mournfully at the pie case on the way out, but I nudged her toward the door.

I couldn't afford to be late for my first club meeting. In that moment, I disappeared and Hammer emerged.

Hammer leaped from the Jeep and sprinted for the side door of the clubhouse, slipping inside with five minutes to spare.

Bash spotted him immediately and crooked two fingers.

"Cutting it a little close, ain't you?" he asked.

"Sorry about that."

Bash didn't smile.

"Every mistake you make comes back on me," he said quietly. "Don't make me think I picked the wrong guy."

He nudged Hammer with his elbow. Not hard. Just enough to remind him that mistakes carried weight around here.

The clubhouse was packed wall to wall. Every chair was filled. Men leaned against walls, crowded around tables, perched on barstools. Voices rolled through the room beneath the music, boots scraping concrete floors sticky with old beer.

Hammer recognized most of the officers gathered near the bar.

All except Bear.

The giant stood at the entrance like a prison guard waiting for trouble.

"It's time," one of the officers called over the noise.

Bear stood and threaded a thick chain through the front-door handles. The heavy links clinked loud enough to cut through the room.

Final.

Hammer felt cold sweat slide down his spine.

Five minutes later and he would've been standing outside looking in.

The atmosphere shifted immediately afterward.

Not with shouting.

Not with orders.

The noise simply thinned out, as though someone had started siphoning oxygen from the room. Conversations faded. Laughter died. Chairs stopped moving. Even the music lowered itself into the background.

Then Hammer felt it.

Attention.

Not aimed toward the officers.

Toward the back.

The door behind the bar opened.

Preacher stepped out like he'd always been there.

Silas Pike didn't look like a cartel boss or a warlord. No flashy jewelry. No giant bodyguards. No theatrics. Black leather vest. Faded jeans. Old boots worn pale by desert roads. His beard was dark, with streaks of iron gray running through it. Neatly trimmed. His expression calm enough to be unsettling. He didn't scan the room. He didn't have to. The room adjusted around him automatically.

Men shifted aside without instruction. Sightlines opened. Conversations stopped completely. Bash moved half a step closer to Hammer without realizing it, instinct overriding thought.

Across the room, Bear gave a single nod toward Preacher.

That told Hammer everything he needed to know.

This wasn't a democracy.

This wasn't just a gang.

It was a court, and Preacher sat on the throne whether he wanted it or not.

Preacher stopped near the center of the room. No raised platform. No stage.

He simply stood where everyone could see him.

When he spoke, his voice wasn't loud.

"Got a job."

Every man in the room leaned in slightly.

"Escort," Preacher continued. "Clean. Professional. No noise."

The word 'professional' hung in the air differently coming from him.

Hammer noticed the reaction immediately. Men straightened. Expressions hardened. Nobody here wanted to disappoint him.

"Pickup's in L.A.," Preacher said. "Drop's here in Kingman. Our guest's important enough that he doesn't want to be seen moving the way he moves."

A ripple passed through the room. Curiosity. Calculation.

Preacher's eyes shifted toward the prospects.

"I want six volunteers," he said. "Three prospects."

Hammer's stomach tightened.

"And their sponsors."

Now he understood.

This wasn't just work.

It was evaluation.

Bash raised his hand immediately. "I'm in."

Two other patched members volunteered just as quickly.

Preacher's attention settled on the prospects.

"Know this," he said evenly. "This job isn't about muscle. It's about discipline. You don't screw up. You don't embarrass me."

He paused.

"You don't embarrass the club."

Service before self. That was the siren call of higher ideals.

Hammer watched several men glance downward for a split-second, like schoolboys being corrected by a principal they respected too much to resent.

Preacher's eyes landed on him.

Only for a second.

But it felt measured.

Curious.

Hammer straightened unconsciously.

"I'm in," he said.

Silence followed.

Preacher studied him carefully, the same way a mechanic might inspect a blade before trusting it.

Then he nodded once.

"Good."

That was it.

No cheering.

No dramatic speeches.

The authority in the room came from certainty. From the simple understanding that every man present wanted Preacher's approval more than they wanted comfort.

"Sponsors," Preacher said, "my office. Prospects, wheels up in one hour. Be ready."

Then he turned and disappeared through the back door again.

The room slowly came back to life, but it felt different now. Sharper. Focused.

Purposeful.

Bash leaned closer.

"Congrats, Hammer," he said quietly. "You just volunteered for something that matters."

Hammer watched the closed office door for another second.

Yeah.

He was finally beginning to understand how power worked inside Deadhand Dominion.

And how easy it would be to die if he misunderstood even one piece of it.

The full patches rose as one and moved toward the backroom where Preacher had disappeared.

The Acne Brothers and I jumped to our feet and hurried for the side exit, only to be stopped by the heavy chain still looped through the door handles—and Bear standing there guarding it like the world's angriest bouncer.

He shifted the cigar in his mouth and waited until he had our full attention.

"Pack for three days on the road," he said. "Bring whatever you need to survive. Bedroll, clothes, tools. Your cuts come off when we cross state lines. California doesn't like guns, so don't get caught with one." He paused. "And wear a damn helmet. Full tank when you get back."

Bear gave the chain a tug. It slipped free with a metallic rattle.

The three of us bolted through the doors.

In my mind, Hammer was still inside reliving what happened.

I sprinted across the lot toward Beyoncé. I hadn't even had time to check on her before the meeting, but there she sat beneath the starlight, black paint gleaming softly.

Beautiful.

The other two prospects already had their Sportsters rolling toward the road by the time I kicked my leg over the saddle and thumbed the starter.

A twist of the throttle put me right behind them.

The motel sat fifteen minutes away.

I made it in ten.

Packing was one thing.

Checking in with Gunny was another.

I'd finally confirmed Preacher. Seen him. Heard him speak. And now, thanks to the prospect cut hanging off my shoulders, I was in position to finish the contract if things escalated.

The motel room door stood wide open.

I dropped the kickstand and stepped inside carefully.

The cleaning woman from earlier froze halfway through making the bed. She backed against the far wall immediately when she saw me.

"I'm sorry," she said quickly. "Melissa told me I should clean now."

She gestured nervously around the room.

The furniture had been restored to its proper places. The broken picture was gone. Fresh sheets stretched across the mattress.

I raised both hands.

"It's okay," I said. "Just give me a minute and I'll stay out of your way."

I grabbed my backpack and yanked open the dresser drawer.

Empty.

"Where're my clothes?"

"I'm washing them," she said quickly. "They'll be ready in an hour. I fold them and bring them back."

I clenched my jaw.

No time.

"Did you see a gun?" I asked.

Her hand flew to her mouth. She nodded slowly.

"Where is it?"

I tried not to bark the question. The poor woman already looked terrified.

She pointed shakily toward the bed.

"Under mattress."

I shoved the mattress aside and grabbed the revolver.

The ugly .357 felt reassuringly heavy in my hand.

Then I moved quickly through the room, mentally checking Bear's list.

Toothbrush.

Toothpaste.

Helmet.

I stuffed two motel blankets into the backpack as a makeshift bedroll.

Good enough.

"I've gotta go," I told her. "Please finish the room and tell the woman in the office I'm leaving town for a few days. I'll pay for everything when I get back. Understand?"

Her hands clasped together in front of her chest like she was praying.

She nodded enthusiastically. I shoved a twenty between her fingers. I wanted her to think of me as a decent guy, respect earned and not from fear.

I headed back outside, fired up Beyoncé, and stopped long enough to top off the tank.

When I checked the time again, my stomach sank.

No chance to call Gunny.

Missing a check-in with Gunny felt a little like stepping on a landmine and waiting to hear the click.

I rolled back into the clubhouse lot just as the other bikes were lining up.

The patched members stood beside their motorcycles waiting for us.

When the last prospect arrived, one of the full patches stepped forward.

He pointed at each rider in turn.

"Dusty. Bash. Pizzaface. Zits. Hammer. I'm Clubfoot." He jabbed a thumb toward the bikes. "Riding order's me, Bash, and Dusty. Prospects ride to the right of your sponsor. This is a quiet job. That means you do what your sponsor says when he says it. No screwing around. No drawing attention." His eyes settled hard on the prospects. "We're crossing into Cali. Who's packing?"

The patched members raised their hands.

So did I.

The other two prospects didn't move.

Clubfoot's expression darkened immediately.

"Why are you unarmed?"

Pizzaface swallowed.

"Bear said not to bring guns."

"No," Clubfoot snapped. "He said don't get caught with one."

Dusty reached beneath his vest and produced a compact backup pistol, handing it to Pizzaface.

At the same time, Clubfoot pulled a tiny revolver from an ankle holster and passed it to Zits.

"You never ride unarmed unless I tell you otherwise," Clubfoot said. "You lose those weapons, I'll beat your ass personally. Understood?"

"Yes, sir," both prospects answered instantly.

Pizzaface shoved the pistol awkwardly into the inner pocket of his cut.

Clubfoot looked at me next.

"And Hammer?"

I patted the revolver hidden beneath my vest.

His eyes narrowed slightly.

Then he nodded once.

"Good."

One by one, engines roared to life.

The sound rolled across the desert night like distant thunder.

For the first time since arriving in Arizona, Hammer realized he wasn't just pretending to be part of Deadhand Dominion anymore.

He was riding with them.

Chapter 9

After a quick stop at the border, we transformed from a rowdy band of bikers bonded by motorcycles and the brotherhood of our MC...

...into a rowdy band of bikers bonded by motorcycles and the brotherhood of our MC with our cuts stuffed into saddlebags.

Some things you just can't wash off.

Even on the interstate, it felt good to be back on Route 66.

The highway twisted through the mountains like it had been grown there. Guardrails vanished beside sheer drops that disappeared into darkness. Massive cliffs rose on either side of us, turning the valley into a stone cathedral.

Our engines thundered through it.

The sound bounced off the rock walls and rolled back over us in waves. By the time we cleared the pass, I could feel the vibration of Beyoncé's pipes deep in my chest.

It was incredible.

The ride changed once we crossed into California.

The patched members grew quieter.

More alert.

Not nervous exactly—but aware.

Even the Acne Brothers stopped screwing around.

Nobody explained why.

Nobody had to.

We stopped at a roadside motel roughly halfway to Los Angeles.

The patched members took one room. I bunked with the Acne Brothers in another.

Before heading inside, I paused near the railing outside the room and looked back east.

The mountains still held the sunrise hostage behind them. The sky above California glowed pale gold, but the Rockies remained dark and cold in the distance.

The wind carried something different here.

Not desert.

Not dust.

Salt.

Faint but unmistakable.

The Pacific couldn't have been more than a few hours away now.

I stretched slowly, joints popping one after another. Every muscle in my body hurt from the ride. My hands still buzzed faintly from gripping the bars all night.

Behind me, Pizzaface and Zits were already arguing over who got the first shower.

I ignored them and dropped onto the motel couch instead, letting my head fall back against the cushion.

Exhaustion settled over me like a heavy blanket.

It had been barely a day and a half since I'd earned my prospect cut.

A day and a half since I'd stopped being alone.

I closed my eyes and listened to the distant ticking of cooling engines outside.

Riding through the night beside those men had felt good.

Too good.

That realization should've bothered me more than it did.

It had been a long time since I'd had brothers. It had been a long damn time since I'd belonged anywhere.

Los Angeles was everywhere.

The highway widened until it felt less like a road and more like a river of steel. Traffic thickened. Smog turned the skyline into a dirty watercolor of concrete and haze. The air lost the sharp desert clarity of Arizona and picked up the smell of exhaust, overheated brakes, and hot asphalt baking beneath the sun.

We rode tight.

Disciplined.

No joking over the comms we didn't officially have. No unnecessary revving. Even the Acne Brothers kept their mouths shut.

This stopped being a ride the moment we crossed into California.

This was business.

We exited onto a feeder road that curved toward a private aviation terminal—the kind of place where rich men arrived specifically to avoid being seen arriving anywhere.

No airline signs.

No crowds.

Just tinted glass, cameras, and quiet money.

Clubfoot lowered one hand, palm down, signaling us to slow.

The formation eased down together.

A matte-black Land Rover idled near the far edge of the lot. Its windows were tinted dark enough to look painted over.

We rolled in and formed a loose perimeter automatically. Bikes angled outward. Engines shut down. Helmets stayed on.

Nobody approached the SUV.

Clubfoot pulled a battered flip phone from his vest and made a short call. Less than a minute later, he waved us closer.

"All right," he said. "Package is in the Rover. Four bikes front, two rear. Same positions. I lead. Bash second. Dusty, tail gunner. Any questions?"

Nobody spoke.

"Mount up."

I swung onto Beyoncé and settled into position between Bash and the Rover.

Bash held out a fist beside him.

"Here's to a quiet ride home."

I knocked my knuckles against his.

We waited another few seconds.

Then Clubfoot circled a finger overhead.

Engines roared alive.

The convoy rolled back onto the highway as one unit.

Clubfoot led us east, climbing steadily toward the mountains. We occupied the middle lane with practiced confidence while the Land Rover stayed exactly two car-lengths behind my rear tire.

Steady and silent.

The rhythm of the road settled my nerves again.

Mile by mile, Los Angeles disappeared behind us beneath a blanket of smog and distance.

The highway twisted as we climbed into the foothills.

That was when the sedan appeared. Black and fast.

It shot up the passing lane on our left, engine screaming.

The moment it cleared the Rover, the driver jerked hard right.

Metal exploded against metal.

The sedan clipped Bash's front tire and slammed into his saddlebag hard enough to shove his bike sideways.

Bash hit me.

My handlebars snapped right. Tires screamed as I rolled onto the rumble strip lining the shoulder.

Ahead of us, Clubfoot and Pizzaface hammered their throttles and surged forward, instinctively opening space around the Rover.

Behind me, the SUV's horn blared.

The sedan driver finally realized what he'd done. His phone slipped from his hand as he yanked the wheel back left and stomped the gas.

Too late.

Bash's bike went into a death wobble.

The handlebars snapped violently side to side while he fought it with everything he had.

For one heartbeat, I thought he might save it.

Then physics won.

The motorcycle pitched sideways and cartwheeled down the highway.

Bash launched into the air.

He hit the pavement hard enough to bounce.

Then rolled to a stop like a broken mannequin.

The Land Rover locked up its brakes behind him.

I slid Beyoncé sideways beside Bash and killed the engine before the bike had fully stopped moving.

I hit the ground running.

Bash lay twisted on the asphalt, blood streaking across torn denim and shredded skin.

I dropped beside him automatically.

Police training took over before thought could catch up.

Airway.

Breathing.

Bleeding.

Spine.

"He alive?" Clubfoot shouted as he sprinted toward us.

"Yeah," I said quickly. "Breathing's good. Arm's broken for sure. Maybe ribs. Could've been worse."

Clubfoot motioned Dusty closer.

When the rear door of the Land Rover cracked open, Clubfoot snapped toward it immediately.

"Stay inside! We don't know if this was an accident or a hit. Be ready to move!" He dropped to one knee beside me. "There's a hospital about fifty miles back. Can you ride him there?"

I looked at Bash.

Then at Beyoncé.

Then back at Clubfoot.

"Yeah," I said. "I can do it."

"Good." His tone sharpened immediately. "Give me anything you don't want cops finding. Hospital name for him is John Smith."

I nodded once and handed over my .357 and my vest; they disappeared into Clubfoot's saddlebags.

The others stripped Bash and his bike. Wallet gone. Phone gone. Cut gone. Anything tying Bash to Deadhand Dominion vanished in seconds.

They strapped him against my back using belts, scarves, and whatever else they could strip loose quickly. Crude but secure.

Pizzaface and Zits moved into traffic, waving cars around the wreck.

Clubfoot grabbed my shoulder before I mounted up.

"If this turns bad," he said quietly, "you don't know us."

Then he stepped away.

I swung onto Beyoncé carefully, feeling Bash's dead weight settle against me.

The bike dipped under the added load.

I throttled hard across the median and pointed west.

Toward Los Angeles.

In the mirror, the club shrank into black dots against the mountains.

The hospital sign finally appeared beside the highway.

Blue H. White floodlights. Civilization.

I was doing ninety when I hit the exit ramp.

Bash's weight dragged against my back with every turn. Every bump in the pavement pulled another low groan out of him—raw, animal sounds that cut straight through the wind and engine noise.

"Stay with me," I muttered. "Nobody dies on my bike today."

The emergency entrance blazed ahead like an airport runway.

I cut across the parking lot, hopped the curb, and rolled straight to the sliding doors.

People scattered.

I killed the engine and shouted.

"Help! He's hurt!"

Two nurses burst outside immediately, followed by a security guard carrying a flashlight like he thought it might stop bullets.

To their credit, the nurses ignored me and went straight to Bash.

"Don't forget his legs," I said quickly. "We had to strap him to the bike."

"What happened?" one nurse demanded while cutting away belts and scarves.

"Car clipped him in the mountains," I answered fast. "Launched him off the bike. He's breathing. Arm's broken for sure. Might have internal injuries."

They moved with practiced speed after that.

A gurney appeared almost instantly.

When they peeled Bash off my back, he sagged bonelessly against them.

One nurse glanced up.

"Name?"

I didn't hesitate.

"John Smith."

Her eyebrows lifted slightly.

"Date of birth?"

"I...don't know exactly. He's forty-two, I think."

That earned me a longer look.

Behind me, tires squealed.

Police cruiser.

Of course.

I didn't turn around.

Didn't need to.

The security guard straightened immediately when the officers stepped out.

Highway patrol.

Two of them.

"Sir," one called. "We need to speak with you."

I kept my voice calm.

"My friend needs help first. Then I'll answer whatever you want."

The staff swept Bash through double-doors before I could follow.

The troopers approached carefully, hands hovering near their duty belts. Their eyes tracked the blood streaking down my shirt and dripping onto the sidewalk behind me.

"Where'd this happen?"

"About fifty miles east. Mountain pass. Black sedan clipped his bike and kept going. I didn't want to wait on an ambulance."

"You get a plate?"

"No."

They spread out naturally, one drifting to either side of me.

"You riding with anybody else?" the second trooper asked.

"Just me and him."

His gaze shifted toward the highway.

"We've had reports of several motorcycles."

I shrugged.

"Yeah, I passed some riders after the wreck. A couple helped me tie him onto my bike."

One of the nurses returned carrying a clipboard.

"Sir, I need forms filled out. Also, if you could move your motorcycle away from the emergency entrance, we'd appreciate it."

I handed the clipboard to the closest trooper.

"Mind holding this while I park the bike?"

He took it with a nod.

I thumbed the starter.

Beyoncé growled back to life beneath me.

As I backed away from the entrance, I considered it.

Running.

Fifty-fifty odds I could disappear before they reacted.

Maybe better.

But then Bash woke up alone in a hospital full of cops with no backup and no story.

I parked in the nearest open space instead.

The trooper handed back the clipboard as I walked over.

"Couldn't help noticing the Illinois plate," he said. "You got ID to match?"

I moved slowly, keeping my hands visible as I pulled out the wallet Gunny had arranged for me.

"You're a long way from home."

"Bad divorce," I said. "Bought a motorcycle and started riding west."

"When'd you buy it?"

"Few weeks ago."

I handed him the folded bill of sale.

"Mind if we verify this?"

I gestured toward the clipboard.

"You've got until I finish this paperwork."

He nodded once and stepped away to make the call.

I filled out what I could.

Left blanks where I couldn't.

The trooper spoke quietly into the phone while I wrote.

"Good morning, sir. California Highway Patrol... Yes, sir, I've got the bill of sale here... Uh-huh... Recovered the title already? That's great... No problem, sir."

He hung up and handed everything back.

"Seller says he found the title and can mail it if you contact him."

I smiled slightly.

"She holding up okay?" he asked.

I glanced toward Beyoncé. "She's solid. Don't know why Polaris ever killed Victory."

That earned the faintest trace of a grin.

"We'll let you get inside. Hope your friend makes it."

"Thanks."

I walked back toward the entrance without hurrying.

Only when the sliding doors shut behind me did I finally breathe normally again.

Inside, I found the nurse and returned the clipboard.

"I'm sorry," I said. "I'm probably not much help. We only met traveling Route 66. Known him maybe a week."

"It's still something," she replied. "Would you like to wait?"

"Yes, please."

She pointed toward a row of molded plastic chairs beneath a muted television.

"We'll come get you once the doctors know more."

I thanked her and sat beneath the fluorescent lights.

For the first time since the crash, there was nothing left to do but wait.

Two hours later, a nurse appeared and led me deeper into the hospital.

"Your friend's on his way," she said. "He had surgery, but he came through like a champ. They'll be bringing him up shortly."

"Thanks."

I switched on the television to keep myself occupied while I waited.

A little while later, Bash rolled into the room on a gurney.

An IV bag hung beside him, fluid dripping steadily into his arm. The other arm was locked in a rigid black brace that looked more like a mechanical exoskeleton than a cast. Bandages covered the worst of the road rash, white islands against angry red skin.

The doctor followed behind the gurney.

"There was internal bleeding," he said. "Getting him here quickly may have saved his life."

I nodded once.

"But," he added, fixing me with a pointed look, "next time, instead of strapping an unconscious man to a motorcycle, call emergency services. We have helicopters. They're faster—and considerably safer."

"Thanks, Doc," I said. "I'll try to remember that. Hard to argue with the results, though."

The doctor smiled despite himself and clapped my shoulder. "Be careful out there."

A few minutes later, Bash and I were alone.

Nothing left to do but wait for Bash to wake up.

I turned the television volume down and let the news chatter in the background.

Los Angeles was on fire.

A mob stormed through a department store and stripped it clean in minutes. The only things left behind were shattered glass, stunned customers, and naked mannequins.

The screen cut to footage of smashed car windows while a reporter reminded viewers to "never leave valuables visible."

Then came the jewelry store.

A sedan crashed straight through the storefront.

Four masked figures jumped out carrying hammers and backpacks. Glass exploded everywhere as they tore through display cases. On the way out, one of them lit a road flare and tossed it in the back seat.

Flames bloomed instantly.

Black smoke rolled through the shattered storefront.

Outside, a crowd stood filming everything on their phones.

Two large marijuana leaves beside three smaller ones.

I leaned forward.

That wasn't decoration.

That was the mark.

Switchblade's car.

The report kept going, but I stopped listening.

The car we'd "borrowed" had just been used in a smash-and-burn robbery in L.A.

Which raised a much bigger question.

Was tonight's escort mission really protection...

...or transportation?

I pulled out my phone.

It was past time to check in with Gunny.

I found a quiet stretch of hallway where I could watch both directions and dialed the memorized number.

The fake business voicemail answered immediately.

"Gunny, I put eyes on him. Silas Pike is in Kingman, Arizona."

I hung up.

Seconds later, my phone rang from an undisclosed number.

"Then why are you calling me from California?"

Gunny's voice was blunt and immediate, steady as bedrock.

"Quick version," I said, shifting so I could keep the hallway covered. "I'm prospecting with the club. Silas sent a team to L.A. on an escort mission. One of the brothers got hit by a car. I brought him to a hospital."

"All right. You pull out," Gunny said instantly. "I'll send another shooter."

"Negative," I replied. "I'm taking the contract."

Silence.

Then, "Rookie, you have sixty seconds to convince me."

"I've been in Kingman over a week. I'm inside the club as a prospect. I've seen Silas exactly once, and only for a few seconds. He's insulated. Careful. He lives inside the clubhouse, and only full-patch brothers get near him without permission. If I walk away now, your next guy starts blind. I'm already inside. I'm the best shot you've got."

The line stayed quiet.

I could practically hear him grinding his teeth.

"You haven't checked in for four days," he said finally. "That stops now. I want contact every twenty-four hours. You confirm with me before you pull the trigger. You build an exit strategy before you even think about taking the shot. No witnesses. No mistakes. Understood?"

"Understood."

"I'll handle the paperwork and attach your name to the contract. This is a serious assignment. Don't rush it. Make it clean."

"Understood."

Another pause.

"Rookie..."

"Yeah?"

"Check in every twenty-four hours."

Click.

The line went dead.

The contract was mine.

I slipped the phone back into my pocket and returned to Bash's room.

He was still unconscious, machines whispering steadily beside him.

On the television, another reporter talked about a wildfire somewhere in California.

Apparently, there was always a wildfire somewhere in California.

Chapter 10

"FUCK ME," BASH GROANED from the bed. "Feels like I got hit by a car."

I stepped over beside him.

"Well, it was one hell of a party. You were dancing with strippers and downing bottles of tequila."

"Strippers?"

"Male strippers," I said. "One of them left his number and asked me to pass it along when you woke up."

Bash barked out a laugh that immediately turned into a groan.

"How bad am I?"

I gave him the short version—the sedan, the crash, strapping him to my bike, the hospital run. I explained how Clubfoot stripped his gear and rolled out with the rest of the club.

"You're checked in under John Smith," I added.

"Did they finish the job?"

"No clue."

"Give me your phone."

He dialed from memory and held the phone to his ear.

"Clubfoot, it's Bash. How'd it go?"

He listened for several seconds.

"Got it. I'll be back as soon as I can." He ended the call and handed the phone back. "Did they bring my clothes?"

"I doubt it. Pretty sure the ER cut everything off. They even swapped my shirt because of all the blood."

"All right," he muttered. "You got a multi-tool?"

I shook my head.

"A knife? Anything sharp?"

"No."

"All right. Find me clothes and something with an edge."

"What exactly are you planning?"

"I'm planning on walking out of this place, stealing a car, and getting back to Arizona before the cops figure out who I am."

He shoved himself upright, ripping monitor leads free from his chest.

"So move, Hammer. Clothes and a knife."

Halfway down the hallway I found the nurses' lounge.

Empty.

Thank God hospitals ran on exhaustion.

I moved quickly.

A row of lockers yielded sweatpants and a zip-up jacket close enough to fit Bash. I grabbed a wallet too—he'd need cash and probably a license to flash if things went sideways.

The kitchenette drawers finally gave up a paring knife.

Not ideal.

Good enough.

When I got back, Bash nodded approvingly.

"Not bad. Help me up."

I wrapped his arm over my shoulders and helped him limp toward the hallway.

"Excuse me," a nurse called. "Where are you two going?"

She stepped out of a nearby room holding a chart.

"I'm helping my uncle stretch his legs," I said casually.

"What room is he assigned to?"

I hesitated.

"Didn't catch the number. We're just walking the floor a little."

"He hasn't been cleared to leave his room yet."

"All right," I said lightly. "One lap and we'll head back."

"No," she replied firmly. "You need to return immediately."

Bash leaned heavily toward her.

"Miss, I'm starving. Missed dinner. My brother is just making sure I don't fall."

"He said you were his uncle."

"Close enough."

Then Bash sagged suddenly.

The nurse stepped forward instinctively to catch him.

He drove her backward into the patient room she'd just exited.

I followed and kicked the door shut behind us.

"What are you doing?" she demanded.

Bash clamped a hand over her mouth.

Even hurt, he outweighed her by at least a hundred pounds.

"Listen carefully," he said quietly. "I don't want to hurt you. But if you scream, this turns ugly fast."

I moved past them and yanked the call-button cord away from the patient in the bed before she could hit it.

The room's occupant—an elderly woman buried beneath blankets—stared at us with wide, terrified eyes.

Bash lowered the nurse into a chair.

"Hammer. Tie her up."

A narrow supply cabinet beside the sink held spare linens.

"This'll work."

I wrapped sheets around the nurse's arms and secured her to the chair as gently as I could under the circumstances. Bash stuffed gauze into her mouth and tied a pillowcase around her head to keep it there.

The old woman trembled beneath her blankets.

Bash stepped closer to her bed.

"That warning goes for you too," he said calmly. "I'll be right outside that door. If you make noise, I come back in here and stop it permanently. Understand?"

The woman nodded frantically.

Bash gave me a look.

We moved back toward the door.

He cracked it open and checked the hallway.

"Come on."

We slipped out and eased the door shut behind us.

"All right," Bash muttered. "Get me to a parking lot."

I led us toward the elevators.

"You weren't really going to hurt them, were you?" I asked quietly.

"Of course not," Bash replied. "But fear buys time. Figure we've got maybe ten minutes before somebody finds them and locks this place down."

"What if they resisted?"

"Fear buys time, but pain buys more."

The elevator arrived with a soft ding.

The ground floor was busier—patients wandering aimlessly, visitors clutching stale coffee, nurses moving fast enough to blur.

Nobody looked twice at us.

In a hospital, everybody looks like they belong somewhere else.

We moved outside into the patient parking lot.

"There," Bash said, pointing toward a faded blue Pontiac that looked old enough to sport a cassette player, maybe even an eight-track.

The farther we walked, the more he folded in on himself.

"You sure about this?" I asked.

"I'll live." Sweat streamed down his face in thick lines.

He grabbed the driver's door handle.

Locked.

Bash stepped back and drove his elbow through the window.

Glass exploded inward.

He stripped off the jacket and used it to clear the remaining shards before reaching inside to unlock the door.

Bash slid behind the wheel and tore open the lower dash panel. Wires spilled out in greasy bundles. Using the paring knife, he stripped two wires and twisted them together.

The engine coughed once—

—then roared to life.

He looked over at me.

"You get your bike. Meet me on the road. If cops show up, you're the rabbit. Let them chase you. I'll head for the clubhouse."

I nodded once.

"Go," he said. "I've got your six."

Beyoncé was still parked near the emergency entrance on the far side of the hospital. About a five-minute jog if nobody stopped me.

I listened hard while I ran.

No alarms.

No sirens.

Not yet.

I swung into the saddle, thumbed the starter, and eased toward the exit.

I caught up with Bash about a mile down the highway.

He flashed me a thumbs-up and a strained grin through the Pontiac's cracked window. Blue smoke rolled steadily from the exhaust, thick enough to leave a trail.

Burning oil.

I held back a few car-lengths and wondered whether the rusted heap would survive the trip back to Kingman.

We still had nearly two hundred miles to cover.

Twenty minutes into the drive, flashing blue lights bloomed in my mirrors.

Adrenaline dumped straight into my bloodstream.

My throttle hand twitched instinctively.

Beyoncé growled beneath me like she'd been waiting for permission.

I couldn't help smiling.

I tapped two fingers against my helmet—the universal sign for police.

Bash stuck his arm out the window and gave me a thumbs-up.

The cruiser gained fast, lights flashing, siren screaming.

Traffic slowed around us. Cars drifted toward the shoulder.

Bash waved once and eased the Pontiac into the breakdown lane with the rest of the traffic.

I rolled the throttle wide open.

Beyoncé answered instantly.

I wasn't completely sure the front wheel left the pavement, but the acceleration in the upper gears made me wonder.

The speedometer rolled into triple digits and kept climbing.

Wind hammered my chest. My beard whipped against my face as the engine thundered beneath me.

In the mirror, the cruiser had fallen back slightly.

More importantly, they'd already passed Bash.

He was clear.

Now I needed to get clear too.

As the police dropped farther behind, I merged into traffic ahead of the siren line—drivers still unaware of what was coming.

I carved between cars like they were parked.

Throttle pinned.

Engine screaming.

I had never felt more alive.

Then I saw it.

A solid wall of brake lights ahead.

"Shit."

I dropped into the narrow shoulder near the median, missing the bumper ahead of me by less than a foot. Both lanes had stopped dead.

I rolled off the throttle and let the bike settle to something vaguely resembling a sane speed.

Around the next mountain curve, I realized the traffic jam stretched at least a mile.

Behind me, flashing blue lights bounced along the opposite shoulder as the cruiser worked its way through the backup.

Ahead sat a tractor trailer.

I eased up beside it and stopped, letting the massive trailer block me from view as the police rolled past.

The truck driver lowered his window.

A thick-bearded man leaned out, grinning.

"Hey, brother, that's a sweet ride. That ain't a Harley, is it?"

"Victory Vegas 8-Ball."

"That is one sexy machine." He nodded appreciatively, then jerked his thumb toward the police cruiser disappearing ahead. "I don't think Smokey was after you anyway. Heard on the radio there's a pileup up down the road. Whole highway's crawling with bears and meat wagons. Play it cool and they'll wave you through."

He was right.

Eventually, my pulse settled back down from the hospital escape and brief sprint from the law.

On the far side of the accident scene, I spotted the blue Pontiac limping along the highway shoulder.

I slipped back into Bash's shadow and followed him home.

By the time the clubhouse fence appeared in my headlights, I could feel the shift.

The lot wasn't empty.

Men stood outside.

Waiting.

That wasn't good.

Bash pulled around the back of the building and killed the engine. I rolled in behind him and let Beyoncé rumble for a second before shutting her down.

For a moment, nobody moved.

Then Bear stepped forward.

He didn't look surprised.

He looked annoyed.

"You're late," Bear said slowly.

Bash pushed his door open and tried to stand.

He made it halfway upright before his legs reminded him he'd undergone surgery twelve hours earlier. I moved fast, sliding under his good arm.

"Easy," I muttered.

Bear's eyes swept over the hospital sweatpants, the bandages, the dried blood.

"You two smell like a felony," he said.

Bash managed a crooked grin. "Good to see you, too."

Bear pressed a folded piece of leather against Bash's chest.

"Clubfoot filled us in on most of the action. There's a nurse in the garage. She'll make sure the docs didn't screw you up worse."

"The garage?" I asked.

"The clubhouse is closed for a private meeting." Bear jerked a thumb toward the matte-black Land Rover parked near the building.

Then he shoved another rolled-up piece of leather against my chest.

I hadn't realized how much I missed my cut until I pulled it over my shoulders.

There was a new patch sewn above the right pocket.

BFFB.

"What's this?" I asked.

"Brothers Forever, Forever Brothers," Bash said. "Clubfoot must've told them how you got me to the hospital. Now help me get to the garage. There's beer in there."

Bash sounded far more concerned about the beer than the surgery.

He leaned heavily against me as we worked our way across the lot.

Inside the garage, one of the vehicle lifts had been cleared out. A gurney sat beneath it, and a woman in dark scrubs waited beside a rolling tool cart covered in medical supplies.

"It's about damn time you got here," she said.

"Hey, Doc," Bash replied. "This is Hammer."

Together, we eased him onto the gurney.

The woman immediately checked his bandages for fresh blood.

"Do you know where they operated?" she asked without looking up.

"They said internal bleeding," I answered.

She peeled back the bandage on his abdomen. "There we go." Her fingers pressed gently around the wound. "Any sharp pain?"

"Nothing a couple beers wouldn't fix," Bash said.

She snorted softly and reapplied the dressing with fresh tape.

"Call me in two days. Sooner if the pain spikes."

She handed him a small orange bottle.

"One a day," she warned. "Any more than that and I stop giving them to you."

"Doc," Bash said solemnly, "you are an angel of mercy."

The woman kissed his cheek and headed for the exit.

As she left, Pizzaface came through the garage door carrying two brown grocery bags.

"Zits and I fetched your stuff," he said.

He handed one bag to Bash and passed the other to me.

I opened mine and immediately spotted my .357 wrapped inside a T-shirt.

"Anything happen on the ride back?" Bash asked.

"Nah," Pizzaface replied. "But we got the guy's plates. Brothers are trying to ID him now. You'll probably hear before I do." He jabbed a finger against the new patch on my cut. "Congrats on that, by the way. Don't think half the brothers have one. Glad you both made it back."

Then he backed out of the garage and left us alone.

Bash took a pull from one of the beers beside the gurney and looked over at me.

"Hammer," he said gravely, "I've got bad news."

"What's wrong?"

"I'm gonna need help getting dressed."

I laughed and slapped him lightly on the shoulder.

"I got you."

It took a while, but before Bash finished his third beer, we were both dressed and ready to limp our way out into the celebration waiting in the parking lot.

Chapter 11

Evelyn Carver reached across the bed but found only empty satin sheets on a mattress far too large for one person.

Bright morning sunlight spilled through floor-to-ceiling windows, bathing her California penthouse in soft gold. For a moment, she simply lay there, staring at her reflection in the mirrored ceiling and enjoying the rare luxury of a morning without an early briefing.

Eventually, Evelyn threw back the sheets and slid from the bed.

Her peach, silk nightgown hung low across her breasts and brushed the tops of her thighs as she moved. She smoothed the fabric along her hips, faintly disappointed there was no one there to appreciate the effort.

Outside, the city was already awake.

But forty stories above it, the noise never quite reached her.

Barefoot, she crossed the apartment toward the kitchen. The coffee machine waited on the counter—an imported chrome monstrosity that looked more like medical equipment than a kitchen appliance.

She pressed a button and placed a simple white porcelain cup beneath the spout.

The machine hummed softly, grinding beans that probably cost more per pound than most people spent on lunch in a week.

Moments later, the rich scent of espresso filled the air. The machine automatically added a splash of chilled cream into the steaming cup.

Evelyn retrieved a cream-filled croissant from beneath a glass-covered dome and carried both breakfast and coffee into the living room.

The couch faced a wall-sized television and an uninterrupted view of Los Angeles sprawling beneath her. The skyline was still wrapped in early-morning haze, turning the city into a watercolor of steel and smoke.

She curled her legs beneath herself and picked up the remote.

The news flickered to life.

"...and last night's premiere brought out some of Hollywood's biggest names."

Footage rolled across the screen.

Flashbulbs.

Red carpet.

Actors smiling like polished mannequins.

Then the camera found her.

Mayor Evelyn Carver stood beside the lead actor from some new action movie she couldn't be bothered to remember, smiling and shaking hands for reporters.

"Mayor Evelyn Carver attended the premiere of *Iron Pursuit*, praising the production for bringing jobs and visibility back to the Los Angeles film industry..."

She sighed softly and sipped her coffee while her televised image waved one final time before disappearing into the theater.

Politics and publicity.

Two sides of the same machine.

The segment transitioned into the weather forecast.

"And today's weather is exactly what you'd expect here in Southern California..." A cheerful meteorologist stood before a glowing digital map. "Sunny skies, seventy-eight degrees along the coast, mid-eighties inland. Light breeze off the Pacific and absolutely perfect conditions across most of the region."

The mayor gave a quiet chuckle.

Perfect.

That word got used a lot on the news.

The broadcast shifted again.

The tone changed immediately.

"...in local news this morning, police are investigating a smash-and-grab robbery at a downtown department store late last night..."

Security footage rolled.

A mob flooded through a department store, sweeping merchandise into bags while stunned employees stood helplessly nearby.

Shelves emptied in minutes.

The camera cut to shattered glass and scattered clothing.

"...authorities say the group disappeared before officers could arrive."

Evelyn's expression tightened slightly.

"...and in a separate incident just hours later, a jewelry store was hit in what investigators are calling a coordinated robbery."

The screen showed surveillance footage from inside the store.

A car smashed through the glass storefront.

Four masked figures jumped out carrying small sledgehammers. They moved with practiced precision, smashing display cases and stuffing jewelry into bags.

The entire robbery lasted less than thirty seconds.

As they fled, one of the thieves tossed something burning into the vehicle.

The outside camera caught flames licking upward from the interior.

"Police say the suspects abandoned the vehicle after setting it on fire. Authorities believe the car had been stolen earlier this week."

The footage zoomed in on the rear of the vehicle just before the flames consumed it.

Marijuana leaf stickers stretched across the trunk like a joke nobody else understood.

Another clip followed.

"...and this morning, protesters gathered near Wilshire and Grand..."

A crowd filled the street.

Signs waved overhead.

Chants echoed against a police line.

Traffic crawled past while demonstrators surged along the sidewalks.

The reporter spoke over the noise.

"...organizers say the protest is aimed at city leadership and current policing policies..."

The mayor muted the television.

She leaned back into the couch, staring at the silent images of the crowd.

Perfect weather.

Movie premieres.

Looted stores.

Protests in the streets.

Los Angeles in a nutshell.

Evelyn took another slow sip of coffee.

Below, the city stretched out forever.

And somewhere inside that sprawling mess, problems were already multiplying.

Her phone buzzed on the table beside her.

She glanced at the screen.

Mayor's Office.

Back to work.

Another day in paradise.

She accepted the call.

"Caroline, you simply missed the event of the year last night. Want to know who I had dinner with? Or maybe who stayed for dessert afterward?"

"Madam Mayor, this is Gregory. Mrs. Mendoza took a few vacation days."

Evelyn frowned slightly into her coffee. She didn't remember approving the request.

"All right. Caroline's out. What's my schedule?"

There was a brief pause while papers shuffled.

"You have a luncheon with Mr. Binnington at the East Side Club at one. He'd like to discuss a housing development initiative within the city."

Evelyn didn't remember his face, but she remembered his donations.

Generous campaign contributions.

And matching donations to her private charity.

"Very well. Confirm it and send a reminder to my phone."

"Of course," Gregory said. "At three o'clock, you have a meeting at City Hall with representatives from the Democratic National Convention. It's marked confidential."

Evelyn sighed softly.

The convention was a necessary evil.

Smile.

Shake hands.

Pretend to care what they thought.

They held the keys to the governor's mansion, and as Mayor of Los Angeles, she was already the favorite if she played the game correctly.

"Fine. Put me back at the office by four. Anything else?"

"There's also a producer from MGM requesting a meeting regarding a project currently in development. He isn't on the official calendar."

"Is dinner open?"

"Yes, ma'am."

"Set something up. Call me once you've finalized the details."

A hesitation.

"Madam Mayor...your calendar says you're having dinner with your husband tonight."

"Cancel it."

The answer came instantly.

"I'd rather spend the evening with the producer. Reschedule my husband for next week."

"Yes, ma'am. I'll make the arrangements."

"Excellent, Gregory."

She ended the call and set the phone aside.

Her first meeting wasn't for hours yet.

Evelyn looked down at the untouched croissant and frowned.

She could practically feel the calories staring back at her.

Two meetings over lunch and dinner already guaranteed she'd exceed her target for the day. The pastry would only make it worse.

She finished the last of her espresso and carried the dishes back into the kitchen.

The trash can opened with a soft hydraulic hiss when she tapped the pedal with her foot.

The cream-filled croissant slid off the plate and disappeared into the garbage.

A small sacrifice to vanity.

Or survival.

It was hard to tell the difference anymore.

She returned to the bedroom and changed into tight athletic shorts and a black sports bra.

Thirty minutes on the elliptical.

Then squats.

Then shower, makeup, and the careful construction of Mayor Evelyn Carver for public consumption.

At times, she thought being a woman in politics was fundamentally unfair.

A male politician could age into power.

Gray hair became wisdom.

Wrinkles became experience.

But a woman?

A woman had to remain flawless.

Strong, polished, attractive, controlled.

Every hour of every day.

She caught her own reflection in the mirror and smiled faintly.

Then again...

If you've got it, flaunt it.

She stepped onto the elliptical and increased the resistance until her legs began to burn.

Then she pushed harder.

Soon, her entire body shimmered with perspiration in the morning sunlight.

Chapter 12

My phone buzzed against the nightstand hard enough to wake the dead.

I rolled over, squinting at the screen. The room was still dark. My brain needed a second to remember where I was.

Kingman.

Motel.

Club.

The name on the screen read Bash.

I answered.

"You awake?" Bash asked.

"I am now."

"Good. Get dressed and report to the garage."

"What's going on?"

"You'll see when you get here."

The line went dead.

I stared at the phone for a second, then swung my legs out of bed. My body was stiff from the ride back yesterday, but for once, there wasn't a hangover trying to split my skull open.

That counted as progress.

Ten minutes later, Beyoncé rumbled across the dirt lot behind the clubhouse. The garage doors were already open, fluorescent light spilling out across the gravel.

Inside, the air smelled like oil, metal, cigarettes...

...and the sharp tang of blood.

Bear stood near the center of the garage, arms folded across his chest like a prison gate. Clubfoot leaned against a toolchest. Dusty smoked beside a cluttered workbench.

Bash sat on a stool, one arm still wrapped in the rigid black brace from the hospital.

Nobody looked happy.

"Morning, Hammer," Bash said.

"Morning."

Then I saw the car.

The black sedan sat beneath the center lift, the passenger side scraped and crushed from the collision that had nearly killed Bash.

Above it, the hydraulic lift hung near the ceiling.

And dangling from the steel frame...

...was the driver.

His wrists were chained overhead, arms stretched tight enough to pull his shoulders out of alignment. His feet hung inches above the concrete floor. One eye was swollen nearly shut, and dried blood crusted the corner of his mouth.

He looked like someone who'd already had a very long morning.

Bear pushed off the wall and walked toward me.

"We had ourselves a little conversation with our friend," he said.

The driver twisted weakly at the sound of Bear's voice. Chains rattled overhead.

Clubfoot flicked his cigarette onto the floor and crushed it beneath his boot.

"Problem is," he said, "he keeps saying the whole thing was an accident."

Dusty snorted smoke through his nose.

"Funny thing about accidents," he muttered. "Usually, they don't involve stolen plates and fake registration."

My eyes drifted back to the man.

He was trembling now.

Bash watched me carefully.

"We want to know if you recognize him," Bash said. "You were closest to the car."

The driver tried to speak.

"Please...listen... I didn't—"

Bear drove a short hook into the man's ribs.

Air exploded from his lungs in a wet gasp.

He folded forward against the chains, choking for breath.

I walked closer.

The fluorescent lights buzzed overhead like angry insects.

The driver's eyes locked onto mine. Bloody saliva clung to his split lip.

"Please," he whispered.

Desperate.

I stopped a few feet away and studied his face.

Bash leaned forward slightly.

"Well?" he asked.

The garage fell silent.

Even the fluorescent buzz seemed quieter somehow.

Every eye in the room settled on me.

Waiting.

The driver's panic leaked through every inch of him now.

"Please," he rasped. "I told them... I didn't mean to—"

The side door opened.

Nobody turned immediately.

They didn't have to.

You could feel it.

Slow footsteps against concrete.

Measured.

Unhurried.

Preacher had arrived.

He didn't look at the driver.

Didn't look at the car.

"What do we have?" he asked.

His voice wasn't loud.

It didn't need to be.

Bear nodded toward the suspended man.

"Driver that hit us in the mountains."

Preacher stepped closer, hands resting loosely near his belt.

"Accident?" he asked.

"That's what he's saying," I answered.

Clubfoot shook his head.

Dusty laughed softly. "He also says he loves his mother."

The corner of Preacher's mouth twitched once, then flattened again.

He stopped beside the sedan and ran his fingers lightly across the damaged door.

Then he looked up at the driver.

The man tried to hold his gaze.

Couldn't.

Preacher turned slightly.

"Which one of you saw him?"

Bash nodded toward me.

"Hammer had the best look. I was busy trying not to die."

Every set of eyes shifted again.

Preacher's gaze settled on me.

Not angry.

Not warm.

Just...evaluating.

"You recognize him?" he asked.

Simple question.

Heavy as concrete.

The driver shook his head violently, chains rattling overhead.

"No, please... I don't know these people, I swear—"

Bear pulled a long-handled wrench from the wall and rested the cold steel against the man's throat.

"Not another word," Bear growled. "You talk when somebody asks."

Silence settled over the garage again.

Preacher never looked away from me.

"This matters," he said quietly. "If this was random, he's unlucky." A pause. "If it wasn't, we've got a problem."

My mouth felt dry.

I stepped closer to the driver. Close enough to smell the fear rolling off him.

Close enough for him to see I wasn't smiling.

I studied him like I was trying to place an old memory.

Truth was, I'd never seen him before in my life.

Didn't matter.

What mattered was what the club believed.

I looked back at Preacher.

"He was driving the car," I said. "But I've never seen him before."

The driver kicked weakly, one heel clipping my leg without any force behind it.

Preacher watched him another second.

Then nodded once.

"Good." He turned toward Bear. "Bleed the truth out of him."

The driver's face went pale beneath the bruises.

"No! Wait... Please—"

Bear stepped toward the lift controls.

The motor whined overhead.

Chains rattled.

The driver started panicking for real now.

"Please! Please don't do this!"

Preacher was already walking toward the door.

He stopped there without turning around.

"If this wasn't random, find out who sent him." A beat passed. "And if it was random..." He glanced once toward the hanging man. "...he picked the wrong day."

The door shut behind him.

The lift motor stopped at full extension.

Dusty grabbed the driver by the jaw and forced him upright until they were face-to-face.

Blood mixed with sweat and tears as the man broke completely.

"I'm sorry," he sobbed. "I didn't mean to hit your guy. I swear it was an accident."

"Easy," Dusty said with a grin. "We ain't done talking. What did you say your name was again?"

The man's eyes widened. You could almost see the gears grinding as he searched through his memory.

"John."

Dusty looked toward Bash.

"Hey, Bash. The man says his name's John. Is that the same lie he told us earlier?"

Bash picked up a notebook from the nearby workbench and flipped a page.

"Nope," he said casually. "Last time, he said his name was Mike."

Bear dragged a steel chair across the floor and planted it beneath the hanging man. The scrape screamed through the garage loud enough to make the prisoner flinch before anyone even touched him.

Then Bear reached into his back pocket and pulled out a pair of heavy metal snips.

Not garden shears.

Industrial cutters.

Short, thick jaws. Long handles.

Built to bite through steel.

"Hammer," Bear said. "Hold his foot."

I stepped forward automatically and grabbed one ankle. Clubfoot caught the other.

"What are you doing?" the man gasped. "My name's John. I swear! It's John."

Bear opened the cutters and slipped the jaws around the man's little toe.

Then he squeezed.

The blades crunched through flesh and bone with horrifying ease.

The man screamed.

His legs exploded free of our grip as he thrashed wildly at the end of the chains. Blood sprayed across the concrete floor.

The severed toe hit the concrete with a wet little splat.

Somehow, Bear caught it before it rolled away.

He shoved it into the screaming man's mouth and clamped a hand over it.

"Swallow," Bear growled.

The prisoner jerked his head side to side, eyes rolling wildly as he searched the room for mercy.

He found none.

Bear grabbed the back of his skull and forced his face upward. "Swallow."

The man finally went limp.

Tears streamed down his cheeks.

Then his throat worked once.

Twice.

I watched the lump slide down his neck and fought hard against the nausea rising in my own stomach.

Bear released him and stared into his eyes.

"So, now you understand the penalty for lying to us," Bear said calmly. "You lie, I cut something off and make you eat it. Understand?"

Clubfoot slapped the back of the prisoner's head.

"Let's try this again. What's your name?"

The man's face had gone corpse-pale.

"I lied before," he whispered. "My name's Jack. Jack Barrett."

I glanced toward Bash.

From where Jack hung, he couldn't see Bash quietly writing the new name into the notebook.

"All right, Jack." Clubfoot grabbed him by the chin. "Do you remember where you told us you got the car?"

Jack squeezed his eyes shut.

"Uh... Uh..."

Bear reached for the next toe.

Jack's eyes snapped open instantly.

"I told you I stole it from a Mexican gang in L.A.!"

"And was that the truth?" Clubfoot asked softly.

"No," Jack whispered.

Bear slipped the jaws around the next toe and crushed downward.

Jack shrieked.

Blood splattered from the wall all the way to Bear's boots.

"Bear," Clubfoot said mildly, "perhaps we should allow Jack a do-over."

Bear grunted and looked down at his boot.

"He got blood on my leather."

"Jack," Clubfoot said patiently, "you should apologize to Bear."

"He cut off my toe!" Jack screamed.

"Yes," Clubfoot agreed. "But you got blood on his boot." He leaned closer. "And he still has the snips. Best not make him angry."

Jack shut his eyes tight like he was praying.

When he opened them again, his voice had steadied slightly.

"Sir...I apologize for getting blood on your boot. I'd gladly clean them if you let me down."

Bear bent, picked something off the floor, and stepped closer.

"Think nothing of it," he said. "Pretty sure there'll be plenty more blood before we're done."

He held up the severed toe between two fingers.

"Although we do still have to address this little issue. If I remember correctly, you know the penalty for lying."

Jack stared at the toe.

Then slowly nodded.

"I'd appreciate the chance to wipe the slate clean and start over," he whispered. "Your buddy said something about a do-over."

Bear waved the toe gently beneath Jack's nose.

"Fair enough."

Jack opened his mouth.

Bear placed the toe onto his tongue like some twisted form of communion.

Jack gagged once.

Then swallowed.

"I agree," Bear said. "Let's give old Jack here a fresh start."

He patted the metal cutters lightly against Jack's groin.

"But no more lying. Understand? Lie again and I start removing parts you'll actually miss."

Jack flinched backward so hard the chains rattled overhead.

The man's eyes bounced from face to face now. Exhausted. Broken. Bleeding onto the floor beneath him.

Clubfoot stepped back into place in front of him.

I glanced at the growing puddle of blood around Jack's feet and briefly imagined myself hanging there instead.

The thought chilled me more than the violence.

"So," Clubfoot said evenly, "let's walk through the accident again."

Jack swallowed hard.

"You sideswiped our brother Bash," Clubfoot continued. "Then you hit the gas and nearly rolled through me and one of our prospects." A pause. "That wasn't an accident, was it?"

Jack closed his eyes.

This time, he didn't reopen them immediately.

"No."

"Someone paid you to hit us?"

"Yes."

"Who?"

Jack's mouth twisted like he'd tasted something rotten.

Then he gave a tiny shake of his head.

"I don't know."

Clubfoot poked him hard in the forehead.

"Open your eyes."

Jack obeyed.

"I don't like repeating myself," Clubfoot said quietly. "But I'll do it once. Who paid you?"

"I swear, I don't know." Jack's voice cracked. "Sometimes, I get envelopes in my locker at work. Directions inside. I do the job. Cash shows up later."

Bear slapped the snips rhythmically against his palm. Smack. Smack. Smack. The sound of a nurse slapping a tool in the surgeon's hand.

"Give us the whole story," Bear said. "And don't leave out a damn thing." He raised the cutters slightly. "Unless you want to leave here missing more pieces."

Chapter 13

EVEN ON SLOW DAYS, the place never really went quiet. Something was always humming, clanking, grinding, or hissing in the background. Jack had worked there long enough that the noise barely registered anymore.

What bothered him was the paycheck.

He wiped grease from his hands with a stained rag and checked the clock hanging above the loading bay.

Ten minutes left.

Too little time to start another job.

Too much time to stand there thinking.

Thinking was dangerous.

Thinking about rent.

Thinking about child support.

Thinking about the alimony payments bleeding him dry while his ex-wife played house with the guy she'd cheated on him with.

The foreman walked past carrying a clipboard.

"Hey, Rick," Jack called.

Rick stopped without much enthusiasm already written across his face. "What."

"You got any extra shifts this week?"

Rick sighed like the question physically exhausted him. "We're cutting hours, not adding them."

"I'll work nights. Weekends. Whatever you got."

Rick flipped a page on the clipboard. "Ain't nothing to give, Jack. Orders are down. You want more money, tell customers to buy more parts."

Jack forced a weak laugh. "Yeah. I'll get right on that."

Rick walked away without another word.

Jack stood there for another second, jaw tight, then tossed the rag into a bin and headed toward the locker room.

Same answer as last week.

Same answer as the week before that.

His locker door stuck like always. He yanked it open harder than he meant to.

Something slid free and hit the floor.

A manila envelope.

Jack frowned.

It wasn't his.

No name. No writing. No markings at all.

Just a plain office envelope folded in half.

He looked around the locker room.

Nobody nearby.

A couple guys were changing at the far end, talking baseball and beer like the world wasn't burning around them.

Jack bent down and picked up the envelope.

Inside was a single sheet of paper.

Typed.

No signature.

No letterhead.

Just instructions.

'Liquor Stop – 1483 Grant Street - Tuesday – 9:15 PM - Cash-only register - No cameras in rear aisle - $500 + whatever is in the till'

Jack stared at the paper for a long moment.

His first thought was that it had to be a joke.

His second thought was worse.

What if everybody in the locker room already knew what it meant?

He checked the envelope again.

Nothing else inside.

No threats.

No explanation.

Just an opportunity.

His stomach tightened.

He looked around one more time, suddenly certain somebody was watching him.

Nobody was.

That almost made it worse.

Jack slid the paper back into the envelope and stuffed it into his jacket pocket.

Every time somebody looked his direction, he wondered if they knew what was in his pocket.

He didn't go the first night.

Didn't go the second either.

But on Tuesday, he drove past the place anyway.

Just to look.

Small corner liquor store. Flickering neon beer signs in the windows. One old guy behind the counter flipping through a magazine like he'd already given up on the evening.

No cop car.

No crowd.

No obvious cameras.

Jack sat at the stoplight across the street, fingers tight around the steering wheel.

Five hundred dollars.

Plus whatever was in the register.

He thought about rent.

Thought about the electric bill.

Thought about the bologna sandwich waiting at home for dinner.

The light changed.

Before he could talk himself out of it, he pulled into the parking lot.

It's probably insurance fraud anyway, he told himself.

Stores did that all the time.

Fake robbery. File paperwork. Everybody wins.

That lie settled into his head easier than it should have.

Jack grabbed the hoodie from the passenger seat and pulled it over his head.

Then he walked inside.

The bell above the door jingled.

The old man behind the counter looked up.

"Evenin—"

Jack pulled the revolver from his waistband.

His hands shook so badly he almost dropped it.

"Open the register."

The old man froze.

Jack's pulse hammered in his ears hard enough to drown out everything else.

"I said OPEN IT!"

The drawer sprang open with a ding.

Stacks of bills.

More money than he expected.

Jack lunged forward, scooping handfuls into his pockets.

The old man raised both hands.

"Take it," he said quickly. "Just take it easy."

Jack turned and bolted for the door.

The whole robbery took maybe twenty seconds.

Twenty seconds to cross a line he'd spent his whole life avoiding.

He didn't stop running until he was two blocks away.

Didn't really breathe until he was back inside the car.

His hands were still shaking when he counted the cash beneath the glow of a streetlight.

Nine hundred and forty-three dollars.

Almost a week's pay.

For twenty seconds.

Jack leaned back against the seat and let out one short, nervous laugh.

Not because it was funny.

Because it scared him how easy it had been.

On the drive home, he bought a pizza.

Extra pepperoni.

First hot meal he'd had in over a month.

He ate three slices standing at the kitchen counter while grease dripped onto the unpaid bills spread beside him.

And for the first time in a long time...

He didn't feel helpless.

Nothing happened the next day.

Or the day after that.

No police.

No detectives knocking on his apartment door.

No squad cars waiting outside the factory.

No grainy security photo on the evening news.

Jack started thinking maybe it really had been insurance fraud.

Maybe the whole thing was some crooked arrangement.

Maybe nobody cared enough to look.

That thought settled into him slowly.

Dangerously.

Two days later, he opened his locker before shift change.

Another manila envelope sat inside.

Same as before.

No name.

No markings.

Just waiting for him.

Jack looked over his shoulder.

Nobody nearby.

He picked up the envelope and opened it carefully.

Cash.

Five hundred dollars exactly.

No note this time.

No instructions.

No explanation.

Just payment.

Jack stared at the bills for a long moment.

His pulse thudded harder with every second.

Because now he understood something important.

The robbery hadn't been random.

Someone had chosen him.

Someone had watched him long enough to know that he was desperate, he was angry, and he was willing.

That realization crawled across his skin like cold oil.

Jack slipped the money into his pocket and closed the locker slowly.

For the first time since the factory started cutting hours...

He didn't feel broke anymore.

He felt owned.

And somehow, that felt worse.

The next envelope showed up three days later.

Jack saw it the second he opened his locker.

Same manila folder.

Same blank exterior.

Same cold feeling settling into his stomach.

This time, he didn't touch it right away.

He just stood there staring at it while the factory thundered around him.

A pallet crashed somewhere out on the floor.

A forklift beeped in reverse.

Compressed air hissed through machinery.

Somebody laughed at a joke that wasn't funny enough to deserve it.

Everything normal.

Except for the letter.

Jack finally reached in and pulled it free.

The envelope felt heavier this time.

Inside sat another single sheet of paper.

Typed.

No signature.

No greeting.

'Blue Honda Civic – Plate FEV-1275 - Lot behind Carver Apartments - Friday – After Midnight - Torch it. - $700 + whatever you find inside'

Jack read the paper once.

And again.

Then, a third time, slower than the others.

His throat tightened.

"Jesus..."

Armed robbery was one thing.

Fire was different.

Fire spread.

Fire trapped people.

Fire killed strangers sleeping behind walls.

He shoved the paper back into the envelope and slammed the locker shut harder than he intended.

The bang echoed through the locker room.

A couple of workers glanced his way.

Jack forced a shrug and headed back onto the floor.

He worked the rest of the shift in silence.

Didn't talk much.

Didn't joke.

Didn't think about the envelope if he could help it.

But every time sparks jumped from a welding station...

Every time he smelled something burning...

The job waiting inside his locker crept back into his head.

That night, he lay awake and stared at the stained ceiling above his apartment.

Listening to pipes knock inside the walls.

Listening to distant sirens somewhere across the city.

And wondering what kind of people sent out jobs like this...

...and how many others were saying yes.

Friday came anyway.

It always did.

He drove past the apartments once around ten.

Just to see.

Big cracked parking lot. Half the lights burned out. Cars were packed in crooked rows like nobody cared where they left them.

He saw the Honda right away.

Blue. Faded. Dented rear bumper.

Looked like it already had one foot in the junkyard.

He kept driving.

Came back an hour later.

Still there.

He parked two blocks away and sat in the car with the engine off.

His hands rested on the steering wheel, but he wasn't really holding it.

Seven hundred dollars.

Insurance job, he told himself.

Had to be.

Nobody asked a factory guy to burn a car unless the owner wanted it burned.

That's how those things worked.

Had to be.

He reached into the back seat and grabbed the tire iron.

From the floorboard, he picked up the bottle.

Old liquor bottle. Rag stuffed in the top. Gasoline smell strong enough to make his eyes water.

He'd made it in the garage twenty minutes earlier with shaking hands.

He sat there another minute.

Then he got out.

The lot was quiet.

No voices.

No movement in the windows.

Just the hum of a distant highway and a dog barking somewhere far off.

Jack walked up to the Honda like he belonged there.

Didn't rush.

Didn't sneak.

He raised the tire iron and smashed the driver's window.

Glass exploded inward with a sharp crack that sounded ten times louder than it should have.

He froze.

Waited.

Nothing.

No lights.

No doors opened.

He pulled the rag out of the bottle, lit it with his lighter, and hurled the Molotov through the broken window.

The bottle hit the steering wheel and burst.

Flames rolled across the inside of the car in a whoosh that sucked the air out of the night.

Jack stepped back fast, heart pounding.

The fire spread quick, licking up the dashboard, crawling across the roof liner.

He turned and walked.

Didn't run.

Didn't look back.

Not until he reached the corner.

By then, the whole car was glowing orange.

He got into his own car and drove home, both hands locked on the wheel.

Didn't turn on the radio.

Didn't think about anything.

Just drove.

The envelope was waiting in his locker on Monday morning.

Same as before.

Same manila folder.

Same blank exterior.

By now, Jack's hands already knew the weight of it before he even touched it.

He looked over his shoulder automatically.

Nobody watching.

Nobody paying attention.

The locker room smelled like sweat, machine oil, and cheap deodorant. Men laughed somewhere near the sinks. Someone cursed at a broken vending machine.

Normal.

Too normal.

Jack opened the folder.

Cash.

Seven hundred dollars.

Underneath it sat another folded stack of smaller bills wrapped tight with a rubber band.

He pulled the bundle free and counted it twice.

Another four hundred and eighty-three dollars.

Whatever had been inside the Honda.

Jack stared at the money in silence.

Nobody had contacted him.

Nobody had congratulated him.

Nobody had threatened him either.

The envelopes simply appeared.

And somehow that made the whole thing feel bigger.

Smarter.

Organized.

He slid the money back into the folder and closed the locker slowly.

Then he looked down the row one more time to make absolutely sure nobody was watching him.

Only after that did he shove the cash deep into his pocket.

And for the first time, Jack started wondering if whoever was leaving the envelopes...already knew he wouldn't say no.

The jobs kept coming.

Small things at first.

Drive here.

Drop this off.

Pick that up.

Cash waiting afterward.

No names.

No faces.

Just envelopes.

Then one of the jobs changed everything.

The note directed him to a U-Haul rental lot outside Los Angeles.

Keys were already waiting inside the cab.

So was another envelope.

'Drive to Seattle. No stops longer than necessary.'

Jack almost walked away.

Almost.

But the envelope held $3,000 up front.

$3,000 to drive a truck.

He climbed in.

The voices started thirty minutes later.

Muffled.

Faint.

Coming from the back of the truck.

Jack gripped the steering wheel tighter and turned up the radio.

He told himself it was animals.

Or workers.

Or something else.

But deep down, he already knew.

Every fuel stop made the sounds worse.

Voices.

Men.

Women.

At least one child was crying.

They shouted in a language he didn't understand.

Banging against the walls.

Begging.

Screaming.

At one gas station outside Sacramento, Jack finally climbed out and walked around to the rear doors.

A thick industrial padlock held them shut.

The banging started the moment he touched it.

"Please!" a woman screamed from inside. "Please help!"

Jack stepped back as if the metal had burned him.

Then he climbed back into the cab and drove.

By the time he reached Seattle, most of the voices had gone quiet.

Only one woman still screamed.

Hoarse.

Weak.

Desperate.

Men with masks unloaded the truck behind a warehouse near the docks.

Jack never saw inside.

Never asked.

A black sedan waited nearby.

The driver never spoke.

He handed Jack another envelope during the ride to the airport.

Two thousand dollars.

And a plane ticket back to Los Angeles.

Jack tried sleeping on the flight home.

Every time he closed his eyes, he heard the woman screaming in the dark.

A week later, another envelope appeared.

This one held the address of an abandoned apartment building in one of the worst neighborhoods in L.A.

Jack drove past it twice.

Condemned.

Boarded windows.

No power.

No water.

But people still lived there.

Squatters.

Candlelight flickered through broken glass.

Shapes moved behind curtains.

Jack drove away.

This had gone too far.

He'd crossed his moral line months ago.

Now, he couldn't even see where the line used to be.

Back at his apartment, he poured himself a heavy glass of whiskey and sat in front of the television in silence.

When he finished the first drink, he made himself a promise.

No more jobs.

No matter what.

The next morning, another manila envelope waited in his locker.

Jack crumpled it immediately without opening it and shoved it into the trash.

He spent the morning welding steel brackets together and trying not to think.

Torch.

Spark.

Steel.

Repeat.

Turn your brain off.

Focus on the weld.

At lunch, he found himself walking back toward the locker room without really deciding to.

The envelope sat untouched in the trash bin.

Jack stared at it for a long moment.

Then reached down and smoothed it flat.

Inside sat a single typed note.

'You missed your appointment yesterday.

If you ever miss another appointment, a note like this will go to one of our other assets.'

Below the warning sat an address.

His ex-wife's house. Beneath that: 'Female – acceptable collateral. Male child – acceptable collateral.'

Jack's knees nearly gave out.

For one terrifying second, he realized how close he'd come to throwing the envelope away unread.

How close he'd come to getting his son killed.

His ex-wife barely registered.

But the image of his little boy lying dead in that house hollowed him out from the inside.

Jack carefully smoothed the wrinkles from the paper with trembling hands.

That night, he returned to the condemned apartment building.

This time, he went inside.

Floor by floor.

Room by room.

He screamed at squatters to get out.

Threatened them.

Kicked doors open.

Most scattered the moment they saw him.

Some cursed him.

Some ignored him.

One old man threw a bottle.

Jack left him there.

Eventually, the building fell silent.

Or silent enough.

In the basement, he found a pile of soaked trash and broken furniture.

Jack lit a match.

Held it for a second too long.

Then dropped it.

The fire caught slowly at first.

Then hungrily.

Jack walked away before the smoke reached the upper floors.

The next morning, the news reported that twelve bodies had been recovered from the ruins of the building.

Most were so badly burned they couldn't be identified.

Authorities believed several may have already been dead before the fire started.

Jack sat alone in his apartment, staring at the television.

And for the first time since the envelopes began...

He understood the truth.

He wasn't working for criminals anymore.

He was working for monsters.

The next envelope didn't show up for almost a week.

Jack opened his locker on Monday morning and found the manila folder sitting on the shelf.

His stomach dropped.

He pulled it out and opened it.

'Cargo van waiting behind Dock 3 - Wednesday – 11:00 PM - Drive to Las Vegas - Leave keys in vehicle - Do not open the back'

At the bottom was something new.

A web address.

Just a URL.

No explanation.

Jack stared at it for a long time.

He didn't own a computer. Didn't have internet at home. Didn't even have a smartphone—just the old flip phone he kept for work.

For the rest of the shift, the machines sounded like they were chewing on metal bones.

When he clocked out, Jack hurried to the library. He had no idea when it closed.

The place smelled like dust and old carpet.

He hadn't been inside one since high school.

A row of computers sat along the wall, half of them empty. A couple of kids wearing headphones played internet games. An old man read the newspaper.

Nothing had changed.

Jack signed in at the desk.

The librarian barely looked up.

"Thirty minutes."

He nodded and walked to the farthest computer.

Sat down.

Rested his hands on the keyboard.

Then he pulled the folded paper from his pocket and copied the URL into the browser.

The page loaded slowly.

Jack slipped the computer headphones over his ears.

White screen. Black text. One link. PLAY.

He swallowed and clicked.

A video started.

Grainy.

Security camera angle.

Liquor store.

Jack's heart stopped.

He watched himself walk through the door in the hoodie.

Watched himself pull the gun.

Watched himself empty the register.

The video cut.

Another angle.

Parking lot.

Night.

The blue Honda.

He watched himself smash the window with the tire iron. Watched the bottle arc through the air. Watched flames bloom inside the car.

His face was clear.

Clear enough for his own mother to recognize him.

Jack leaned closer to the screen, breathing shallow.

The video cut again.

Him walking away from a U-Haul, face visible, plates clear.

Another cut.

Him running from the condemned apartment building.

The footage fast-forwarded until flames crawled up through the structure.

Another clip.

Another crime.

His sins played one after another in a silent march.

Then the sound in his headphones changed.

A low, flat, computer-generated voice filled his ears.

"You work for us. Drive the van or the police get the video."

Jack's hands started to shake.

He looked over his shoulder.

Nobody was paying attention.

He turned back to the screen.

More clips played.

Different angles.

Different cameras.

Too many.

Way too many.

A hand tapped his shoulder.

Jack jumped so hard that the headphones slipped off one ear.

He spun around.

The librarian stood behind him, arms crossed, glasses low on her nose. She looked more annoyed than concerned.

"You can't watch that here," she said.

Jack blinked.

"What?"

"That movie." She pointed at the screen. "It's not appropriate for the library."

He looked back at the monitor.

The video had already closed.

Just a blank white page.

His reflection stared back at him.

"I— I wasn't... Sorry."

She cut him off. "You need to turn it off and leave."

Jack swallowed.

"Okay."

He clicked the mouse once, and the screen went black.

He pulled off the headphones and set them carefully on the desk.

His legs felt weak when he stood.

The librarian stepped aside so he could pass.

Jack walked out of the library without looking back.

Outside, he stood on the sidewalk for a long time with the folded paper in his hand.

'Cargo van.

Las Vegas.

Do not open the back.'

Jack closed his eyes.

The machine had him now.

The last envelope had shown up three days earlier.

Jack opened it immediately.

'Follow instructions exactly

Vehicle provided'

Directions.

Times.

Highway numbers.

And one line that made his hands start to sweat.

'Stay behind the motorcycles - Wait for the signal - Take them out - Do not hit the SUV'

Jack read it again.

And again.

Take them out.

Not scare them.

Not block them.

Not follow them.

Kill them.

He looked around the locker room.

Nobody watching.

Nobody cared.

Same as always.

He folded the paper and shoved it into his pocket.

For the rest of the shift, he worked like a machine.

Didn't talk.
Didn't joke.
Didn't ask questions.
Because he already knew the answer.
If he didn't do it...
Someone else would press play.
The car was exactly where the note said it would be.
Parked behind an old strip mall on the edge of town.
Black sedan.
Engine cold.
Keys balanced on the front tire.
Jack stood there for a long moment before picking them up.
His hands felt numb.
He opened the door.
The interior smelled like cigarettes and cheap air freshener.
A prepaid phone sat on the passenger seat.
The kind sold beside gas station registers.
It buzzed the second he picked it up.
A text message appeared.
'Drive. Follow directions.'
Jack swallowed.
Then he started the engine.
The drive west felt longer than it should have.
Miles of highway.
The mountains rose ahead like jagged teeth.
The phone buzzed every so often with fresh instructions.
Exit here.
Stay on this road.
Slow down.
Speed up.
No names.
No explanations.
Just orders.
After a while, the phone buzzed again.
'They're coming.

Stay behind them.

Wait.'

Jack tightened his grip on the steering wheel.

A few minutes later, he saw them.

Motorcycles.

Six of them.

Spread across the lane like they owned the highway.

And in the middle—a black SUV.

Large.

Blacked-out windows.

Land Rover.

Jack's mouth went dry.

That was the target.

He stayed back like the instructions said.

The phone buzzed again.

He didn't want to look.

He did anyway.

'Next pass.

Do not hit the SUV.

Take the bikes.'

His foot froze on the gas pedal.

"No..." he whispered.

He shook his head.

"No, no, no..."

The road curved through the mountains.

Guardrail on one side.

Rock wall on the other.

Nowhere to run.

The phone buzzed again.

'NOW'

Jack's vision tunneled.

His hands moved before his brain caught up.

He floored the accelerator.

The sedan roared forward.

He pulled into the passing lane, heart hammering against his ribs.

He came up beside the Rover.

Couldn't see inside.

Couldn't see who was watching him.

The phone buzzed one final time.

'DO IT'

Jack jerked the wheel.

The sedan slammed sideways into one of the motorcycles.

Metal screamed.

The formation exploded apart.

One bike fishtailed.

Another shot toward the shoulder.

Jack fought the steering wheel, trying not to spin out.

Trying not to hit the SUV.

One of the motorcycles went into a violent wobble.

The rider lost control.

Jack saw him launch into the air.

He heard the impact even over the engine noise.

"Oh God—"

He yanked the wheel straight, punched the gas, and shot forward.

Didn't stop.

Didn't slow down.

Didn't look back.

The phone buzzed again.

Jack ignored it at first.

Then finally looked.

One message.

'You only got one of them, but good enough for now.

Wait for payment.'

Jack dropped the phone onto the passenger seat like it had burned him.

His hands wouldn't stop shaking.

For the first time since the envelopes started showing up...

He realized something worse than being broke.
Someone else was driving his life.
And he had no idea who was behind the wheel.

Chapter 14

My throat went dry as the dangling man replayed the events that had brought him here.

The similarities between our paths weren't lost on me.

When he finished, he licked his bloody lips as if they'd gone dry.

"Is that everything?" Clubfoot asked. He poked the man in the ribs with a long-handled wrench for emphasis.

"I hid out at a motel," Jack whispered. "Too scared to go home. Too scared to find another envelope in my locker. That's where you guys found me."

"Any last words?" Bear stood, pulled a snub-nose revolver from the back of his belt, and pressed it against Jack's temple.

"Wait," I snapped, stepping forward before I realized I'd moved.

The room shifted.

Bear turned toward me but didn't lower the gun.

Jack hung limp in the chains, as if he'd already accepted how this ended.

"Can I talk to you guys outside for a minute?" I looked at Bash, hoping he'd back me.

Bash pushed himself off the workbench with a grunt.

"Sure," he said. "I need a smoke anyway."

One by one, the others followed him outside.

The garage door slammed shut behind us.

"All right, Hammer," Bash said. "What're you thinking?"

"I think we keep him alive."

"This fucker tried to kill us," Bear growled. "Almost killed Bash."

"Yeah," I said. "But listen to the story. The people in the Land Rover—the VIP—we thought they were the target." I shook my head. "They weren't. We were."

That got everyone's attention.

"When Jack got the message to move in for the attack, it came in real time. Somebody saw what happened up there in the mountains. Somebody knew the hit had gone sideways before he even got clear."

Clubfoot crossed his arms.

"You're saying the orders came from inside the Rover?"

"I think so," I said. "Or from somebody watching the convoy live."

Bear frowned.

"That's a hell of a reach."

"Maybe," I admitted. "But if I'm right, killing him cuts off our only line back to whoever's running this."

Bash rubbed his jaw and shook a cigarette from the crumpled pack tucked into his cut.

"I think we keep him breathing," I continued. "Use him as an inside voice. Next time he gets one of those envelopes, he calls us first."

Bash lit the cigarette and exhaled slowly through his nose.

"That's smart," he admitted.

Bear didn't look convinced.

Bash slapped my shoulder.

"Let's bring it to Preacher." He nodded toward the garage. "You stay with our friend. Make sure he doesn't go anywhere."

I glanced toward the building.

"Pretty sure he's not running."

That earned a small grin from Clubfoot.

The others headed toward the clubhouse.

I stayed behind.

Inside the garage, Jack hung unconscious, head slumped forward.

Blood had dried in long streaks down his chest. The puddle beneath him had spread wider across the concrete.

I stepped closer.

His lips were moving slightly.

Mumbling.

"Hey," I said quietly. "You still alive?"

Jack blinked hard and looked around the garage.

Panic flashed across his face before memory settled back in.

"You thirsty?"

"Yeah," he croaked.

His voice sounded like sandpaper dragged across concrete.

I grabbed a beer from the refrigerator against the back wall, twisted the cap off, and held it to his mouth.

He winced when the cold bottle touched the split in his lip, but he drank greedily.

Halfway through the beer, I pulled it back.

"Do you have even the slightest idea who's behind the messages?" I asked. "The envelopes. The phone. Any of it?"

Jack closed his eyes.

"I told you everything." His voice shook. "I swear to God, I told you everything I know." He swallowed carefully. "Are they going to kill me?"

I hesitated.

Then answered honestly.

"I don't know."

He didn't react.

"It depends on whether they think you're worth more alive than dead."

I raised the beer again, but Jack shook his head.

"What more can I give you?"

"I suggested you become our inside man," I said. "Next time the great beyond sends you a message, you call us first."

Jack let out a weak laugh that sounded close to breaking. "I could do that."

"Good," I said quietly. "Because right now, that's probably the only thing keeping you alive."

Only a few minutes passed before one of the rear garage doors rolled open.

A flat-black Harley-Davidson rolled out into the darkness.

What would've been chrome on another bike was coated in black pearl so deep that the machine looked almost unreal beneath the night sky. The motorcycle moved like a shadow given wheels.

The rider was unmistakable.

Preacher.

Even though I'd only seen him clearly a handful of times, there was something about the way he carried himself that stood apart from everyone else.

Calm.

Controlled.

Dangerous.

He rolled toward the road without looking back.

Other bikes followed in his wake, forming two clean columns behind him.

Bash emerged from the clubhouse and waved the Land Rover forward. The SUV pulled into the center of the formation like a protected animal moving through a pack of wolves.

Five more motorcycles brought up the rear.

The rumble of engines eventually faded into the desert night.

When the last taillight disappeared over the horizon, Bash limped back toward the garage.

He was moving more slowly than before. A crutch was tucked beneath one arm, and sweat rolled heavily down his face by the time he reached me.

I shoved a rolling mechanic's stool toward him.

He sat with a grunt.

I grabbed two beers from the fridge, twisted the caps off, and handed him one while he caught his breath.

"Preacher decided to personally escort our guest back," Bash said finally. "The club's riding them to the edge of L.A." He took a long drink. "I told him what we figured out. The club—not the Rover—was the real target."

I nodded slowly.

"I think that's why he moved early," Bash continued. "Didn't want whoever's behind this getting another shot lined up."

He drained half the bottle.

"What about him?" I asked, nodding toward Jack.

Bash didn't hesitate.

"Cut him down. He leaves now."

I stared at him for a second.

Then I hit the lift controls.

The chains rattled as Jack descended.

The moment his feet touched the concrete, his legs buckled beneath him. He collapsed to his knees, arms still stretched overhead until I unlocked the restraints.

The second the chains came loose, he crumpled into a bloody heap on the floor.

"Get the hell out of here," Bash said flatly.

I stepped forward and pulled Jack partly upright, dragging one arm over my shoulder to help him.

"Not you, Hammer," Bash said. "Just him. If he can't walk out on his own, he dies where he falls."

Then Bash reached beneath his cut and pulled out a black 1911.

The garage suddenly felt very quiet.

"Now move," Bash said.

Jack stumbled barefoot across the lot, leaving bloody footprints behind him in the dirt.

For one brief second, I actually thought Bash was letting him go.

Then the gun fired.

The shot cracked through the morning air.

A spray of red mist burst from the side of Jack's head.

He collapsed into a rag doll before he hit the ground.

For half a heartbeat, I saw myself lying there instead.

Face-down.

Blood spread beneath me.

I blinked, and it was Jack again.

"What the hell, Bash?" I shouted, one hand pressed against my ringing ear.

Bash calmly lowered the pistol.

"Stuff that piece of trash in the trunk of his car."

"I thought we agreed to use him as an inside man."

"No, you suggested it." He pointed the pistol toward the body. "But he was a package mule. He never knew enough to matter." Bash grimaced as he shifted on the stool. "Hell, his handler probably already knew we grabbed him. They'd never use him again."

I looked back toward the corpse.

"You're missing the biggest mistake he made."

"What's that?" I asked quietly.

Bash met my eyes.

"He tried to kill a brother."

The words landed like that last gunshot.

"You even think about killing one of us," Bash continued, "that's a death sentence." Then he jerked his chin toward the car. "Now get him in the trunk."

Afterward, Bash had me scrub the blood out of the concrete.

Said it was part of being a prospect.

An hour later, he drove the club pickup while I followed in Jack's sedan—with Jack zipped into the trunk like forgotten luggage.

We drove deep into the desert.

The sun sat low on the horizon by the time Bash finally flashed his brake lights.

I pulled over behind him.

Dawn broke almost instantly out there.

One second, darkness.

The next, the desert erupted in harsh gold light.

Bash climbed stiffly out of the truck.

"Take the gas can from the bed," he said. "Torch the car." He handed me a road flare. "Let's get this done. Then we'll grab breakfast at Miss Tilly's."

I took the can without answering.

Half the gasoline went across the seats and dashboard.

The rest I dumped into the trunk.

Over Jack.

I cracked the flare alive against the pavement.

Red sparks hissed.

Then I tossed it through the driver's window.

The car ignited with a heavy whump.

Flames curled out through the shattered windows.

I backed away fast.

The gas can in the trunk detonated a second later with a muffled boom.

Another fireball rolled upward.

"Jesus," I muttered, retreating another few steps.

Then the fuel tank went.

The explosion hit like a punch from God.

The blast knocked me flat onto my back.

Heat rolled over me as burning debris spiraled into the air.

I scrambled backward on all fours while thick black smoke clawed upward into the morning sky.

"Damn!" Bash shouted from beside the truck. "Hammer, you alive?"

I waved at Bash and climbed to my feet.

He pulled the truck alongside me.

"Get in," he said. "On the off chance somebody comes out here to see what all the fireworks were about, I'd rather not still be standing next to a burning corpse."

He shoved the passenger door open.

I climbed in.

"Well," Bash said as he pulled onto the dirt track, "breakfast is on me. You've earned it."

He pushed the pedal halfway to the floor, and the truck surged forward, spraying dust and gravel behind us.

A blues station crackled through the radio.

Bash turned it up.

I shifted in the seat and closed my eyes, trying to settle my nerves while the music rolled through the cab.

All I could see was Jack.

The gunshot.

The body dropping.

The fireball rising into the desert sky.

And underneath all of it was a quieter thought. How long until somebody did the same thing to me?

How long until I ended up stuffed into the trunk of a car, dumped in the desert, and burned down to bone and ash?

Lost in the desert.

Forgotten before the fire even cooled.

"Well, Prospect," Bash said after a while, "you handled yourself good tonight."

I opened one eye.

"You've been solid since the day you showed up," he continued. "Thanks for having my back."

I nodded once.

"After breakfast, I need to start rebuilding my bike. Get her roadworthy again." He glanced over at me. "You know how to wrench?"

"Nope," I admitted. "But if you point at what needs doing, I'll figure something out."

Bash laughed softly.

"That's the spirit."

Breakfast at Miss Tilly's was her usual combination of legendary breakfast burritos and coffee strong enough to remove paint.

Neither of us talked much.

Exhaustion had settled too deep for conversation.

When we finished eating, Bash finally shook his head.

"Bike can wait," he muttered. "I need sleep more than I need chrome."

He dropped me off at the motel just after sunrise.

I stumbled inside, kicked the door shut behind me, and collapsed onto the bed fully dressed, boots still laced tight around my ankles.

I blinked once.

Then the world disappeared.

Sometime later, my phone buzzed against the nightstand.

I surfaced slowly from the darkness, disoriented and heavy-limbed.

The room was dim.

The clock beside the bed told me I'd slept nearly twelve hours.

My mouth tasted like old whiskey and motel air.

The phone buzzed again.

Unknown Number.

I squinted at the message.

'Call your mom.'

That was it.

No signature.

No explanation.

Just three words.

And somehow, they scared me.

I knew it was a dream because nobody was bleeding.

For as long as I could remember, blood had become part of the landscape—a constant reminder of where I was and the danger surrounding me.

This time, I walked along a dirt road beside a burbling stream. No clouds. No gunshots. Just sunlight spilling across green fields while unseen birds sang somewhere overhead.

I carried a fishing pole in one hand and a dented metal lunchpail in the other.

Beside me, Andy Griffith strolled along whistling a familiar tune.

A breeze rolled across the field.

I breathed deep.

For a second, all I smelled was fresh grass and river water.

Then the stink of sweat and cigarettes drifted in underneath it.

Andy looked over at me and smiled.

"Come on, Hammer," he said. "I'm not waiting all day for you."

The whistling stopped.

I rolled onto my back.

A muscular man sat in a chair beside the bed.

Salt-and-pepper hair tied back beneath a black bandana. Black leather vest. One-percenter diamond. Skeletal-hand patch flipping the world off.

And across his chest, a single word:

PRESIDENT.

I came upright instantly, heart pounding.

Silas Pike sat alone in my motel room.

The target of my contract.

A man tied to murders, rackets, disappearances, and enough violence to fill a graveyard.

And he was sitting ten feet away from me.

I slid toward the edge of the mattress.

Preacher lifted one hand slightly.

I stopped.

"Hammer," he said calmly, "I have a problem."

A black .45 pistol spun slowly across the small table beside him like some dark version of a fidget toy. Every time the barrel pointed my direction, another bead of sweat rolled down my back.

I tried to remember the room.

I'd passed out fully dressed.

Had I taken out my .357?

A fuzzy memory surfaced—dropping it on the dresser near the door before collapsing into bed.

I fought the urge to look.

No reason to make him nervous.

"What can I do to help?" I asked carefully.

Preacher rubbed his beard with one hand while the other kept the pistol spinning.

"You see," he said slowly, "before I took the club on our little joy ride, I left a man hanging in the garage."

The pistol spun.

"A man who tried to kill one of my brothers."

Spin.

"A man you argued we should keep alive."

Spin.

"Imagine my surprise when I got back and found out he was gone."

"What?"

"He's gone," Preacher repeated patiently, like he was explaining something to a child. "Do you know anything about that?"

Relief hit me first.

This was about Jack.

Not me.

"Yeah," I said quickly. "I took him out to the desert and torched him."

The pistol stopped spinning.

"So, you killed him and disposed of the body?"

"No. Well...yes."

Preacher tilted his head. "Which is it?"

I swallowed.

"No, I didn't kill him. Yes, I helped dispose of the body."

"Who killed him?"

I stared at him.

Surely Bash had already explained this.

"Bash shot him," I said. "He said the guy deserved it for trying to kill him."

"And that's your answer?" Preacher asked quietly. "Bash killed him?"

"Yeah." I spread my hands slightly. "I don't understand what's going on. Ask Bash. He was there."

Preacher studied me for a long moment.

"Bash is gone."

That hit me harder than the pistol.

"What?"

"He disappeared."

"No," I said immediately. "We had breakfast this morning."

"Bash doesn't have a bike anymore," Preacher replied. "This is a motorcycle club. No bike. No membership."

"We were supposed to work on his bike later today."

Preacher shook his head slowly. "He's in the wind."

The words settled heavily into the room.

Then he leaned forward slightly.

"You know what else?" he asked. "He was your sponsor."

I didn't answer.

"If he's gone," Preacher continued, "he can't sponsor you anymore."

The pistol rested motionless beside his hand now.

"That means you aren't a prospect."

A cold knot formed in my stomach.

"What are you saying?"

I shifted toward the edge of the bed again.

This time, the .45 came up smoothly.

The barrel settled directly on my chest.

"You're staying in a club motel," Preacher said evenly. "Wearing a club prospect cut. My prisoner disappears. You're the last man seen with him." A pause. "And now your sponsor vanishes."

His eyes stayed locked on mine.

"Am I missing anything?"

I couldn't speak.

Preacher stood.

The pistol remained loose at his side, but somehow that felt worse.

"Take off the cut," he said.

I stared at him.

"You have thirty seconds to get out of town."

My heartbeat hammered in my ears.

"If I hear your name anywhere west of the Mississippi again," Preacher said quietly, "I'll have your head."

He pointed toward the door with the pistol.

"Now move."

I stood and peeled off the club's cut.

It hurt more than I expected.

For a little while, I'd had brothers. A family. A place where I belonged.

The cut hit the floor.

And just like that, I was alone again.

A glint caught my eye.

The .357 sat on the dresser beside the door.

"Don't even think about it."

The words were punctuated by the click of a hammer being pulled back.

"You have five seconds."

"My bike's at the clubhouse."

"Three...two..."

I ripped the motel-room door open.

The world exploded.

The entire parking lot erupted in cheers.

Motorcycles lined the gravel from one end of the motel to the other. Headlights burned through the darkness. Brothers shouted, laughed, and pounded fists against gas tanks.

For half a second, my brain couldn't process what I was seeing.

Then Bash appeared beside me and slammed a wad of leather against my chest.

I caught it reflexively and stared down at it in confusion.

A massive skeletal hand flipping the world off.

Full back patch.

Full brother colors.

I looked up slowly.

"What the hell?"

Bash grinned. "You earned it, Hammer."

I pulled the cut on before anyone could change their mind.

The crowd roared louder.

Bash wrapped me in a crushing hug and pounded my back hard enough to drive the air from my lungs before spinning me around.

Suddenly, I was face-to-face with Preacher.

He holstered the .45 and pulled me into another rough embrace.

More back-slaps.

More laughter.

Then the rest of the brothers came forward one at a time.

Bear.

Clubfoot.

Dusty.

Switchblade.

Every one of them hugged me, hit me on the back hard enough to bruise ribs, and welcomed me into the club.

The prospects came last.

For a moment, I wondered how they'd take me getting patched over them.

No resentment.

No jealousy.

Just grins and rough congratulations.

Zits nearly tackled me into a parked bike.

"All right," Preacher finally barked over the noise, "I hate to interrupt this beautiful love story, but I've got steaks being delivered."

A cheer rolled through the parking lot.

Preacher grabbed the front of my cut and yanked me back into the motel room.

Bash followed us inside and shut the door behind him.

The noise outside muffled instantly.

Preacher leaned against the dresser and folded his arms.

"All right, Hammer," he said. "I've never seen somebody patched in this fast."

I didn't know what to say. What could I say?

"You impressed me," he continued. "Time and time again." He pointed toward Bash. "What I told you earlier was true. He's got until the end of the month to get another bike, or he loses his patch. He's too damn proud to ask for help, but I don't like losing good soldiers."

Bash rolled his eyes but stayed quiet.

"Report to Clubfoot from now on," Preacher continued. "He handles paying jobs." He stepped closer. "And understand this part real clear—I wasn't lying. If Bash lost his patch before tonight, you'd have lost yours too."

I nodded, just a small movement.

"But you earned this," Preacher said. "Glad to have you in the brotherhood."

"Yes, sir," I said honestly. "That's the first thing on my list."

Preacher smirked. "Maybe not the first thing." He held up my phone. The text message glowed on the screen.

'CALL YOUR MOM.'

"I don't want to hear you're ghosting your mother," he said as he handed the phone back.

Then he stepped past me and headed for the door.

Bash held out a fist.

I bumped knuckles with him.

"I'll be in the truck," he said. "Talk to your mom. Then we'll head to the clubhouse. I'd bet money Sally's already waiting for you."

"Thanks, man. I'll only be a minute."

"No rush." Bash grinned. "Half the guys in the club don't even know where their moms are. The brothers can wait." He opened the door. "But the steaks might not."

He disappeared outside, laughing.

The room suddenly felt much quieter.

I stared down at the phone in my hand.

Then I dialed Gunny.

The call went to voicemail.

"Mom," I said, "sorry I missed my check-in."

I hung up.

Two minutes later, my phone rang.

"Damn straight you are, Rookie."

There was the sound of a car horn in the background, and what might have been a Taylor Swift song turned low on the radio.

"Are you driving?" I asked.

"Grocery run. Getting low on supplies. Now report in."

I leaned against the wall and glanced at the new patch on my chest.

"I had Preacher in my motel room."

"And?"

"He patched me into the club. Full member."

Silence.

Then, "Well, shit."

"The whole MC was outside waiting. I'm in."

Gunny's voice hardened immediately.

"There's a complication."

My stomach tightened.

"The contract got updated. You've got two weeks."

Two weeks.

Jesus Christ. I stared down at the skeletal hand stitched across my chest.

"Can you make that happen?" Gunny asked.

I took a slow breath.

"Yeah," I said with confidence I didn't feel. "I'm your man."

"And you need to get out clean," he continued. "Nobody can suspect it was you."

"Understood."

Even as I said it, my mind raced through impossible scenarios.

How do you kill the president of a motorcycle club...while he's living inside the club, surrounded by soldiers twenty-four/seven?

"All right," Gunny said. "Check in every twenty-four hours. Don't make me call you again."

"You see, current situation suggests that might not work for me. Preacher saw your message. They're waiting outside. I'll call when I can call."

The line clicked dead.

I slipped the phone into my pocket.

On the way out the door, I picked up the .357 from the dresser and tucked it into the back of my jeans.

Then I headed out to join my brothers.

Chapter 15

MAYOR EVELYN CARVER SAT alone in her office, the city spread out beyond the floor-to-ceiling windows.

The sky glowed a near-perfect blue, broken only by a handful of soft white clouds drifting lazily between the skyscrapers.

Eventually, she pulled her attention away from the view and back to the document sitting on her desk.

It was over a hundred pages thick.

She had counted.

Maps. Graphs. Spreadsheets. Environmental reports. Economic projections dressed up to appear certain.

And page after page of legal language nobody actually read unless they were paid by the hour to pretend they enjoyed it.

The thing sat on her desk like a cinder block.

Thick. Bound. Tabbed for easy reference.

As if anyone honestly expected her to read it all.

Evelyn flipped open the cover page.

Turned another five pages without reading a word.

Environmental impact assessments.

Zoning amendments.

Traffic studies.

Projected revenue forecasts.

She closed it again and pushed the document toward the edge of the desk like distance alone might make it disappear.

Then she leaned forward and rested her forehead against the binder.

For one hopeful moment, she wished information could seep into her skull through osmosis.

After a minute, she decided chai tea was probably the more realistic solution.

She pressed the intercom button.

"Gregory, could you—"

The office door opened before she finished.

Caroline Mendoza strode into the room carrying a tray with two China cups of chai tea balanced perfectly in one hand.

Officially, Caroline was the president of the city council.

Unofficially, she was the closest thing Los Angeles had to a vice mayor.

Caroline crossed the room like she owned the office and set the tray on the desk.

"Sorry, I'm late."

"Oh, were you gone?" Evelyn asked dryly. "I barely noticed."

Caroline handed her a cup and settled into the leather chair across from the desk.

"Family issue," she said with a dismissive wave. "Nothing important. How were things here? I saw you at the movie premiere." A sly smile tugged at the corner of her mouth. "Who was the gorgeous slab of man escorting you down the carpet?"

Evelyn sighed dramatically.

"Some Hollywood actor. I don't even remember his name."

Caroline raised an eyebrow.

"Did you take him home?"

"You are evil," Evelyn said, laughing despite herself. "God, I missed this. Gregory's efficient, but you can't discuss the important things with him."

"Should I replace him for you?"

"No," Evelyn replied. "But you're never allowed to take another vacation."

Both women laughed softly.

For the first time that morning, Evelyn relaxed.

She leaned back into her chair, cupping the warm tea between both hands while breathing in the cinnamon and spice.

Then she slid the thick document across the desk.

"Did you have a chance to look through this?"

Caroline glanced at the title page.

"I did."

"Thank God. What do you think?"

Caroline opened the binder to one of the marked tabs. "The developer wants a reclassification of protected parkland," she said. "On paper, it looks minor. Peripheral acreage. Low-traffic sections. They're presenting it as underutilized space."

"And in reality?"

Caroline looked up.

"In reality, it creates precedent." She closed the binder gently. "Once you open that door, you never really get to close it again."

Evelyn nodded slowly.

"That's what I was thinking."

"But..." Caroline added carefully, "You should consider giving it to him."

Evelyn leaned forward, elbows resting on the desk, fingertips steepled beneath her chin. "Why?"

Caroline lowered her voice slightly—not because anyone might overhear, but because quieter words carried more weight.

"He's positioned to make a very significant contribution," she said. "Not directly, of course. But adjacent interests."

Evelyn smiled faintly.

"Significant?"

"A generous donation to the Democratic Party of California would help quite a bit this election cycle."

"Nothing closer to home?" Evelyn asked. "My reelection campaign, perhaps?"

Caroline smiled over the rim of her teacup.

"No. Anything that obvious invites reporters to start connecting dots. Besides..." She tilted her head slightly. "I thought you had your eye on the governor's mansion."

Evelyn's smile widened slightly.

"So that's what this really is?" she asked. "A fundraising opportunity?"

"It's leverage," Caroline corrected.

"And the park?"

Caroline gave a small shrug. "People don't notice the edges of things disappearing. They only notice when you take something central." She tapped the binder lightly. "This isn't central."

Evelyn turned back toward the massive windows overlooking Los Angeles.

From forty stories up, the city looked clean.

Orderly.

Manageable.

"That's how it starts," Evelyn said quietly. "A little piece around the edge."

Caroline didn't respond.

She didn't need to.

Evelyn turned back toward her desk and pulled the thick report closer again. Her fingertips rested lightly against the cover.

"Set up a meeting with the developer," she said. "All three of us. Somewhere private." Now, Evelyn looked up. "I want to hear him say it out loud."

Caroline gave a small nod. "Of course."

She crossed toward the office door, heels clicking softly against polished stone.

At the threshold, she paused.

"One more thing."

Evelyn flipped the binder open again without looking up.

"Yes?"

Caroline's voice stayed calm. Almost casual. "Los Angeles doesn't run on ideals," she said. "It runs on momentum."

Evelyn turned a random page and stared at paragraphs she had no intention of reading.

"Hm."

Caroline smiled faintly to herself and stepped out of the office.

The door closed softly behind her.

Caroline returned to her own office a few floors below City Hall.

Unlike the mayor's office, her window didn't dominate the wall. The view wasn't inspiring.

From Evelyn's office, Los Angeles looked limitless.

From Caroline's, it looked crowded.

Concrete.

Steel.

The sides of other buildings pressing inward from every direction.

The bright California sky had been reduced to a narrow strip of blue overhead.

A paper cup of sweet mocha coffee waited on the corner of her desk, left there by her secretary.

Caroline slipped into her chair and unlocked the bottom drawer.

Inside sat a simple prepaid phone.

Cheap.

Forgettable.

Disposable.

She powered it on and pressed the first speed-dial number.

The line clicked.

"Angela Dickenson," a woman answered.

Angela Dickenson was a freelance journalist specializing in political corruption.

Depending on which party she investigated, she used different names.

"Miss Dickenson," Caroline said smoothly, "the mayor's office is quietly selling protected city reserve land in exchange for political donations." A pause. "You may want to look into Washington Residential."

Caroline ended the call before the reporter could ask questions.

One minute later, she pressed another saved number.

"Yeah?"

"I have a job for you."

The voice on the other end stayed silent.

"I want a fire set in the southern section of the city reserve," Caroline continued. "Burn everything along Pine Street."

"What's the timeline?"

"I want it done before next week."

"That costs extra."

"Done."

She disconnected the call and leaned back slowly in her chair.

Almost time.

She powered off the prepaid phone, returned it to the drawer, and locked it away.

Then she reached for the official office phone on her desk and dialed another number.

The California Democratic Party headquarters.

"You've reached the office of Bryan Thomas," a woman answered pleasantly. "Who may I say is calling?"

"This is Caroline Mendoza from Los Angeles."

"One moment, please."

Soft jazz filled the line while she waited. Piano and saxophone drifting together in polished little circles.

A minute later, a man picked up.

"Caroline," he said. "Do you have news for me?"

"Yes," she replied calmly. "It's time for Evelyn Carver to go."

Silence.

Caroline smiled faintly.

"And I can deliver her to you gift-wrapped."

Another pause.

Then, "Very well. Do that and you'll have the party's support." His tone shifted slightly. "You'll be the next Mayor of Los Angeles."

Caroline looked out at the gray canyon of buildings beyond the glass.

For the first time all day, she smiled for real.

Chapter 16

Two days had passed since I earned my patch, and the fog from that night was finally starting to clear.

The celebration had already become the kind of story brothers exaggerated into legend—though Sally's private congratulations back at the motel probably deserved most of the credit for that.

The next two days consisted mostly of Gatorade, aspirin, bland food, and sleep.

Sally woke early that morning and said she had to work a shift. She disappeared with a kiss before I even realized I had no idea what she actually did for a living.

With the Arizona sun hammering the streets outside, the clubhouse felt like a blessed reprieve. Cool. Dark. Safe in the way caves probably felt safe to hunted men thousands of years ago.

I stepped through the door and waited for my eyes to adjust to the dim light.

Bash sat at one of the tables, his arm still wrapped in the black brace from the hospital. He waved me over.

I snagged two beers from the bar on my way across the room.

"How's the arm?" I asked as I handed him one.

"Good enough," he said. "How's your head?"

"Good enough," I agreed.

Another chair scraped across the floor.

Clubfoot dropped into the seat beside us.

"The two guys I was looking for," he said.

Bash raised an eyebrow.

"What's up?"

Clubfoot didn't answer immediately. He tipped his bottle back, drained half of it, then slowly rolled the glass between his palms like he was organizing his thoughts.

Finally, "Got a job."

"What kind of job?" Bash asked.

Clubfoot glanced at me first, then back to Bash.

"One that pays."

"How much?"

Clubfoot set the bottle down. "Five."

Bash blinked. "Hundred?"

Clubfoot shook his head. "Thousand."

The noise level in the clubhouse dipped as one song ended, and another started.

"That'll get me back on two wheels," Bash muttered.

"That's the idea," Clubfoot said.

I leaned forward, resting my elbows on the table. "What's the job?"

Clubfoot's expression stayed flat. "Brush fire."

"Where?" Bash asked.

"L.A."

That tightened something in my chest.

"That's not smash-and-grab nonsense," I said quietly.

"No," Clubfoot agreed. "It's not."

Bash finished his beer.

"Timing?"

"Tonight."

That got his attention.

"Tonight?" Bash said. "Come on, L.A. is four hours away. We'd have to leave now."

"That's the requirement," Clubfoot replied. "Client wants it done fast."

"Controlled?" Bash asked. "Or chaos?"

Clubfoot gave a slight shrug. "Client didn't ask for subtle. Just asked for results."

That told us everything.

I felt my stomach tighten.

A wildfire in Los Angeles wasn't some insurance scam or desert meth lab. Fires like that swallowed neighborhoods. Burned through mountainsides. Put people on the news crying in front of ashes.

Investigators would crawl all over it.

The damage could hit billions.

I looked toward Bash.

His bike.

His patch.

His future in the club.

He met my eyes and held them.

"The bike keeps your cut," I said quietly. "What's your deadline?"

Bash smirked.

"Tomorrow."

I nodded once, then looked back at Clubfoot.

"What's the play?"

We leaned in close until our heads nearly touched over the table.

Clubfoot lowered his voice—not because anyone could overhear us, but because this kind of conversation always happened low and close.

"The southern point of the city reserve," he said. "Burn everything along Pine Street. Make sure the fire doesn't die early."

He leaned back and reached into his vest.

An envelope hit the center of the table.

"Half now," he said. "Half when it's done."

Bash grabbed the envelope immediately and thumbed through the cash.

"Yeah," he muttered. "It's real."

"Has to happen tonight," Clubfoot added. "Clock's running."

Then he stood and disappeared into the back office, where Preacher handled club business.

Bash stared at the money for another moment before stuffing the envelope inside his vest.

"Brush fire in L.A.," he said. "That's not exactly low-profile."

"No," I agreed.

He looked at me.

"You in?"

I took a slow breath.

"Yeah."

Bash grabbed the keys to one of the club trucks parked out back—a faded work pickup with mismatched body panels and enough dents to disappear into any traffic jam in America.

He tossed me the keys.

An hour later, we were on the road.

Neither of us talked much.

The radio filled the silence instead.

The sun was sinking toward the Pacific by the time we crossed into Los Angeles.

Traffic thickened immediately.

Noise.

Smog.

Congestion.

Kingman felt a thousand miles away.

We rolled along the edge of the city reserve before turning onto Pine Street.

On one side of the road, rows of multi-million-dollar homes sat behind stone walls and decorative iron gates.

On the other side—

Wild scrubland.

Dry grass.

Dead brush.

And farther back, dense trees climbed into the reserve like a wall of waiting fuel.

The reserve stretched along Pine Street for nearly a mile.

Bash stared out the windshield.

"Shit," he muttered. "That's a long burn."

"You got any ideas?" I asked.

Bash scanned the edge of the road while I drove.

Dead brush. Dry hills. No irrigation.

"Yeah," he said. "But first, we ditch the truck."

I followed his directions deeper into the rougher parts of town. We left the pickup behind a row of abandoned storefronts with boarded windows and graffiti-tagged brick walls.

Then we slipped into our disguises—black hoodies and baseball caps.

Half a mile down the road, a twenty-four-hour grocery store buzzed under fluorescent lights that sounded like angry insects.

Bash found an old gray Ford parked near the edge of the lot.

Unlocked.

He slid behind the wheel, reached under the steering column, and yanked out a fistful of wires. A few quick cuts with his pocketknife, two sparks—

The engine coughed to life.

I jogged around and jumped into the passenger seat.

We hit three different gas stations over the next hour.

At the first, I grabbed several plastic gas cans while Bash topped off the Ford's tank.

At the second, I filled the cans while Bash came back carrying a half-dozen road flares.

At the third, we bought even more gas.

Each stop followed the same pattern: park far from the building, keep our heads down, and stay off camera as much as possible.

No doubt grainy images of our faces had landed on somebody's security footage somewhere.

If the cops wanted us, they were going to have to earn it.

By the time we rolled back toward Pine Street, the back seat sloshed with gasoline.

Bash killed the headlights and eased the Ford onto the shoulder.

"This is the plan," he said. "You take one can over to those trees. Light a flare and set the can on top of it."

I stared at him.

"That's the plan?"

He ignored the tone.

"We do the same thing at the other end of the reserve. Then we dump the car into the trees and torch it too."

I looked at the gas cans stacked in the back seat. "You're seriously putting a plastic gas can on top of a burning flare?"

"Well, not the burning end," Bash said patiently. "As the flare burns down, it melts through the plastic. Gives us about five minutes before ignition." He pointed farther down Pine Street. "I'll drive up a bit and set another one. Meet me back at the car. Then we spread the rest out."

I grabbed a can and a flare and slipped into the tall grass.

The dry brush whispered against my jeans as I moved toward the tree line.

I started counting fires in my head.

The meth trailer.

Jack's car.

Now this.

Arson was becoming a disturbing addition to my résumé.

Espionage. Murder. Arson.

What the hell had happened to me since leaving the police force?

At the base of the tree, I cracked the road flare to life.

Red light hissed through the darkness.

I set it carefully on the ground, then stretched my arm out as far as possible and lowered the gas can onto the far end of the flare like I was placing an explosive in a war movie.

When nothing immediately exploded, I backed away quickly and turned into a sprint through the grass.

Farther down the reserve, I spotted Bash's flare glowing red between the trees before disappearing again.

I pushed harder toward the car.

I had just yanked open the passenger door when a fireball erupted behind me.

Orange flames blasted upward through the trees.

"What the hell did you do?" Bash snapped. "That should've taken five minutes."

A second explosion roared somewhere behind him.

Another plume of fire rolled into the night sky.

Bash slid into the driver's seat and twisted the ignition wires together.

"Cheap Chinese flares," he growled. "Burned too fast. Let's move. Those fires are gonna draw attention."

The Ford rolled forward in darkness with the headlights still off.

A hundred yards later, Bash jerked the wheel hard right and drove straight into a cluster of trees.

"Change of plans," he said. "I'll light the car. You take two more cans farther down Pine. We need this burning before the cops arrive." He shoved two gas cans into my hands. "Spread them out a couple hundred yards."

I grabbed two more flares and stuffed them into my back pockets.

Across the street, lights had started coming on inside the mansions.

Backyard floodlights clicked alive one by one as the flames climbed higher through the reserve.

Somebody was definitely calling 911.

I glanced back over my shoulder.

The Ford's windows glowed orange as the fire inside the car spread.

The trees around it had already started to catch.

I popped the flare and carefully balanced the gas can at the very edge of the burning stick.

The eruption was immediate.

A massive fireball rolled upward, lighting the night blood red.

The smell of burning gasoline hit me hard enough to taste.

I staggered backward, heart hammering, trying to convince myself I was fine—that it had been the car's gas tank exploding, not the can sitting three feet from my boots.

In the ugly red glow, I spotted Bash moving through the tall grass.

He lurched more than ran, his busted arm clamped tight against his stomach.

Back at the end of Pine Street, flashing blue lights appeared.

I still couldn't hear sirens over the roar of the fires.

I cut back toward the tree line and ran.

One more setup.

One more ignition point.

Two trees stood close together farther down the reserve. I cracked the final flare alive and dropped it between them, then balanced the gas can across the far end.

Hands empty now, I sprinted toward the corner of Pine Street.

I glanced back once toward the fields but didn't see Bash anywhere.

The police had arrived near the burning car.

Then a spotlight exploded across the darkness and locked onto me.

"You! Stop where you are!"

Instead, I dove into the grass.

Dry stalks slapped against my face as I scrambled forward on my hands and knees. Sweat soaked the inside of my hoodie.

I moved blind, heading toward our meeting point.

Off to my right, I heard tires crunching slowly over gravel.

The tops of the grass flashed blue under police strobes.

The spotlight swept over me once—close enough that I felt naked beneath it—then moved on.

I froze.

Waited.

The cruiser rolled by only yards away.

Heading straight toward the end of the road.

Toward Bash.

The spotlight drifted farther ahead.

I started crawling again, slower this time.

"Hey! You there! Stand up and put your hands in the air!"

I eased upward just enough to peek through the grass.

The spotlight had stopped ahead of me, fixed on something low in the field.

I couldn't tell what.

I dropped back down and kept crawling toward the light, careful and slow.

Close now.

Very close.

Close enough that I doubted they could see anything beyond their own spotlight.

Then behind me—

BOOM.

Another gas can detonated inside the reserve.

The spotlight jerked away instantly.

Officers shouted.

The cruiser turned toward the explosion.

A few seconds later, the final can ignited.

Flames rolled upward through the trees like a living thing waking up angry.

The police car crept back along the road as the officers searched the darkness.

I was moving again.

Fast now.

The line of grass finally broke, and I reached the roadside ditch.

"Bash!" I shouted once the cruiser moved far enough away.

"Hammer!"

His voice came back strained and tight with pain.

"Where are you?"

A hand lifted weakly from a thick patch of grass farther ahead.

I sprinted over and hauled him upright.

He nearly collapsed against me.

"Let's go," he hissed through clenched teeth.

Sweat poured down his face and dripped from the end of his beard.

I slipped under his good arm and took his weight.

"We need somewhere to hole up," I said. "Then I'll circle back for the truck."

Bash nodded tightly while sucking air between gritted teeth.

We both looked back one last time.

The police stood beside their cruiser with blue lights silently pulsing across the smoke and trees.

The grove where Bash torched the car had become a solid wall of flame.

Still no fire department.

Not yet.

A thought crawled into my head.

What if they stopped it?

What if the fire crews contained the blaze before it did enough damage?

What happened if we failed?

A hot wind rolled down from the mountains.

The flames surged higher.

Bash patted my shoulder.

"Don't worry about it," he said, like he'd read my mind. "We did the job. Now let's disappear."

We staggered across the street toward the line of expensive homes bordering the reserve.

Eight-foot brick-and-steel privacy fences blocked the yards from view as we moved along the dark sidewalk.

The third house we passed sat completely dark.

I looked at the wall.

"What do you think?" I asked quietly. "If I boost you, can you make it over?"

Bash pushed away from me and leaned heavily against the brick, breathing hard.

"Yeah," he muttered. "Just give me a minute. All that crawling might've pulled something loose."

His broken arm stayed clamped against his side while sweat continued streaming down his face.

I glanced back toward the road.

The police cruiser still sat near the edge of Pine Street.

Beyond it, the reserve burned brighter every second.

Still no fire trucks.

Just wind.

And flames.

"Looks like the cops are staying busy with the fire," I whispered. "Your call. We keep moving along the houses, or we jump a fence and hide."

Bash pulled in a deep breath, held it a few seconds, then slowly let it out.

"We go over," he said. His voice sounded steadier now. "I'll need a boost."

"All right," I said. "Let's do it."

I pressed my back against the wall and laced my fingers together for a step.

Bash rested a hand on my shoulder.

"Lower."

I slid down farther until my legs braced hard against the brick.

Bash stepped into my hands and reached for the top of the fence.

I grunted under his weight as I lifted.

His boot landed on my shoulder.

Then he climbed me like a ladder.

A second later, he disappeared over the top and landed with a heavy thud on the other side.

We both froze.

No alarms.

No lights.

No screaming homeowners.

Everything stayed quiet.

I backed up a few steps, sprinted forward, and launched myself at the wall.

My boot caught a lip in the brickwork just long enough to throw me upward.

I barely caught the top with my fingertips.

For one horrifying second, I hung there, kicking at empty air before finally dragging myself higher.

I scrambled over the wall about as gracefully as a drunk raccoon falling through a dumpster.

By the time I dropped onto the other side, I was breathing hard enough to pass out.

Flat on my back, I stared toward the house.

Still dark.

Still quiet.

Bash extended a hand toward me.

"That was graceful."

"I didn't have a ladder," I wheezed.

"Well," he said, hauling me upright, "I hope you learned something."

"What's that?"

"Never be the last man over the wall."

We started toward the rear of the house.

Halfway there—

CLICK.

Motion lights exploded across the backyard.

"Shit!"

Bash grabbed my shoulder, and we bolted around the side of the house, using the corner to shield us from the street and the police.

Three steps later, we slammed directly into a chain-link fence.

The impact bounced both of us onto our asses.

That's when the growl started.

Low.

Deep.

The kind of sound you feel in your spine before your ears recognize it.

A giant black dog stared at us through the fence with sleepy eyes.

The beast looked like someone had stitched loose skin over pure muscle.

Wrinkles hung from its body in heavy folds.

It blinked once.

Then slowly unfolded itself onto all four legs.

Drool hung from its jaws in thick ropes.

I scooted backward a couple of feet automatically, suddenly very aware of how flimsy chain-link fencing actually was.

The dog shook itself once.

Skin and slobber flapped in every direction.

Then it stopped, sucked in a deep breath, and unleashed a single thunderous bark that echoed between the houses.

"Let's move," I hissed, dragging Bash upright.

We squeezed between the kennel and the side fence, giving the dog as much room as possible.

The beast glared at us the entire time but didn't bark again.

It didn't need to.

Its opinion on trespassers had been made very clear.

With Bash leaning against me again, we followed the fence line until we finally reached the front gate.

"We need to find somewhere for you to rest," I said. "Then I'll circle back for the truck."

"No," Bash grunted. "Keep moving. The truck can't be more than a couple of miles."

It turned out to be closer to five.

But by the end of it, Bash was walking under his own power again.

When we finally reached the truck, I slid behind the wheel while Bash collapsed into the passenger seat with a groan.

Then we put Los Angeles in the rearview mirror.

I flipped through radio stations until I found an AM news channel.

For the first hour, there was nothing about the fire.

Finally, Bash groaned and switched the station over to classic rock.

A few miles later, he was snoring against the window.

We smelled like gasoline, smoke, and exhaustion.

It was nearly a four-hour drive back to Kingman.

Other than one quick stop at a Gas & Go for fuel and coffee, we drove straight through the night.

By the time we crossed back into Arizona, the first light of dawn was crawling over the desert.

Chapter 17

Clubfoot knocked on the truck window hard enough to wake the dead.

I jerked upright and nudged Bash with my boot.

He groaned but didn't open his eyes right away.

The fact we'd both slept through the night in the pickup explained two things.

We were exhausted...and those bench seats were a hell of a lot more comfortable than they looked.

Clubfoot knocked again and spun his finger in a circle.

I cranked the window down.

"If you two are done cuddling," he said, "come inside. Scotch has coffee brewing, and Preacher wants to talk to you about the L.A. job."

Cool air drifted through the clubhouse doorway as Bash and I stepped inside.

Bear sat at his usual table beside the entrance.

Instead of his standard bucket of beer bottles, a plate of steak and eggs sat in front of him beside a massive mug of coffee.

I honestly wasn't sure the man ever left that seat.

"Morning, Bear."

I held out a fist.

He bumped knuckles without looking up from his breakfast.

"Preacher's in the back," he said. "Get coffee first."

Bash was already limping toward the bar, his busted arm pressed tight against his side.

Watching him move, I couldn't help wondering if he'd torn something internally during the fire job.

I was going to have to convince him to let the club nurse re-examine him.

The clubhouse felt strange this quiet.

Scotch moved through the room, collecting empty bottles and straightening furniture, rebuilding the place after the previous night's celebration.

The prospect gave me a nod and pointed toward the coffeepot behind the bar.

Bash had already poured two mugs.

The smell alone told me this wasn't Miss Tilly's infamous motor-oil sludge.

This was actual coffee.

I grabbed one and followed Bash toward the back hallway.

The office door carried nothing except the club patch painted across it in massive detail:

A skeletal hand with its middle finger raised high.

No nameplate.

No title.

Didn't need one.

Bash knocked once and cracked the door. "Preach."

"Come in."

It was my first time seeing the inside of the room.

I expected something bigger.

Meaner.

Maybe lined with guns or stacks of cash.

Instead, it looked more like a military holding cell than an outlaw king's office.

A scarred wooden table sat in the middle of the room with four mismatched chairs around it.

An old Army surplus desk rested against one wall, its surface carved with scratches, gouges, and what looked suspiciously like knife marks.

Beside it sat an Army cot with a thin mattress wrapped in a plain green blanket.

A faded U.S. stamp was still visible near the foot.

That was it.

No decorations.

No trophies.

No luxury.

Preacher sat at the table with a steaming mug in front of him.

He waved us toward the empty chairs.

Bash sat first.

The moment he leaned against the table, one leg shifted, and the entire thing rocked sideways.

My coffee sloshed dangerously close to the rim.

Preacher held up a finger.

"Hang on."

He bent down, shoved a folded piece of paper beneath one of the legs, then tested the wobble with both hands.

Satisfied, he sat back down.

"Sorry, Preacher," Bash said.

"Don't worry about it," Preacher replied. "Club's needed new tables for years. I've just been dragging ass about fixing the place up."

He reached into his cut and pulled out a white envelope.

Setting it between us, he tapped it once with a finger.

"Second half," he said. "Got a call last night. The job caused a hell of a stir, but the client was happy. Real happy."

Bash tried to hide a grin behind his coffee mug.

"Nice work," Preacher continued. "Especially on short notice." Then his expression shifted slightly. "Tomorrow's the first of the month."

Bash's smile faded.

"Club bylaws say if you don't ride, you don't belong," Preacher said calmly. "You got a bike yet?"

Bash leaned back carefully and sighed. "I'm working on it."

"You're out of time," Preacher replied. "But I found something."

Now, Bash looked interested.

"Buddy of mine's selling a Harley Fat Boy. Clean title. Good shape." He paused. "He'll let it go for eight."

That got Bash's full attention.

Preacher sipped his coffee while Bash did the math in his head.

Finally, Bash exhaled slowly.

"Eight..." He glanced down at the envelope. "I'm still short. I took the first payment," he said quietly. "That one belongs to Hammer."

"Pass," I said immediately.

Both of them looked at me.

I shrugged.

"You sponsored me. Backed me. Put your neck on the line getting me into the club." I pushed the envelope toward Bash. "I owe you."

For a second, Bash just stared at me.

Then he slowly pulled his own envelope from inside his cut and placed it beside the other one.

From his back pocket, he retrieved an old leather wallet attached to his belt by a chain.

He opened it, thumbed through a stack of hundreds, and added fifteen more bills to the pile.

The money sat in the middle of the wobbling table like a down payment on survival.

"Fifteen hundred short," Preacher said.

I stood and pulled my wallet from my pocket.

"Sit."

Preacher's voice came out flat and cold.

"Do you think there isn't a man in this club who'd loan him the money in a heartbeat?" he asked. "That's not how we do things. If a man can't handle his own ride, we don't need him."

I sat back down slowly, my wallet still in my hand.

Bash didn't move.

He stayed hunched over the table, eyes fixed on the envelopes of cash.

I took a sip of coffee.

"Let me ask something," I said finally.

Nobody interrupted.

"Can I buy a favor?"

Preacher's eyes narrowed slightly, like he was trying to pry open my skull and inspect what was rattling around inside.

"From Bash," I continued. "Favor to be named later."

The room went quiet.

Again.

Nobody looked at me now.

They looked at Preacher.

Waiting.

Preacher took a slow sip of coffee and let the silence stretch.

Then, finally, he shrugged one shoulder and looked at Bash.

"You serious?" Bash asked me.

"Sure," I said. "Sooner or later, I'm going to need help with something. When that happens, you owe me."

Bash thought about it.

"It's got to be real," he said. "Not some bullshit like passing ketchup across the table. A real favor. Something a patched brother would ask."

"I understand."

He held my eyes for another second.

"Then yeah," he said quietly. "I owe you."

I opened my wallet and counted out $1,500.

Still more cash than I'd had on me the day I rolled into Kingman.

Preacher gave a slow nod.

"I'm a witness to the deal," he said. His eyes shifted to Bash. "Make sure you earn every penny."

From inside his cut, Preacher pulled a set of keys hanging from a Harley-Davidson keychain and tossed them across the table.

Bash snatched them out of the air.

A grin spread across his face before he could stop it.

"I knew you'd find a way," Preacher said.

Then he stood.

Bash and I immediately rose with him.

"I'll have my guy handle the paperwork," Preacher added. "Title will be here tomorrow."

He stepped around the table and pulled Bash into a quick, rough embrace.

"Don't let it get this close again."

The words landed with a hard slap between Bash's shoulder blades.

Bash nodded once.

"Understood."

Preacher stepped back and looked at me.

Really looked at me.

Finally, he held out his hand.

I took it.

His grip was strong enough to hurt.

"That was a good thing you did," he said. "Almost too good." His eyes locked onto mine. "I've got my eye on you, Hammer."

Then he released my hand.

"All right. Get out of here. It's about time for my breakfast."

Bash and I grabbed our coffee mugs and headed for the door.

The moment we opened it, Scotch stood on the other side carrying one of Miss Tilly's breakfast burritos on a paper plate.

We stepped aside so he could deliver food to the king.

Out at the bar, Bash drained the last of his coffee and dropped the Harley keys onto the counter.

"You didn't have to do that," he said quietly.

"Yeah," I said. "I did."

He stared down at the keys. "I could've figured something out."

I slapped him on the shoulder. "I know you would have." I finished my coffee and set the mug down. "I'm heading back to the motel for real sleep, and you should go see the doc. The way you're guarding that side makes me think you tore something loose."

"I'll do that," Bash said. "But first, I'm checking out my new ride." He grinned slightly. "You coming?"

"Pass," I said. "I'm so tired I can barely keep my eyes open."

Bash grabbed my forearm before I turned away.

"Tomorrow. Mandatory club meeting. Eight-thirty sharp."

"I hear you."

"You're full patch now," he added. "Don't be late."

I nodded once.

"Wouldn't dream of it."

Outside, the Arizona sun hit like a furnace blast.

I threw a leg over Beyoncé and settled into the saddle.

The leather seat burned through my jeans, but I ignored it and thumbed the starter.

The engine roared to life beneath me.

I'd been honest with Bash.

I was running on fumes.

I woke slowly, reluctantly.

Not because of noise.

Because of warmth.

Soft fingers traced across my chest, light as breath, moving with practiced purpose. The kind of touch that knew exactly how to pull a man out of sleep and into temptation.

I didn't open my eyes right away.

I stretched slightly as blood rushed south, abandoning whatever higher functions my brain had left.

"Hello, stud," Sally whispered against my ear.

I could hear the smile in her voice.

I exhaled slowly, reached for her waist beneath the sheet, and pulled her on top of me.

"Hello, beautiful," I murmured. "What did I do to deserve this kind of visit?"

"I stopped by the clubhouse," she said. "They told me you were sleeping in." Her lips brushed mine. "I figured that probably meant you hadn't eaten today."

Only then did I catch the smell.

Hamburgers.

My stomach growled beneath her.

Sally laughed softly.

"Oh, I was right," she said. "Or was that growl for me?"

I shifted beneath her and slid one hand along her back, pulling her closer until I could steal a long, slow wake-up kiss.

When we finally broke apart, I answered, "Yes," I said. "And yes."

She slipped off the bed and grabbed a paper bag from the dresser.

When she bounced back onto the mattress, her body kept moving for an extra second in ways that made concentrating difficult.

She reached into the bag and pulled out a burger wrapped in paper already stained through with grease.

Taking a small bite herself, she raised an eyebrow.

"Want some?"

I held out a hand.

"Nah." She shook her head mischievously. "Open your mouth. I want to feed you."

I leaned up on one elbow and obeyed.

She held the burger to my mouth while I took a bite.

Before I could even finish chewing, she kissed me again and lightly licked the tip of my nose.

The burger was incredible.

At least I assumed it was.

Hard to focus on food with Sally draped across me.

I winked at her while I chewed.

"See?" she said smugly. "I know exactly what you need."

She reached down beside the bed and lifted a milkshake from the floor, then dug a few fries from the bag.

Using one like a spoon, she scooped up some ice cream and held it toward me.

"Trust me."

Fries dipped in a milkshake sounded criminal.

Then she popped it into my mouth.

Sweet.

Salty.

Perfect.

Apparently, Sally really did know what I needed.

We polished off the food together until the last fry disappeared.

Then she rolled across my chest and murmured something about missing a crumb.

Her lips traced slowly downward, teasing and playful.

With a dramatic flourish, she yanked the sheet away and grinned.

"Well now," she purred. "Looks like dessert survived."

Her fingers wrapped around me, and I groaned despite myself.

When she started licking me, my eyes rolled back into my skull.

When lunch was over, we lay sprawled naked across the bed.

Hamburger wrappers and empty cups littered the floor around us like the aftermath of a very strange battlefield.

I was still trying to catch my breath.

For the first time in days, I actually felt alive.

Sally stretched beside me and smiled lazily.

"Care to join me in the shower?"

"I think I can manage that," I said.

"It'll have to be quick."

She rolled off the bed and disappeared into the bathroom.

A second later, the shower hissed to life.

I followed her on shaky legs, feeling like a newborn giraffe trying to survive its first day on Earth.

The hot water felt incredible.

We took turns soaping each other up, teasing and laughing while steam filled the tiny bathroom.

After a few minutes, Sally slipped back into the bedroom while I stayed behind, letting the water pound against my shoulders.

For a little while, I forgot about the club, the contract, the bodies, and the fire. Everything was just hot water and silence.

When I finally stepped out wearing nothing but a towel, Sally was already dressed and leaning toward the mirror, applying fresh makeup.

"Where are we going?" I asked.

"You're not," she said. "I've got work tonight."

Something in the way she said it made me pause.

Then she picked up her purse and pulled out a thick roll of cash wrapped in a rubber band.

"Could you do me a favor?" she asked.

"Sure."

"You're going to the clubhouse tomorrow, right? Monthly meeting?"

"Yeah."

She held out the money. "Would you give this to Preacher for me?"

I didn't take it right away.

"What is it?"

For the first time since I'd met her, Sally hesitated.

Only a little.

But enough.

She looked up at me, confusion flickering across her face like she hadn't expected the question.

Then realization hit her.

A hand touched her mouth.

"Oh," she whispered softly.

Her expression changed.

Not shame.

Not exactly.

Just...tired.

"Half," she said.

A slow knot tightened in my stomach as the pieces clicked together.

"Half of what?"

She gave me a small smile that never quite reached her eyes.

"Of me."

That one landed hard.

I took the roll of cash and turned it over in my hand.

"You work for him?" I asked quietly.

Sally nodded.

"Not just me," she said. "Most of the girls around the club do." She shrugged lightly. "Girls come through. Guys come through. Out-of-town business. Parties. Deals." Another shrug. "Whatever they want to call it."

"And Preacher organizes it."

"He keeps it safe," she corrected gently. "Safe and controlled."

"For a price."

"Half," she confirmed.

Silence stretched between us.

I looked down at the money.

Then back at her.

"You okay with this?"

Sally leaned back against the dresser and looked toward the motel window.

"'Okay' doesn't really factor into it," she said. "I'm saving up."

That surprised me.

"For what?"

This time, her smile looked real.

"Nursing school."

I blinked.

"You're serious?"

"Yeah." She laughed softly. "Turns out I don't actually want to spend my whole life around drunk bikers and cheap motel rooms."

I smiled despite myself.

She stepped closer and rested her hand over mine.

"This is what I've got right now," she said quietly. "Until I can get somewhere better."

I studied her face.

For a second, I thought I saw moisture gathering in the corner of one eye.

Or maybe I just wanted to.

"You'll take it to him?" she asked.

"Yeah," I said. "I'll take it."

She let out a slow breath, relieved.

"Thanks. Everybody settles up on the first."

I tucked the cash into my pocket.

"Anything I should tell him?"

She shook her head. "He'll know."

Then her expression shifted slightly.

A little of the old Sally came back.

"Besides," she added, "he already knows about you."

That made me look up fast enough that she laughed.

"Is that a problem?" I asked.

Sally stepped in close and rested her hands lightly on my shoulders.

"Depends," she murmured.

Then she kissed me.

Slow.

Deliberate.

Not playful this time.

Like she was reminding us both exactly what this was...

...and exactly what it wasn't.

When she pulled away, she smiled softly.

"Try not to get yourself killed, Hammer."

"No promises."

She laughed under her breath and headed for the door.

I stood there dripping water onto the carpet long after it closed behind her.

The room still smelled like burgers and shampoo.

But underneath, it was something heavier now.

Something harder to wash off.

I pulled my cut from the dresser and set Sally's roll of cash beside it.

Right next to the skeletal hand on the patch...still flipping the world the bird.

Chapter 18

I SPENT THE EVENING alone in my motel room with a case of beer and the television humming in the background.

Mostly, I spent it trying to figure out how I felt about Sally. She was fun. Smart. Dangerous in bed. And that last part led my brain into places I didn't especially want it going.

How many men had there been before me?

How many nights like ours had she sold just to survive?

That thought should've bothered me more than it did.

Instead, what bothered me was realizing I was jealous.

Which was ridiculous.

I wasn't exactly boyfriend material.

I was an undercover assassin embedded in an outlaw motorcycle club so I could eventually kill its president.

Not exactly husband material either.

I checked in with Gunny before midnight.

He reminded me that the clock was ticking.

The contract had a new deadline, which was a bunch of bullshit. That change should have doubled my fee. I had value. My efforts came at a great personal cost amid the moral ambiguity of the actions I'd been a part of for just this one hit. Murder, theft, arson, and a long list of other crimes that I'd committed for the opportunity to get close. *Make sure no one knows it was you.* Famous last words.

Funny how easy it was to forget that around the clubhouse.

By the time the beer ran out, my brain had gone pleasantly numb.

Sleep came easily after that.

A spear of sunlight punched through the motel curtains and landed directly across my face.

I groaned and rolled over.

Afternoon.

Today was the meeting.

I showered off the stale beer smell and found the cleanest T-shirt I owned.

My jeans still carried grease stains and desert dust, but I couldn't bring myself to care.

Lunch at Miss Tilly's only made my mood worse.

I sat alone in a booth, pushing fries around my plate while the burger slowly cooled in front of me.

The food tasted fine. I barely noticed.

The third time Miss Tilly wandered over asking if everything was okay, I finally got the message.

I dropped a twenty beside the untouched fries and left.

I didn't really want to go to the clubhouse.

But there wasn't much else left to do.

I pointed Beyoncé toward the edge of town and arrived nearly two hours early.

When I stepped inside, the first thing that hit me was wrongness.

Bear wasn't at the door.

"Hammer!" he called from the middle of the room. "Get over here and make yourself useful."

Bear and Scotch were rearranging tables into long rows stretching across the clubhouse floor.

At the far wall, another line of tables formed a raised section where the officers would sit during the meeting.

The whole setup reminded me of a church social mixed with a prison cafeteria.

I grabbed a table and helped line things up.

"Appreciate it," Bear said once we finished. "Grab yourself a drink."

"Actually, I need to see Preacher."

Bear jerked a thumb toward the hallway.

"He's in the office. Go knock."

Behind the bar, Scotch cleaned glasses while the prospects hauled bags of ice toward the beer wells.

I nodded to the Acne Brothers as I passed.

The skeletal hand painted on Preacher's office door seemed to mock me while I stood there gathering my thoughts.

Finally, I knocked twice.

"Who is it?" a voice called from inside.

"Hammer. Got something for Preacher."

The door opened.

Inside, Preacher and the club officers sat around the wobbling table. Coffee mugs. Ashtrays. Stacks of paper.

For a second, it looked less like organized crime and more like a city council meeting for violent felons.

"Hey, Hammer," Preacher said. "What can I do for you?"

I stepped forward and placed Sally's roll of cash beside his coffee mug.

Preacher looked down at it but didn't touch it.

"What's this?"

"Half," I said. "From Sally."

A small grin tugged at the corner of his mouth.

Without counting it, he picked up the roll and tossed it toward one of the officers standing in the corner.

"Thanks for bringing it by." He studied me for a second. "Anything else?"

I shook my head. "No."

Another short pause.

"This your first meeting as a patched member?"

"Yeah."

Preacher nodded once. "Good. See you out there."

That was it.

Dismissed. No questions. No lecture. No warning.

I stepped back into the clubhouse, wondering if I'd just passed some kind of test without realizing it.

The place filled quickly after that.

By sunset, the room was packed shoulder-to-shoulder with patched members, prospects, women, and enough cigarette smoke to stain the walls another shade darker.

Then Bash walked in.

I spotted him the second he came through the door. Same grin. Same swagger.

Though he still rolled one shoulder carefully, like his ribs were reminding him not to get too cocky.

I grabbed his hand and pulled him into a quick shoulder-slap.

"So," I said, "how's the bike?"

Bash's grin widened immediately.

"Fucking amazing," he said. "Runs like a dream. Only fifteen thousand miles on her. Great shape." He shook his head. "Always wanted a Fat Boy."

"Yeah," I said. "Takes one to own one."

He barked out a laugh.

"Swear to God, I've heard that joke a thousand times already." He shook his head. "Pretty sure that's why the last guy sold it."

"How's the arm?"

Bash shrugged carefully. "Doc says nothing major. Couple weeks and I'll forget it ever happened." Then he leaned in closer and tapped his pocket with a crooked grin. "She also gave me something for the pain. Good stuff."

"Careful with that."

Bash smirked. "I'm always careful."

We both knew that was a lie.

At precisely 8:30, the back door opened, and the officers stepped into the room.

Bear moved to his usual spot beside the entrance.

"All right," he barked. "Anyone without a full patch get outside. Prospects are on bike watch tonight. Bar's closed till the meeting's over, and this might take a while."

The hang-arounds shuffled reluctantly toward the door while patched members took seats at the long rows of tables.

The officers moved to the front of the room.

Preacher stood at the center table.

"We're riding," he said.

He never raised his voice.

He never had to.

Every man in the room leaned toward him automatically.

"Los Angeles," he continued. "We've been invited for a week."

A few low chuckles rolled through the room, but nobody looked amused.

Preacher's eyes swept slowly across the crowd.

"Client wants the city lit up," he said. "Wants it loud. Wants it messy." He paused. "Wants it to look like the world's falling apart."

My stomach tightened.

Two men had nearly started a forest fire on their own.

What the hell would happen if the entire club got involved?

Preacher rested both hands on the table.

"Anything goes."

That came as a surprise. Looting. Arson. Violence. No limits.

I glanced toward Bash.

The grin was gone from his face now.

Something colder had taken its place.

Something eager.

Preacher straightened.

"We ride Sunday. That gives you six days to prepare." He paused. "Only bring what you need. We roll out at fourteen hundred hours." His gaze swept the room one final time. "There will be no mistakes."

Silence followed him.

Not nervous silence.

Focused silence.

The kind soldiers carried before deployment.

The meeting broke a few minutes later.

Chairs scraped. Voices rose. Beer bottles opened.

Bash slapped me on the shoulder.

"Back to L.A.," he said. "Can you believe this? I swear I could make that trip blindfolded now."

"Yeah," I said, forcing a grin. "Starting to feel personal."

Bash shook his head immediately. "No, it's business." He pointed toward the officers' table. "It's always business."

Bear reopened the doors and let Scotch return to the bar.

Someone carried buckets of beer out to the prospects watching the bikes, while others started dragging tables back into place.

I paced around pretending to help while my brain raced.

I needed to contact Gunny.

Before I could slip outside, Bash shoved a cold beer into my hand.

"Come on," he said. "You've gotta see the new ride."

He wasn't wrong.

The Fat Boy looked incredible under the parking lot lights.

Gloss-black paint. Chrome polished bright enough to mirror faces. Aftermarket pipes and upgraded engine work that Bash claimed brought it close to 150 horsepower.

"She's beautiful," I admitted. "Perfect bike for you."

We clinked bottles.

"It was all you," Bash said. "Your money pushed me over the edge. Kept the cut on my back."

Then he pulled me into another one of those crushing bear-hugs.

The man smelled like leather, smoke, gasoline, and painkillers.

"You would've figured it out," I said once he let go.

"Maybe," Bash answered. "Maybe not." He looked at the bike again. "I'm not forgetting this."

"I hope not," I said. "I bought myself a favor."

Bash laughed.

"I'll add it to the pile." He pointed at me. "That includes dragging my busted ass through the desert and getting me to a hospital. Don't think I forgot that one, either."

I slapped him lightly on the shoulder.

"I'm not counting favors," I said. "But if I'm ever stranded in the desert without a gas can, I expect priority treatment."

"Always, brother."

That word meant something.

Brother. Not prospect. Not outsider. Brother.

Bash headed toward the clubhouse while I drifted toward the bike line with my phone already in my hand.

"Hammer!" one of the prospects called out.

It was Zits.

"You mind watching the bikes for a minute?" he asked, shifting side to side like a little kid trying not to piss himself. "Clubfoot's hogging the bathroom, and I'm about to die."

I laughed. "Go. I've got it."

He jogged around the side of the building toward the rear lot.

The second he disappeared, I pulled out my phone and dialed Gunny's number.

Voicemail.

Perfect.

"Gunny," I said after the beep, "don't call back. I'm still inside and still moving forward, but the club's planning coordinated attacks in Los Angeles next week. Fires, riots, maybe worse. If something goes sideways... I wanted you to know before it happens."

"Who are you talking to?"

I nearly jumped.

Zits stood a few feet away, holding his stomach.

Apparently, his bathroom emergency wasn't quite as urgent as advertised.

I lowered the phone casually.

"Old lady," I said. "Told her if my laundry isn't done when I get back, I'm trading her in."

Zits snorted. "Ain't you with Sally?"

"Yeah. Why?"

He grinned. "I heard housewife skills aren't exactly her specialty."

I forced a laugh.

"They're not," I admitted. "But I'm trying to train her."

Zits laughed harder and wandered back toward the clubhouse.

I slipped my phone into my pocket and stared out across the sea of motorcycles.

The laughter. The music. The engines cooling in the dark.

A week from now, these men were planning to turn Los Angeles into a warzone.

And somehow...

I was becoming one of them.

We laughed about that until Pizzaface returned. With the bikes covered again, I slipped back inside the clubhouse for a minute, then took the first chance I could to disappear.

I climbed onto Beyoncé and pointed her out of town. I needed air. Distance. Time.

One thing I'd learned riding Route 66 was that motorcycles gave a man space to think. Wind roared in my ears as I wandered the empty roads outside Kingman, turning at random until I found myself on a long stretch of desert highway that disappeared into darkness.

I twisted the throttle.

The speedometer climbed into triple digits.

The night swallowed me whole.

Wind clawed at my cut until it snapped behind me like a flag. The engine thundered beneath me, steady and alive. At a hundred miles an hour during daylight, a rider needed complete concentration.

At night?

It bordered on suicide.

My eyes strained against the darkness, knowing if anything appeared in my path, I probably wouldn't have time to react.

Didn't matter.

For the first time in days, my head was clear.

My heart pounded in rhythm with the engine. Wind forced itself into my lungs. Bugs drawn to the headlight exploded against my face and jacket.

I didn't care.

For a little while, the night belonged to me.

Then I saw it.

A gray blur in the middle of the road.

My body reacted before my brain did.

I rolled off the throttle.

The roar of the engine dropped into a sharp mechanical whine as compression fought to slow the bike. The front suspension dipped hard.

A split-second before impact, I leaned and shoved the handlebars.

Beyoncé snapped sideways.

The obstacle missed my leg by inches.

I coasted another hundred yards before easing off the throttle completely and making a slow U-turn.

The armadillo had curled itself into a tight gray ball in the middle of the road.

I pulled up beside the trembling little creature and nudged it gently with the toe of my boot.

It unrolled instantly and scampered off into the desert on tiny, frantic legs.

I laughed softly under my breath.

With the bike idling beneath me, I could hear my pulse hammering in my ears. I was breathing hard, adrenaline still racing through my veins.

Alive.

For the first time in a while, I felt in control again.

I reached down and patted Beyoncé's gas tank.

Didn't say anything.

Didn't need to.

She understood.

Far off on the horizon, I could see the soft orange glow of Kingman against the night sky.

With my thoughts finally untangled, I pointed the bike back toward town and rolled on the throttle again—this time at a saner pace.

Somewhere out there in the desert, I'd managed to outrun everything chasing me. The club. Gunny. The contract. Sally. Los Angeles.

At least for a little while.

I wasn't in any hurry to catch those problems again.

By the time I rolled into the motel parking lot, the low-fuel light glowed bright orange on the console bar.

That would be tomorrow's problem.

Tonight, I felt good.

Tired—but calm.

For months now, I'd been running flat out until exhaustion finally knocked me unconscious. I'd been terrified that if I slowed down long enough, my thoughts would catch up with me.

Tonight, they didn't.

I stripped down, slid beneath the cool motel sheets, and closed my eyes.

For the first time in longer than I could remember...

I slept peacefully.

And dreamed happy dreams.

Chapter 19

"MISS CARVER, THE REPRESENTATIVES from the California Democratic Committee are here," a disembodied voice announced.

Mayor Evelyn Carver rose instantly from behind her desk.

She smoothed the front of her blouse as she crossed the office, then subtly adjusted the fabric until her cleavage bordered on scandalous without quite crossing the line.

Politics were perception.

And perception started before the first word was spoken.

She opened the office doors with a bright, practiced smile.

"Gentlemen. Ladies. I'm so glad you could make it." She stepped aside gracefully. "Please, come in and make yourselves comfortable. Gregory can arrange refreshments if anyone would like something."

One of the men paused beside her.

"Coffee service would be appreciated," he said. "I suspect this may be a lengthy discussion."

"Of course."

Evelyn nodded toward Gregory, who immediately disappeared to handle the request.

The committee members filtered into the office.

Introductions followed as everyone settled into chairs around the conference table, but Evelyn barely listened.

Names didn't matter, and neither did titles.

They all knew who she was.

And that was what mattered.

Once everyone was seated, a bald Black man near the center of the group folded his hands together and spoke.

Anthony Cross.

President of the California Democratic Committee.

Kingmaker. He mattered.

For nearly twenty years, no Democrat had reached the governor's mansion without his blessing.

"I always enjoy our meetings, Evelyn," Cross said smoothly. "As you know, we've been watching your progress for several years now. Los Angeles represents the largest voting bloc in the state. Naturally, we cultivate leadership here carefully."

Evelyn smiled while discreetly wiping damp palms against the sides of her skirt beneath the table.

This was it.

The moment she'd been building toward since the day she took the mayor's office.

The governor's mansion in Sacramento.

Maybe beyond.

"Yes," she said confidently. "And I'm proud of what this administration has accomplished. Los Angeles has grown substantially under my leadership, and I believe I can bring that same vision to the entire state."

Cross gave a thin smile.

"Yes... Well." He waved a hand dismissively. "Let's skip the campaign speech and get to the interesting part."

He nodded toward one of the aides.

The man pulled a laptop from a briefcase and set it on the conference table.

A news report flickered onto the screen.

Wildfire footage.

Burned hillsides.

Smoke.

A reporter's voice filled the office.

"...more than five hundred acres of protected reserve land destroyed in last month's fire. Following the disaster, the damaged property was quietly rezoned and sold to private developers at a fraction of its estimated value..."

The footage shifted.

Construction renderings.

Political donation records.

"...weeks later, the developer responsible for the purchase donated two-point-five million dollars to the California Democratic Party..."

The aide paused the video.

Across the screen, bold red letters screamed: L.A. CORRUPTION

Evelyn leaned forward immediately.

"That's completely out of context," she snapped. "Those events were unrelated. What exactly was I supposed to do with burned land? Replant the entire reserve myself? The donation was simply support for—"

Cross smiled faintly.

Not kindly.

Just enough to silence her.

"Relax," he said. "That report will never air."

He paused.

"At least...not as long as you remain useful."

A knock interrupted the silence.

Gregory entered, carrying a polished silver tray topped with a coffee service. Another assistant followed with pastries arranged beneath glass covers.

Nobody spoke while the staff moved around the room.

Nobody touched the food.

Once the door clicked shut again, Evelyn leaned forward slowly.

"I'm not sure I understand what this meeting is about."

Cross rose from his chair and poured himself a cup of coffee.

He considered the pastries briefly before deciding against them.

Then he sat back down.

"Mayor Carver," he said calmly, "I'm not here to discuss old headlines. I'm here to discuss your future." He gestured lightly around the office. "You've built a strong profile here. Executive experience. National recognition. The kind of political résumé that translates well at higher levels."

His eyes drifted toward the frozen image on the laptop screen.

"But this?"

He tapped the table once.

"This doesn't scale."

Evelyn followed his gaze toward the words: L.A. CORRUPTION

The headline suddenly felt less like journalism and more like a loaded gun resting on the conference table.

"You want the governor's office?" Cross asked. "Then people need to believe you can control the city you already have."

"I am controlling it," Evelyn replied sharply.

Cross took another sip of coffee. "The public disagrees."

"They always disagree," she shot back.

"I don't need universal approval," Cross replied calmly. "I need stability. I need confidence. I need voters believing tomorrow will be better than today." He leaned back slightly. "Right now, the narrative writes itself. Crime. Corruption. Civil unrest. Instability." He shrugged. "That's not a launch platform. That's ballast."

Evelyn's jaw tightened.

"What exactly are you asking me to do?"

"Fix it," Cross said. "Or distract from it."

"Distract?"

"You don't need perfection; you need optics." He gestured toward the paused report again. "Fewer bad headlines. Different headlines. A shift in tone." He spread his hands slightly. "Use your imagination. Just change the narrative."

"And if I can't?"

Cross smiled again.

This time, there was absolutely no warmth in it.

"Then we find someone who can."

Silence settled across the office.

Outside the windows, Los Angeles sprawled endlessly beneath the afternoon sun.

Beautiful from a distance.

Rotting underneath.

Evelyn leaned back slowly in her chair.

"How much time do I have?" she asked quietly.

Cross didn't even blink.

"Not much."

He stood, and with that, the alleged "long" meeting was over. It had been a quick and quiet dismantling of everything she'd done based on what was completely out of her control. Arson. But the donations... She had let that camel nose under the tent.

"We'll be watching your progress," he said smoothly. "Don't let us down."

Evelyn rose quickly, but the delegation was already moving toward the door.

One of the younger aides paused beside her on the way out.

"Los Angeles is your audition," he said quietly. "Don't let it fail you."

Then he disappeared into the hallway.

Evelyn realized she didn't even know the man's name.

Gregory stepped carefully into the office once the others were gone.

"Ma'am," he asked cautiously, "should I clear away the coffee service?"

"Shut the door," Evelyn snapped. "I don't want to be disturbed."

The door clicked shut behind him.

The second she was alone, Evelyn grabbed Cross's coffee cup and hurled it across the office.

It shattered against the window in an explosion of ceramic shards.

The saucer followed an instant later.

Fragments scattered across the carpet.

She stood there, breathing hard, fists clenched at her sides, fighting the urge to scream.

No.

Not here.

Not where someone might hear.

There wasn't time for anger.

Only damage control.

She snatched up her phone and dialed Caroline.

If anyone could salvage this situation, it was her vice mayor.

Several floors below, Caroline Mendoza sat calmly behind her desk, reviewing spreadsheets.

The city's water aquifer was critically low.

The fire department's deputy chief had become increasingly vocal about the amount of dead underbrush spreading through the reserve land. Apparently, the recent fires had convinced him the city was sitting on a powder keg.

Caroline skimmed the latest email.

She typed a quick response:

'I'll address your concerns with the mayor at the earliest opportunity.'

Then she hit send.

Her personal phone rang almost immediately.

Evelyn.

Perfect timing.

Caroline answered brightly.

"Evelyn! How wonderful to hear from you. So, tell me, which movie star did you throw out of your bed this morning?"

"Caroline," Evelyn said sharply, "not today. I need your help."

Even through the phone, the panic was obvious.

Caroline smiled slightly.

"Of course," she said gently. "What happened?"

"Anthony Cross came to my office this morning. The committee says they're watching me for governor, but they think the city's becoming a liability."

Caroline leaned back in her chair, careful to keep the satisfaction out of her voice.

For over a year, she'd been quietly feeding information to Cross.

It looked like the seeds were finally sprouting.

"They expect you to fix Los Angeles overnight?" Caroline asked sympathetically.

"No, of course not," Evelyn replied. "But he said I need to change the narrative. Shift public perception. Give the press something else to focus on."

"How much time do you have?"

"None," Evelyn admitted. "I need something immediately."

Caroline let a thoughtful silence stretch for a moment.

Then, "What if you divorce your husband?"

A pause.

"Don't joke. I'm serious."

"So am I," Caroline replied. "Announce that you've discovered he's been cheating on you. Say he's been exploiting your political position for personal gain." She stood and slowly crossed toward the office window. "Instantly, you become the victim. No reporter wants to attack a woman publicly humiliated by her husband. Sympathy buys time."

Evelyn was quiet.

Thinking.

"That...might actually work."

"Of course it will," Caroline said smoothly. "Then reach out to your studio contacts. Let Hollywood help shape the coverage. You've spent years doing favors for those people; it's time to cash some in."

"You're brilliant," Evelyn breathed. "I knew you'd know what to do."

Caroline smiled.

"When I make governor," Evelyn continued, "I'm taking you with me."

The call disconnected.

Caroline laughed softly after the line went dead.

While she scrambled to protect herself, she'd never notice the city collapsing around her.

Caroline crossed the office and pulled aside a decorative curtain, revealing a hidden restroom door behind it.

Inside, the lights remained off.

She preferred darkness for these conversations.

She reached into her purse and removed a prepaid burner phone.

The glowing keypad reflected faintly across her face in the mirror, giving her features a ghostly underlit look.

She turned away from the reflection and dialed from memory.

The line rang twice.

Then a male voice answered.

"Yeah."

"It's me," Caroline said. "I want action."

"What kind of action?"

"I need your club here now."

The man sighed.

"Relax. We'll be there on Saturday. A couple extra days won't matter."

"I'm not paying for delays," Caroline snapped. "I want destruction. Fires. Violence. Panic. I want the city scared."

Silence.

Then, “You’re asking for a warzone.”

“I’m asking for results.”

“You’ll get attention.”

“That’s the point.”

“And when that attention turns?”

Caroline smiled into the darkness.

“That’s not your concern,” she said. “I’ll decide where it lands.”

The voice hesitated.

“We’re talking about moving a lot of men. Weapons. Supplies. We can’t magically appear overnight.”

Caroline’s eyes narrowed. “It’s exactly like that,” she said coldly. “There’s another million dollars waiting if your people arrive tomorrow.”

This time, the silence stretched longer.

“...yeah,” the man said finally. “We’ll move.”

“Good.”

“Make sure the safehouse is ready.”

The line went dead.

Caroline slowly lowered the phone.

Then she turned back toward the mirror.

The faint glow of the keypad illuminated her grin from below, twisting it into something inhuman.

For the first time, she didn’t look away from her reflection.

“It’s time,” she whispered softly, “to give this city a facelift.”

Chapter 20

I WOKE WITH THE sun, feeling refreshed and strangely satisfied.

The devil on my shoulder whispered that it wouldn't last.

I ignored him.

A hot shower washed away the desert dust from the night before. As I dried off and pulled on my clothes, one thought settled into my brain stronger than anything else.

Coffee.

Real coffee.

Not Miss Tilly's sludge that could strip paint off an engine block.

And I wasn't ready to head back to the clubhouse yet.

As I laced up my boots, I could almost smell fresh coffee in the air. Now all I had to do was find it.

I opened the door.

Sally collapsed inward.

She'd been asleep against the doorframe.

My hands shot out to catch her—

Then froze.

Her face was bruised.

One lip split open.

I slowly removed the oversized sunglasses from her face.

Two black eyes stared back at me.

My stomach dropped.

I looked her over quickly.

Bruises circled both wrists.

More around her ankles.

Rope marks.

Someone had tied her down.

Someone had hurt her.

A dark pressure built in my chest so fast it almost made me dizzy.

Carefully, I scooped her into my arms and carried her to the bed. She didn't wake.

I pulled the sheets up to her chin and stepped back outside.

Her Jeep sat crooked in the parking lot.

The keys were still in the ignition.

A small black purse covered in glitter lay on the passenger seat.

I hadn't seen it before, but somehow, I already knew what was inside.

I opened it.

Ten one-hundred-dollar bills wrapped in a red rubber band.

My jaw tightened.

I climbed into the Jeep and drove to the nearest drugstore.

I bought peroxide, aspirin, bandages, gauze, and a basic first-aid kit.

The cashier recommended the grocery store down the street for coffee and doughnuts.

Turned out she was right.

The place had a small coffee counter with fresh pastries stacked behind glass displays.

I bought two large coffees and half a dozen assorted doughnuts.

Then I returned to the motel room to wait for Sally to wake up.

And while I waited...

I thought about Preacher.

My mind had already decided who was responsible.

It was time to stop drifting around this assignment.

It was time to focus.

Preacher had to die.

Sally slept until nearly afternoon.

While she slept, I drank both coffees, ate half the doughnuts, cleaned my .357, and sharpened my knife.

The metallic scrape of the whetstone filled the room in slow, steady strokes.

Finally, Sally whimpered softly and opened her eyes.

She stared blankly at the ceiling.

I slid the knife back into its sheath and holstered the revolver behind my back before moving to the bed.

I sat carefully beside her and brushed damp strands of hair from her face.

"Hey, girl," I said softly. "Anything I can do?"

She shook her head.

Tears gathered at the corners of her eyes and rolled silently into the pillow.

"I grabbed some first-aid stuff," I said. "But I'm not exactly a nurse."

Truth was, I was afraid touching her would hurt her worse.

"Do I smell coffee?" she asked weakly.

I gave her a guilty smile.

"You did," I admitted. "But I drank it while you were sleeping. I've still got water and doughnuts, though."

"How about aspirin?"

I handed her the bottle and some water.

She shook four tablets into her palm and swallowed them with a long drink.

"I need a shower," she whispered.

But she didn't move.

She just stared upward.

"Want me to get lunch?" I asked. "Anything you want."

"Not yet." Her voice cracked. "I...don't want to be alone."

I lay beside her carefully and rested a hand against her hip.

"How bad was it?" I asked quietly.

"I don't want to talk about it."

She rolled against me and buried her face against my chest.

A few seconds later, I felt her crying again.

Silent tears soaked through my shirt while I wrapped my arms around her and waited.

Eventually, the crying slowed.

When she was ready, she took the first-aid kit and one of my cleaner T-shirts into the bathroom.

At her request, I waited outside the door while she showered.

While the water ran, I texted Gunny my update.

'Mission is still on track. It'll be finished by the end of the week.'

I still had no idea how I was going to pull it off.

But one thing felt certain now.

Preacher was never leaving Kingman alive.

When Sally finally stepped out of the bathroom, she was wearing my oversized T-shirt.

Her wet hair hung down past her shoulders.

A bandage covered one cheek.

And her eyes stayed fixed on the floor like she couldn't bear to look at me.

I stepped closer and gently lifted her chin.

Then I kissed her softly.

Fresh tears spilled down her face instantly.

I wrapped her against my chest and held her there until the shaking stopped.

By sundown, she finally admitted she was hungry, but she still didn't want me leaving the room.

Fortunately, Kingman had pizza delivery.

And once I mentioned I was with the club, the delivery driver agreed to pick up a case of beer too.

Sally climbed back beneath the blankets while we waited for the food.

She pulled the sheets all the way up to her chin like armor.

I sat beside her quietly for a while before speaking.

"At some point," I said carefully, "I'm gonna want to know what happened."

She stared toward the television without really seeing it.

"And I'm gonna want to know who did it."

Her fingers tightened slightly around the blanket.

"It doesn't have to be tonight," I continued. "But whoever did this..."

I paused.

"...I'm going to make it right."

Sally only shrugged and looked away.

"It was just some guys," Sally whispered. "They were from out of town. I don't even know their names."

"How many?" I asked.

"Three."

My jaw tightened.

"I need to talk to Preacher about this. He'll get me their names."

Sally shook her head immediately.

"Don't. I don't want this spread all over the club. Just let it go."

"You told me he keeps the girls safe," I said. "Well, it's time he steps up."

She looked exhausted.

"Wait until after we eat," she said quietly. "Then I'll take you to his place."

I frowned.

"What? I thought he lived at the clubhouse."

"He's got a trailer outside town," she said. "He's only there a few hours at a time. That's where he meets the girls."

I pulled a chair over beside the bed and sat down beside her, holding her hand gently.

A trailer.

So, Preacher wasn't untouchable after all.

The pizza wasn't much better than the beer.

I'd ordered the carnivore special.

Sally had gone with pineapple, ham, and jalapeños.

That alone should've counted as a felony.

The beer was generic light stuff that tasted like somebody had filtered water through stale bread. Probably whatever had been cheapest at the grocery store.

Still, the food helped.

The beer helped more.

Sally downed three fast ones before slowing. By the fourth, some of the tension had finally started to leave her shoulders.

Once she finished eating, I brought the conversation back around.

"I want to go talk to Preacher," I said carefully. "You said you'd give me the address."

She closed the pizza box and stared at it for a long moment before answering.

"I don't want you to go."

"It'll be fine," I said. "He needs to know what those pieces of shit did to you."

She laughed once. Cold. Bitter.

It sent a chill straight through me.

"He already knows."

I stared at her. "What?"

"He knows."

"Did you already tell him?"

She shook her head slowly.

"No. He sets up the dates. You think he doesn't know exactly what every girl is walking into?"

The room suddenly felt smaller.

"He runs the club," she continued quietly. "That's why nobody messes with the girls. Everybody knows what happens if someone hurts one of us." Her eyes found mine. "This wasn't random."

The words landed like a pile driver.

"This was punishment."

My stomach turned.

"Punishment for what?"

"When I gave you that money for him," she said softly, "I told him I was thinking about getting out."

I felt my heartbeat slow. Cold. Controlled. Dangerous.

"This was supposed to be my last job."

For a second, I couldn't speak.

"Welcome to the MC," she whispered. "Once you're in...you're in for life." She rested a trembling hand against my chest. "That goes for you, too."

I stared at her bruised face while anger built quietly inside me.

"You wear his patch," she said. "He owns you."

"You want out," I said. "I'll explain that to him."

She shook her head violently.

"He'll kill me."

I pulled her into my arms.

"I'm not letting that happen."

"How?" she whispered. "He'll kill you."

I couldn't stop the grim smile that touched my face.

The irony almost made me laugh.

"I don't think so," I said.

I looked into her swollen eyes.

"What's the address?"

She hesitated.

Then, finally, she gave in.

"It's east of town. Off Route 66. There's a red mailbox beside the road with no numbers on it."

I listened carefully.

"You turn there and follow the dirt road about a mile. White single-wide trailer with a beige stripe running the length of it." She swallowed hard. "There's a shed out back. That's where he keeps his bike."

Tears rolled down her cheeks again as she gave me the directions.

I stood and moved toward the door.

Then she grabbed my arm.

"Don't do this," she pleaded. "Please." Her fingers tightened around me. "Stay here. I'll take care of you."

That settled it.

Because the moment she said that, I realized something ugly.

There was no version of this where I walked away.

Not while Preacher still owned her.

Not while he could send her out again.

Not while he could hurt her whenever he felt like making a point.

I paused beside the door and stared at my cut hanging over the chair.

The skeletal hand flipped me off beneath the dim motel light.

I picked it up slowly.

This might be the last time I ever wore it.

I swung onto Beyoncé and brought her to life.

The engine rumbled beneath me like an angry animal.

The low-fuel light glowed bright orange on the instrument panel.

One more delay before I handled business.

I pulled onto Route 66 heading east, searching the darkness for a red mailbox beside the road.

And somewhere out there...

Preacher waited.

I spotted the red mailbox and rolled past it.

A few hundred yards farther down Route 66 stood an old billboard advertising Kingman to tourists chasing the nostalgia of the Mother Road.

Perfect place to stash Beyoncé.

I parked the bike behind the sign, where she'd disappear into the shadows, and started hiking down the dirt road.

The .357 rested heavy in my hand.

Sally said the trailer was only about a mile in.

The desert was dead quiet except for the crunch of gravel beneath my boots and the distant hum of highway traffic.

Eventually, I spotted it.

A white rectangle against the gray desert night.

No lights.

No movement.

I circled around the trailer carefully, keeping low.

The front door stood slightly open.

My pulse kicked up.

I eased closer and listened.

Nothing.

I slipped inside.

The trailer was empty.

I checked the time and grimaced.

Only ten o'clock.

If Sally was right, Preacher might not show up for hours.

And even then there was no guarantee.

He could've decided to spend the night at the clubhouse instead.

Still... Since I was already here, I figured I might as well learn something useful.

The trailer looked exactly like his office. Minimal. Controlled. Almost sterile.

The living room held only a couch and a television. Nothing else.

The kitchen had place settings for two.

The fridge was stocked with beer and frozen Chinese dinners.

The bedroom was the only space that looked remotely lived in.

An unmade bed.

Shelves stacked with neatly folded clothes.

No photographs. No decorations. No books. No keepsakes. Nothing personal.

The place felt temporary.

Like Preacher existed there but didn't actually live there.

I slipped back outside and climbed a low hill overlooking the trailer.

Far enough away to stay hidden.

Close enough to watch the place.

I lay down on the back side of the hill and stared up at the stars while I waited to kill the president of my motorcycle club.

At some point, I must've drifted off.

The sound of a motorcycle engine snapped me awake.

I eased up to the crest of the hill and spotted a single headlight cutting through the darkness.

I drew the .357 and waited.

The motorcycle swung around to the far side of the trailer and killed the engine.

About a hundred yards out.

Easy shot with a rifle.

Hard shot with a pistol.

I'd have to get closer.

Preacher stepped around the trailer with a woman hanging off him like a second skin.

They disappeared inside, and a light flicked on.

Bad move.

The light wrecked their night vision.

Mine stayed intact.

I crouched low and sprinted toward the trailer, keeping to the shadows.

When I reached the side window, I knelt beneath it and listened.

Honestly, it felt less like surveillance and more like peeping through a stranger's bedroom window.

Even if I got a clean angle...

The girl was still a witness.

This was never going to be tidy.

I settled in and waited for an opening.

Then I heard more engines.

Headlights rolled down the dirt road.

I cursed under my breath and slid beneath the trailer.

Three motorcycles pulled up hard in the driveway.

Bear, Clubfoot, and the vice president.

"Preacher!" Clubfoot hammered on the door.

"What the hell's going on?" Preacher snapped as he opened it.

The other bikers shoved their way inside.

"Something's off with that crazy L.A. broad," someone said.

"What does she want now?"

"I was on the phone with her. She wants us there tomorrow. And she doesn't want a *little* chaos." A pause. "She wants us to torch the city."

I shifted beneath the trailer, listening hard.

"Well," Preacher said, "that's what I told everybody at the meeting. She's just moving up the timeline."

"I don't think you understand," Clubfoot shot back. "She wants the city burning. Not a few houses or storefronts." His voice sharpened. "She wants the beachfront torched. The docks burned. Factories. Warehouses." A beat. "There's over a hundred locations on the list."

"And?" Preacher asked.

"And people are gonna die."

Silence.

Then, Preacher answered calmly, "Yeah, I know what she wants."

That chilled me worse than the desert air.

"We won't hit every target," he continued. "If the heat gets too big, we pull out and disappear." He laughed once. "But this kind of payday?"

I could practically hear him grinning.

"Every man riding out there could come home with a million dollars in his saddlebags."

"Money won't matter if we're dead," the VP said.

"Fine," Preacher snapped. "Make it voluntary. Anybody too scared can stay home." His voice rose. "But nobody staying behind gets a cut."

"You need to think about this."

"No," Preacher barked. "You're doing too much thinking."

The trailer shook slightly as somebody slammed a hand against a wall.

"This is the job. If you don't want it, stay home."

Silence.

Then Preacher again, "Unless there's something else, get the hell out."

The trailer door slammed open.

Bootsteps crunched across gravel.

"I think this needs to go before the whole club," the VP said outside.

"You should've brought it up at the meeting," Preacher shot back. "Too late now."

"This isn't a one-man club."

"We'll discuss it tomorrow."

Preacher banged on the trailer door.

"Candy! Get out here. Looks like business just ruined our evening."

A blonde woman stepped outside carrying her cowboy boots.

She paused long enough to kiss Preacher hard.

"Can I get a raincheck for tomorrow?" she asked.

"Maybe," Preacher said. "Depends how long L.A. keeps me busy."

She laughed softly and turned toward the bikes.

"Who's making room for little old me?"

"Hop on," Bear answered.

Candy climbed onto the back of Bear's bike.

A second later, engines roared to life.

The motorcycles disappeared into the darkness in a cloud of exhaust and dust.

And suddenly...

I was alone with Preacher in the middle of nowhere.

Chapter 21

I SLIPPED OUT FROM beneath the trailer and circled around to the rear shed where Preacher kept his bike.

Now that I finally had the president of this insane motorcycle club alone...

I wasn't about to let him disappear into the desert.

I crouched beside the Harley and yanked the spark plug wires loose.

It wouldn't stop him forever.

But it might buy me a few seconds if things went bad.

And right now, a few seconds sounded priceless.

I slid back beneath the trailer with the .357 resting heavy in my hand.

If Preacher came out for the bike...

I'd shoot him.

If he went to sleep...

I'd make sure he never woke up.

The night dragged on.

My arms and legs stiffened from lying motionless.

Occasionally, I heard movement inside.

A floorboard creaking.

A cabinet door.

The muffled sound of footsteps.

But mostly, the desert stayed silent.

I checked my watch and frowned.

Three in the morning.

At this point, I was starting to wonder if the man ever slept.

Enough waiting.

If I wanted this done, I'd have to make my own opportunity.

I eased myself out from beneath the trailer and moved toward the back door.

The .357 led the way.

I paused beside the window and listened. Nothing. No voices. No television. No movement.

I crept to the door and slowly tested the handle.

Unlocked.

I almost laughed.

The president of a violent outlaw motorcycle club didn't even bother locking his own front door.

Either that was confidence...or insanity. Maybe both.

I eased the door open an inch and froze, listening for any reaction from inside.

Nothing.

Another inch.

Still nothing.

From my angle, the living room looked empty.

This was it.

I opened the door just wide enough to slip through.

Then, it slowly closed behind me.

Every movement measured.

Every breath controlled.

When the latch finally clicked softly into place, I allowed myself one careful breath.

The trailer looked exactly the same as earlier.

Open living room. Tiny kitchen. Dead silence. No sign of Preacher.

Which probably meant he was in the bedroom.

Hopefully asleep.

Hopefully stupid enough to leave the light on.

I crossed the room slowly, keeping to the shadows, making sure mine never stretched beneath the bedroom doorway.

The .357 stayed raised in both hands.

No sound. No movement. No breathing.

I reached the bedroom door and stopped.

My hand hovered over the knob while I steadied my nerves.

Then, I slowly turned it.

The door cracked open barely an inch.

Light spilled through the gap.

Still no sound.

I pushed it open another fraction and leaned forward just enough to look inside.

I found myself staring straight down the barrel of a .45.

Close enough to see the rifling spiraling into darkness.

"Welcome to hell," Preacher growled.

My blood turned cold.

"Be real careful what you do next," he said quietly. "One wrong move and your life's over... Even I can't miss from this distance."

The gun never moved.

Not even a tremor.

"Pass me your revolver," he said. "Butt first."

For half a second, I considered it. Push through the doorway. Pull the trigger. Maybe we both die.

Instead, I reversed the .357 and handed it over.

Preacher snatched it from my grip and tossed it onto the bed behind him without taking his eyes off me.

"Nice and slow," he said. "Back up."

I obeyed.

"We're going into the living room."

The .45 followed my face every step of the way.

I tried to answer, but my mouth had gone completely dry.

I swallowed hard.

"I understand."

My voice sounded weak even to me.

When we reached the couch, Preacher motioned with the pistol.

"Take the fucking cut off."

I slipped out of the vest and tossed it onto the cushions beside me.

"Any other guns?"

"No."

He studied me for another second and then nodded toward the couch.

"Sit."

I lowered myself carefully onto the cushions.

Preacher grabbed my cut and flung it across the room like it disgusted him.

Then he pulled a kitchen chair around backward and sat facing me.

The .45 rested casually in his hand.

But the barrel never drifted far from my chest.

"You know something, Hammer?" He leaned back slightly. "I never trusted you."

The room felt smaller by the second.

"You were too eager," he continued. "Too willing."

He shook his head slowly.

"Young probies? That makes sense. Kids always want to belong to something." His eyes narrowed. "But you?" A long pause. "A man your age doesn't work this hard to join a club like ours."

He studied me carefully, squinting like he was trying to peel my face apart layer by layer.

"I told the others you were moving too fast."

I forced myself not to look away.

My heartbeat pounded in my ears.

"So, what now?" I asked quietly.

"We're going to have ourselves a little chat," Preacher said. "And if I think for even one second that you're lying to me..." He let the sentence hang. "The interview's over." Then he smiled. "Where are my manners? Want a beer? Might be the last one you ever drink."

I licked my lips again.

Still dry.

"Yeah," I said quietly. "I could go for a beer."

Preacher motioned toward the kitchen with the pistol.

"Fridge."

I stood slowly.

Every movement deliberate.

No sudden motions.

No clever ideas.

I turned my back on the gun and walked toward the kitchen.

One step. Two. Three. I counted every one of them. Seven steps to the refrigerator.

I opened the door carefully and reached inside for two bottles.

Still alive. That felt important.

I turned around slowly.

The .45 pointed straight at my chest.

Five steps back.

I handed him one of the beers.

He took it without lowering the gun.

Then I walked back to the couch.

Somewhere along the way, I forgot to keep counting.

After I sat, we both twisted off the caps and took a drink.

The beer was ice cold.

Cold enough my fingers stuck slightly to the glass.

Cold enough to hurt my teeth.

It tasted better than any beer I'd ever had in my life.

Probably because I thought it might be my last.

I forced myself to stop after one swallow.

Every part of me wanted to drain the bottle.

"Taste good?" Preacher asked.

"Yeah."

He nodded slowly.

"Funny how much we appreciate the little things when we're standing at the edge of the grave."

He took another drink and smacked his lips.

Then his eyes locked onto mine again.

"So," he said. "Business."

The pistol rested casually across his leg.

Still pointed in my direction.

"Why are you here?"

"To end it."

The words slipped out before I could stop them.

Preacher raised an eyebrow.

"Go on."

"You," I said. "The club. Violence follows you everywhere. Bodies pile up behind you."

The smile faded slightly.

His eyes narrowed into slits.

For a second, I thought this was it.

That I'd finally said the wrong thing.

Then the smile slowly returned.

He leaned back in the chair.

"That's a hell of an accusation, but honestly?" He shrugged slightly. "You're not exactly wrong."

The pistol stayed loose in his hand.

"So tell me something," he continued. "Did I do something to you personally?"

"No." I swallowed hard. "An assassin. Pay me enough and I put bad men in the ground."

Preacher exploded with laughter. Deep. Violent. Genuine.

But even while laughing, the pistol rose back toward my face.

I stared at the barrel while he laughed.

Part of me wondered if I'd see the muzzle flash before I died.

"So..." he finally said, wiping tears from one eye. "Who wants me dead?"

I closed my eyes, trying to recall the contract details Gunny had shown me months ago, a name I wasn't supposed to know.

"Caroline Mendoza."

Everything changed.

Preacher shot to his feet.

"That bitch!"

The rage in his voice rattled the walls.

He grabbed the kitchen chair and hurled it across the trailer. It exploded in the corner.

"Son of a bitch!"

The gun came up.

BOOM.

The shot deafened me.

Beer bottles shattered across the floor.

Foam splashed across the linoleum.

Stuffing drifted lazily from the bullet hole punched through the cushion beside me.

I gripped the edge of the couch and stayed perfectly still.

Preacher kicked the wall hard enough to shake the trailer.

My heart hammered so violently, I thought it might burst.

"When?" he barked.

"When what?"

He pointed the pistol at my face again.

The barrel trembled with fury.

"When did she hire you?"

"At least six months ago."

He slapped the pistol against his leg.

"That bitch!"

He paced across the trailer like a caged animal.

This time, he didn't fire.

"How do you keep a secret?" he snapped.

Then answered himself.

"You kill everybody who knows it."

I must have looked confused, because he shook his head angrily and kicked the wall again. "Of course you don't get it. She's behind all of this."

He stormed to the refrigerator, kicked it once for good measure, then ripped the door open and grabbed two more beers.

He tossed one at me.

I caught it automatically.

Before I realized what I was doing, I'd already drained half the bottle.

"That bitch," he muttered again as he dropped back into the chair.

Finally, I spoke.

"I don't understand."

Preacher leaned forward, elbows on his knees.

"It started about a year ago," he said. "She contacted me out of nowhere. No idea how she got my number." He shook his head. "For some stupid reason, I answered."

The .45 dangled loosely from his fingers now.

"She wanted chaos." His eyes drifted toward the dark window. "She wanted fear. Violence. Fires. Riots. Pressure. She wanted Los Angeles turned into a warzone." He looked back at me and laughed bitterly. "And I helped her do it."

"Why?" I asked.

"Fuck if I know," Preacher snapped. "Something about a hostile takeover. We were the hostile part while she handled the takeover."

He drained the beer and hurled the empty bottle against the wall.

Glass exploded across the trailer.

I finished mine more carefully and set it beside the couch.

"She's been playing me from the beginning," he muttered. "Hell, she's got the club fighting itself now." He pointed toward the door with the pistol. "I heard the boys outside earlier. You heard them too." His eyes narrowed. "Where were you hiding?"

He paused.

A grin slowly spread across his face.

"No...not the desert." He pointed the barrel of the gun toward the floor. "You were under my damn trailer."

My jaw dropped before I could stop it.

Preacher barked out a laugh.

"Don't look so surprised," he said. "You think you're the first man to come after me?" He tapped the side of his head. "Motion detectors. I knew you were inside the trailer the second you opened the door."

He slapped the pistol lightly against his thigh again, though most of the rage had burned itself out.

"You know," he said, "you're not the first assassin somebody's sent after me." He studied me for a long moment. "But you're the one who got the closest."

Silence settled over the trailer.

Then, "Take your shirt off."

"What?"

The pistol lifted slightly.

Not threatening.

Certain.

"Why?"

He just stared at me.

I pulled the shirt over my head.

"Turn around."

I stood and turned my back to him.

"Pant legs too. Let me see the tops of your boots."

I rolled them up slowly.

"Good enough."

Then, to my surprise, he ejected the magazine from the .45 and tossed it into the kitchen.

The chambered round slid across the floor after he racked the slide.

A second later, the pistol disappeared into the bedroom.

Then he pulled the hunting knife from his belt.

The blade flashed silver under the trailer lights.

"Did you bring a knife?" he asked.

I reached into my pocket and pulled out my folding knife.

Thumb on the stud. Flick. The blade snapped open with a metallic click.

Preacher nodded once.

"Good."

"We don't have to do this," I said carefully. "I didn't know she was playing both sides."

"It doesn't matter."

His voice went cold again.

"I'm guilty of every crime you came here to stop."

He rolled his shoulders once.

"You're an assassin."

The knife tilted toward me.

"I'm a killer."

A grim smile spread across his face.

"So, this?"

He widened his stance.

"This is exactly how it ends."

Sweat broke across my skin instantly.

The trailer suddenly felt ten degrees hotter.

"Well, Hammer," Preacher said softly. "It's been real."

Then he lunged.

Fast.

Way faster than a man his size should move.

I slipped right, staying barely outside his reach.

"Don't do this," I warned again.

He circled the trailer and kicked a second kitchen chair out of his way.

It skidded across the floor between us.

"You came into my house to kill me," he growled. "Now you want to walk away peaceful?" He shook his head. "I don't think so."

He prowled sideways.

Knife low.

Eyes locked onto mine.

"Some lessons have to be taught the hard way."

He came at me again.

This time, I dodged left and slapped his knife-arm wide.

The blade sliced downward anyway.

Pain flared across my forearm.

A shallow cut.

Not serious.

But enough.

Blood rolled toward my wrist.

Preacher smiled.

"First blood."

He suddenly reversed direction, circling the opposite way.

I mirrored him.

Then he kicked an empty beer bottle across the trailer.

Instinct made me glance toward the movement.

That was the mistake.

He exploded forward.

A left hook smashed into my jaw.

My head snapped sideways.

I grabbed his wrist with my free hand and yanked him past me.

He bounced off the wall and turned back, grinning.

My turn.

I drove forward with a fast left-right combination.

The first punch hammered into his ribs.

He rolled with it.

My knife missed his face by inches.

He answered with a brutal elbow to my temple.

Stars burst across my vision.

I stumbled backward.

Too slow.

His knife slashed across my side, scraping a rib.

Hot pain tore through me.

I spun away instinctively.

Preacher smiled wider and licked the blood from his blade.

The sight sent a chill crawling down my spine.

"What's wrong, Hammer?" he taunted. "Never gone toe-to-toe with a real killer before?"

He stalked toward me slowly.

"I bet you're the kind of man who works from a distance."

Another step.

"Behind a scope."

Another.

"But this?"

He spread his arms slightly.

"This is personal."

He attacked again.

This time, I was ready.

His knife shot toward my stomach.

I twisted sideways and slashed hard across his forearm.

Blood opened instantly along the outside.

He jerked back.

I surged forward before he could recover.

Not with the knife.

With my boot.

I drove a hard kick straight into him.

He slammed into the trailer wall and crashed to the floor.

The print of my boot sat square in the middle of his chest.

Preacher swung wildly with the knife, keeping me back while he climbed to his feet.

"So the boy can fight," he said, breathing harder now. "Guess I don't have to take it easy on you anymore."

Then he launched himself at me.

His roundhouse kick glanced off the side of my head.

I never saw it coming.

The world spun sideways, and I crashed onto the couch.

Preacher came after me instantly.

Knee driving toward my chest.

Knife raised overhead.

Looking for the kill.

I rolled off the couch at the last second.

His knee slammed into the cushions hard enough to shake the trailer.

I shoved his leg sideways to keep him off balance and scrambled across the floor.

Make space.

Get up.

Don't die.

Pain exploded across my back.

I rolled until I hit the wall.

Preacher was already back on his feet.

His boot slammed into my ribs.

"Come on," he growled. "Get up. I don't kill men lying on the floor."

He stepped in for another kick.

I exploded forward.

Shoulder low.

I tackled both his legs and drove through him with everything I had left.

He crashed backward onto the floor.

His knife missed my spine by inches.

I landed on top of him.

Knee in his stomach.

Both hands clamped his wrist to the floor.

Preacher hammered a hook into my ribs.

The punch drove the air from my lungs.

I gritted my teeth and drove my rear knee into his side, but the strike lacked power.

I couldn't get leverage while fighting his knife-arm.

Another hook smashed into my gut.

Black spots burst across my vision.

I yanked his arm upward, trapped it against my chest, and dropped backward.

My leg whipped over his shoulder as I fell.

Armbar.

His elbow locked tight against my hips.

I pulled hard.

Preacher roared in pain, but he still refused to let go of the knife.

His legs kicked violently.

His free hand grabbed his own wrist, relieving pressure before I could break the arm.

We rolled across the trailer floor in a tangled mess of limbs and blood.

My leg slipped free.

His arm came loose.

Move.

Create distance.

Get up.

Don't die.

I kicked him hard in the face and shoved backward across the floor.

We both scrambled to our feet. Both breathing hard. Both bleeding.

Preacher switched the knife into his left hand.

I raised my fists automatically.

One came up red with blood.

I hadn't even felt him cut me.

Blood streamed down my forearm and dripped from my fingertips.

I stepped forward.

My legs felt heavy now.

Like concrete blocks tied to my boots.

Preacher moved slower too.

That viper-like speed was gone.

I reversed my knife grip.

Blade down along my pinky.

Then lunged.

Knife high.

Driving down toward his collarbone.

Preacher's blade snapped upward to block, and my left fist smashed into his face.

Crunch.

His nose broke under my knuckles.

He staggered backward into the wall.

His knife drifted wide.

Mine came down hard.

The blade sliced along the side of his face, opening his cheek nearly to the ear before burying deep into his shoulder.

The knife stuck fast.

Preacher roared and shoved me backward.

My knife stayed buried in him.

His own knife stayed low.

Still hunting my stomach.

He charged.

I caught his wrist, spun him sideways, and hammered two punches into his kidneys.

He stumbled toward the far side of the trailer while I leaned against the wall, sucking air into burning lungs.

I was hurt.

But he was hurt worse.

Preacher leaned back against the wall and laughed through bloody teeth.

"I don't believe it," he rasped. "You might actually get me."

He flipped the knife in his hand and caught it by the blade.

My eyes widened.

Then his arm snapped forward.

The knife flew at me like a bullet.

I tried to dodge.

Too slow.

The blade slammed into my bicep and buried itself to the bone.

White-hot pain exploded through my arm.

Before I could react, Preacher was already digging inside his cut for something else.

Gun.

I ripped the knife from my arm and charged him before he could clear leather.

His hand came free with a short-barreled pistol.

The gunshot detonated inside the tiny trailer.

Then I hit him.

We crashed to the floor together in a bloody heap.

Pain tore through my leg like molten steel.

I looked down and saw a hole punched through my jeans.

Blood poured down my calf.

Shot.

I'd been shot.

I looked over at Preacher.

The hunting knife protruded from his stomach.

His eyes locked onto mine.

Pure fury.

He raised the pistol toward my face.

I kicked out desperately and smashed his wrist.

The gun flew free, skidding across the trailer toward the kitchen.

"Well..." Preacher coughed.

Blood spilled from the corner of his mouth.

"...fuck me."

He spat a mouthful of blood onto the floor between us.

"Damn."

The side door exploded inward.

Bash stormed into the trailer with a pistol already drawn.

Chapter 22

Bash stepped into the trailer, pistol raised.

The barrel moved between Preacher and me before finally settling on my chest.

"What the hell is going on?"

How had I missed the sound of the Fat Boy pulling up?

Then again, I'd been a little busy fighting for my life.

I raised my empty, blood-covered hands.

"Easy, Bash," I said. "This isn't what it looks like."

Preacher gave a wet laugh and spat another mouthful of blood onto the floor.

"So, it doesn't look like he shoved my own fucking knife into my gut?"

Bash's expression darkened instantly.

"Hammer..." he said slowly. "Is that true?"

"Hold up," Preacher rasped. "Put the gun down first. We're gonna talk before you decide whether or not to kill him."

Blood spread wider beneath him with every second.

Bash lowered the pistol slightly but kept both hands locked on the grip.

"Hammer," he repeated. "Did you do this?"

His voice sounded softer now.

Hurt.

"Oh yeah," Preacher growled. "Turns out the prospect you sponsored is a cold-blooded killer." He waved weakly toward me. "Boy came here in the middle of the night to end me. Sit down," Preacher ordered. "I don't have enough time left to crane my neck looking at you."

Bash slowly lowered himself onto the couch.

The pistol rested across his lap.

Still ready.

Still dangerous.

Preacher's eyes shifted back to me.

There was hatred there.

And something final.

"I'm dead," he said flatly, blood bubbling at the corner of his mouth, "so you've got two choices. One..." he wheezed, "...we go to hell together." He coughed hard and pointed weakly at me. "Or...you do a job for me."

"What job?"

"I want you to kill the bitch who hired you."

I stared at him.

"It doesn't work like that."

Preacher gave the faintest smile. "Maybe not." His eyes drifted toward Bash. "But he can shoot you right now."

I looked over.

Bash said nothing.

The tears building in his eyes came as a surprise.

"The people I work for are careful with contracts," I said quietly. "We target the worst people we can find."

Preacher's head sagged forward.

He sucked air through bloody teeth before forcing himself upright one last time.

"In my desk..." he whispered. "Clubhouse."

His breathing rattled now.

"Taped under the top drawer."

He swallowed hard.

"Thumb drive."

Another wet cough.

"I didn't trust her."

Blood dripped from his chin.

"I kept copies..."

He fought for another breath.

"Everything."

His eyes found mine again.

"Take it to your people."

A long pause.

"Key's in my cut."

Then his head lowered.

This time, it stayed there.

Bash and I sat in silence while Preacher's breathing slowed...

...and stopped.

The trailer suddenly felt impossibly quiet.

Finally, I spoke.

"I need to go."

Bash looked at the body.

"You killed Preacher."

"Yeah."

He sat up slowly and raised the pistol again.

"You have five minutes to disappear."

I slid sideways across the floor toward my shirt.

The movement sent pain tearing through my leg.

I ripped the shirt in half and tied it around the bullet wound as tightly as I could.

I wrapped the other half around my bleeding forearm.

Using the wall for support, I forced myself upright.

My leg held.

Barely.

Automatically, I reached down and grabbed my cut from beside the wall.

"No."

Bash's voice cracked like a whip.

"You don't deserve that."

I froze.

"Leave it."

The pistol stayed fixed on me.

Tears rolled silently through his beard now.

"You killed two brothers tonight," he said. "Preacher..." His voice tightened. "...and Hammer."

That was no surprise. After what happened to Sally, I wasn't among a brotherhood.

"I don't even know who the hell you are," Bash continued. "But I owed Hammer." He wiped angrily at one eye. "I'll bury this for the brothers. I'll tell them what they need to hear."

The pistol never moved.

"But you do the job Preacher asked for."

Silence stretched between us.

Then, "If I ever see you again..." His jaw clenched. "...I'll kill you myself."

I nodded once.

No argument.

No excuses.

I limped toward the door.

"Wait."

I turned carefully.

Bash knelt beside Preacher's body and dug through the cut until he found a ring of keys.

He tossed them toward me.

I caught them awkwardly one-handed.

"Now get the fuck out of here," he said quietly. "Before I change my mind."

I stepped out into the desert night.

And left the club behind me.

My leg burned with every step. A mile walk had been nothing earlier, but now it was going to be one more trial in a long line of them.

The bullet wound pulsed hot inside my thigh.

My bicep throbbed where Preacher's knife had buried itself to the bone.

Everything hurt.

But my body still worked.

So I kept moving.

Head down.

Faster.

Because Bash was balancing on the edge of something ugly.

And if he changed his mind...

...I wanted as much desert between us as possible.

Somewhere off the roadside, something large moved through the brush.

Branches rattled softly.

Following me.

If it was a predator drawn by blood, I was finished.

All my weapons were still back at the trailer.

And there was no chance in hell I was going back.

The brush shook again.

Closer this time.

I pushed harder.

The main road appeared ahead through the darkness.

Maybe a hundred yards away.

Then the trailer exploded.

A massive red fireball punched into the night sky behind me.

Heat rolled across the desert.

The blast echoed off the distant hills like thunder.

The world turned blood red for a moment.

Whatever creature had been stalking me vanished instantly into the darkness.

Coyote.

Maybe a mountain lion.

Didn't matter.

I kept moving.

A few minutes later, I slipped behind the billboard where Beyoncé waited in the shadows.

I threw my leg over the saddle, twisted the throttle, and pointed her toward the clubhouse one final time.

I took Beyoncé around the back and parked beside the rear entrance.

The eastern horizon was just starting to turn pink.

Dawn.

I checked my phone. 4:45 a.m.

Too early for most of the club to be moving around. Good.

I slipped off the bike and limped toward the door.

My leg had stiffened badly during the ride over, but I didn't have time to baby it.

I pulled the keyring from my pocket and worked the lock.

Only two keys sat on the ring. One full-sized. One small silver key.

The larger key slid perfectly into the lock.

I slipped inside and quietly shut the door behind me.

The clubhouse felt dead at this hour. Dark. Silent.

The office looked exactly the same as before.

Military surplus furniture. Bare walls. Minimalist. Functional.

I collapsed into Preacher's desk chair and took a moment to breathe through the pain.

Then I crossed my fingers and pulled open the top drawer.

Paperwork. Envelopes. Receipts. Licenses. Everything it probably took to keep a semi-legal biker bar running.

I reached underneath the drawer.

My fingers brushed duct tape.

Then plastic.

Thumb drive.

I peeled it free and shoved it into my pocket.

If Preacher told the truth...

...this might blow the whole thing open.

The chair squealed softly as I leaned back.

That's when I noticed the bottom drawer.

Every instinct told me to leave it alone.

Instead, I grabbed the handle and pulled.

Locked.

I looked at the small silver lock mounted beside the drawer.

Then at the tiny key on the ring.

No way.

The key slid in perfectly.

I unlocked the drawer and pulled it open.

My breath caught in my throat.

Cash.

Stacks and stacks of cash.

Packed tight to the top of the drawer.

I grabbed one bundle and thumbed the edge.

Hundreds.

All hundreds.

This was escape money.

Real escape money.

I scrambled around the office looking for a bag but found nothing.

Desperate, I ripped the green Army blanket off the cot and spread it across the floor.

I dumped the drawer into the center.

Bundles of money piled onto the blanket.

I rolled the whole thing tight and tied the ends together.

Time to disappear.

I grabbed the bundle, kicked open the door, and froze.

A motorcycle engine roared around the corner.

Bash.

His Fat Boy rolled into the alley and stopped beside Beyoncé.

"Why are you still here?" he asked.

His eyes dropped to the blanket roll instantly.

Then his hand disappeared under his cut.

Gun.

"I'm leaving," I said quickly. "Like Preacher told me to."

Bash pulled the pistol free.

"I'm gonna find the bitch who put the contract on him," I continued, "and I'm gonna finish the job that he gave me."

It took everything I had just to swing my leg back over the bike.

Pain ripped through my thigh.

I dropped the blanket roll across my lap and thumbed the starter.

Beyoncé roared to life.

For half a second, I thought I might actually get away.

Then Bash fired.

The first bullet slammed into the engine block.

The second ripped through the gas tank.

Two more punched into the motor.

"What the hell?!"

I jumped off the bike as blue smoke poured upward.

Gasoline streamed across the blacktop beneath her.

The engine coughed once.

Twice.

Then seized solid.

Dead.

I stared at the motorcycle in horror.

"You killed Beyoncé."

The words came out broken.

My stomach twisted painfully.

I thought I might actually throw up.

Bash stepped off the Fat Boy slowly.

"That was my brother's bike," he said quietly.

His eyes stayed hard.

"You aren't half the man he was."

He raised the pistol again.

"Now get the fuck out of here."

The barrel pointed straight at my face.

I took several slow steps backward.

Then turned away.

I didn't want him to see my face.

Didn't want him to see what that just did to me.

I shuffled around the corner, clutching the blanket full of cash under my arm.

Every time I heard a motorcycle in the distance, I ducked behind parked cars until it passed.

When I finally reached the motel, Sally's Jeep was still parked outside.

First, I stashed the blanket roll in the back seat.

Then I headed inside.

Sally lay curled beneath the blankets with the sheets pulled up under her chin.

"Honey," I said softly. "Wake up. We've gotta go."

She groaned and stretched.

"Can't we just do coffee and donuts again?" she mumbled sleepily. "I don't wanna go out looking like this."

Then she opened one eye.

Saw me.

And instantly sat upright.

"Oh my God." She scrambled off the bed. "What happened? Did you talk to Preacher? Did he do that to you?"

The questions came fast and panicked.

But even while talking, she was already pulling clothes on.

"Where are we going?"

Her eyes dropped to my leg.

"Oh God..." Her voice cracked. "You're bleeding. Is that a gunshot wound?" She grabbed my arm. "Why aren't you answering me? How much trouble are we in?"

"Bathroom," I said quietly. "I need help cleaning this up."

I led her into the tiny motel bathroom.

Then lowered myself carefully onto the toilet and eased my jeans down over the wound.

"What do you mean, help you clean this?"

"You told me you wanted to be a nurse," I said. "Time to prove it."

I unwrapped the blood-soaked shirt from around my thigh.

Pain exploded through my leg, reminding me it was still attached.

Fresh blood immediately started running down my calf and pooling on the bathroom floor.

"Oh God. Oh God. Oh God," Sally whispered.

But to her credit, she went right to work.

She grabbed a wet washcloth and carefully cleaned the blood away from the wound. Fortunately, it wasn't bleeding as badly as before.

Once she got a better look at it, she swallowed hard.

"Bullet went through," she said quietly. "That's good... I think."

"Yeah," I grunted. "Could've been worse."

Together, we packed the wound with folded washcloths and tied it tight using strips torn from a pillowcase.

After my leg was mostly under control, she cleaned the cut on my arm.

By the end of it, I'd decided I was in piss-poor condition but probably still among the living.

Sally disappeared for a minute and returned with clean clothes.

She helped me dress slowly and carefully.

"All right, that's as good as we're gonna get." I grabbed the edge of the sink and forced myself upright. "Help me to your Jeep. I need you to get me the hell out of town."

Sally grabbed her purse and slipped under my arm to support me.

I pushed open the motel room door, painfully aware that I was completely unarmed.

Fortunately, the parking lot was empty.

No bikes.

No club members.

No trouble.

We made it to the Jeep without anyone spotting us.

"Where are we going?" Sally asked as she dropped the vehicle into drive.

"Nearest city."

"It's only a couple of hours to Flagstaff," she said. "Would that work?"

"Perfect."

She stomped on the gas pedal, spraying gravel behind us as we pulled out of the motel parking lot.

As we drove east out of Kingman, we passed the little red mailbox marking the road to Preacher's trailer.

Or what used to be Preacher's trailer.

I glanced down the dirt road.

No smoke.

No flashing lights.

Nothing.

Like the desert had already swallowed the thing whole.

For the first time in days, I felt the faintest flicker of hope.

Maybe we were actually getting out.

"I'm wiped out," I muttered.

I reclined the passenger seat and closed my eyes.

"Straight to Flagstaff. Wake me if there's a problem."

Chapter 23

IT WAS LATE IN the day when Caroline Mendoza got the call.

She had just returned from another late meeting with Evelyn Carver, the Mayor of Los Angeles. Together, they'd spent the afternoon reviewing "strategies" for redirecting the city's worsening news coverage.

Caroline knew it would never work.

But as long as she played along, the mayor would never suspect her real agenda.

Caroline wanted the mayor's office for herself.

She opened the door to her apartment.

It wasn't as extravagant as the mayor's penthouse, but it had everything she needed.

She hung her jacket beside the door and crossed into the kitchen.

The room was sleek and modern. A massive imported gas stove dominated one wall. The refrigerator was large enough to belong in a restaurant kitchen. But the centerpiece—the thing Caroline truly loved—was the climate-controlled wine cabinet.

One hundred and twenty bottles.

Separate temperature zones.

Custom shelves for chilled crystal glasses.

Today had been a red wine day.

Most days spent with Evelyn turned into red wine days.

Caroline selected a chilled glass and pulled a bottle at random from the cabinet.

She fed the neck into a sleek opener mounted on the counter. Seconds later, the foil had been stripped away and the cork cleanly removed.

She poured half a glass before returning the bottle to an open cooling shelf, only briefly glancing at the label.

Napa Valley.

Cabernet.

Expensive.

She carried the glass to the couch and held it toward the light.

Dark garnet filled the center of the bowl while hints of ruby flickered along the edges.

She brought the wine to her nose.

Blackcurrant.

Blackberry.

Cherry.

A faint trace of vanilla.

Closing her eyes, she took the first sip.

Plum and dark fruit rolled across her tongue.

Smooth.

Balanced.

Perfect.

She swallowed with a satisfied sigh.

With her free hand, she slowly unbuttoned the top of her blouse as the tension of the day finally began to slip away.

Shoes discarded.

Feet up.

Glass in hand.

For a few precious minutes, the city ceased to exist.

She was nearly finished with the glass when the burner phone buzzed.

Caroline stared at it in annoyance.

More than anything, she wanted to ignore it and pour herself another glass.

But she'd been expecting confirmation that the club had arrived in Los Angeles.

By sunrise, her plan was supposed to be in motion.

She dug through her purse and answered the phone.

"You're late," she snapped. "I told you I wanted your people in L.A. first thing in the morning."

"Shut the hell up," the voice answered.

Caroline blinked. "What?"

"You heard me. I'm just giving you this as a courtesy call."

The voice paused.

"It's over."

Her expression hardened.

"We had a deal."

"No," the man replied. "You had a deal with Preacher. He's dead. Your deal ain't worth rat shit."

Caroline sat upright.

"What do you mean he's dead?"

"As in somebody blew up his place with him in it. The rest of us voted and decided you ain't worth the trouble."

A harsh chuckle crackled through the line.

"So, like I said, this is a courtesy call. We ain't coming. And if you're smart, you'll lose this number."

The line went dead.

Silence filled the apartment.

Then Caroline smiled.

A moment later, she laughed.

She raised her wine glass in salute toward the empty room.

"Well fought, Preacher," she murmured. "You were fun while you lasted."

She drained the rest of the wine in a single swallow and slowly spun the empty glass between her fingers.

The wine really was excellent.

She refilled the glass and returned to the couch.

"Now..." she whispered. "Who else can help me implement a hostile takeover of the city?" She took another slow sip. "Or... I could simply eliminate Evelyn."

That thought lingered.

"If I had Evelyn killed, Cross would probably install one of his own people instead." She swirled the wine gently as a smile spread slowly across her face. "But if I break her...then she'll have no choice but to support me."

That idea earned another sip.

She needed the city burning.

Needed panic.

Needed chaos.

Fear changed elections faster than policy ever could.

Her contacts at the docks were an option, though risky. Most of the people on her payroll were locals. If any of them realized who they were actually working for, things could become complicated very quickly.

Then there were the cartels.

Reliable.

Violent.

Efficient.

And always willing to do more for the right price.

Her fingers reached for the wineglass again, only to discover it was already empty.

She considered pouring another.

Decided against it.

Too much indulgence led to mistakes.

And Caroline Mendoza did not believe in mistakes.

That was the difference between her and Evelyn.

Evelyn made mistakes.

Hiring Caroline had been one of them.

The mayor had assumed she was a harmless diversity appointment.

A poor Hispanic woman elevated into city politics because it looked good in photographs.

She'd never bothered looking deeper.

Never realized Caroline was smarter than her.

More ambitious than her.

And infinitely more ruthless.

Caroline picked up the burner phone again and scrolled to another number.

The cartels would do.

She needed results.

And she needed them immediately.

Hell, she thought as the phone began to ring, half their people were probably already inside Los Angeles anyway.

Chapter 24

"HAMMER, WAKE UP. WE'RE in Flagstaff."

Sally's voice sounded far away.

Distant.

Like it was coming through water.

I tried to open my eyes, but they wouldn't cooperate.

Something heavy crushed down on my chest.

It felt like someone parked a truck on top of me.

Every breath came shallow and tight.

My arms and legs felt pinned beneath invisible weight. Numb. Useless.

I tried to say Sally's name.

Nothing came out.

The world tilted sideways.

Spun.

My stomach rolled as darkness crept in around the edges of my vision.

I reached for consciousness and missed.

The last thing I felt was the Jeep swaying beneath me.

Then I was floating.

Weightless.

Falling backward into the dark.

And then there was nothing.

"Mr. Smith, can you hear me?"

I didn't recognize the voice.

The truck was off my chest, and breathing came easier now, but I still couldn't find the strength to open my eyes.

Or answer.

Everything felt heavy.

Distant.

Like I was buried under wet concrete.

I tried once to move my hand.

Nothing happened.

The voice drifted farther away.

Silence settled over me again.

And I slipped back into the dark.

Over time, I realized I was awake.

My whole body ached.

My arms and legs felt heavy.

My eyelids opened.

A hospital room.

Dim.

Quiet.

The only sound was the slow, steady beep of a machine somewhere behind me.

I shifted my arm and found a tube taped beneath a bandage.

Above me hung two IV bags.

One clear.

One red.

Blood.

The hospital meant one thing.

I was alive.

A deep breath confirmed it.

Half a dozen cords disappeared beneath my blanket. I turned my head slowly, tracing them back to the monitor beside the bed.

Green lines crawled across the screen in steady little waves.

One tracked my heartbeat.

The others?

No clue.

Years of watching hospital dramas on television hadn't taught me nearly as much as I thought.

But one thing on the monitor did catch my attention.

FLAGSTAFF MEMORIAL HOSPITAL

The memories came back in a rush.

Preacher.

Bash.

The money.

Sally.

Running.

The desert.

The trailer exploding behind me.

I must've been in worse shape than I realized.

I pulled the blanket aside and checked my leg.

A thick bandage wrapped around my thigh where the bullet had gone through.

Still attached.

Good enough.

The knife wound in my arm came back next.

Another bandage.

More cuts covered with strips of tape and gauze than I remembered earning.

Apparently, I'd lost more blood than I thought.

On the table beside me sat an envelope.

Sealed.

JOHN SMITH was written neatly across the front.

I opened it and pulled out a bright yellow get-well card covered in sunflowers.

Inside was a folded sheet of paper.

The handwriting was precise and careful.

I told the hospital your name was John Smith.

When we got to Flagstaff, I couldn't wake you up, so I brought you here. The seat and floorboard were covered in blood. The nurses kept asking questions, but I'm pretty sure it doesn't matter whether they believed me or not. By law, they had to treat you anyway.

I told them you were my boyfriend, and we got jumped by a gang downtown.

I'm sorry I couldn't stay.

But I know what you did to Preacher, and I know you did it for me.

I'm not a good person, Hammer.

I wish things could've been different.

I wish I'd never gotten involved with the club.

I wish I'd met you somewhere else, at some other time.

I found the money in the back of the Jeep.

I'm sorry, but I need it if I'm going to disappear. If anyone from the MC ever finds me, they'll kill me.

By the time you read this, I'll already be gone.

Don't follow me.

You're dangerous. Maybe for good reasons. Maybe not. I honestly don't know anymore.

But I spent too much of my life letting dangerous men decide things for me.

I'm done with that.

Maybe I'll finally make it to nursing school.

Maybe I'll end up waitressing somewhere in Nevada.

Maybe I'll dye my hair, change my name, and pretend none of this ever happened.

Honestly?

Any of those sounds pretty good right now.

For what it's worth...

Those weeks with you were the happiest I've had in a long time.

Don't die.

— Sally

I stared at the letter for a long time.

Not really reading it anymore.

Just sorting through how I felt.

She was fun.

The first real fun I'd had since my wife died.

But our whole relationship had been built on lies.

She was a prostitute.

I was an assassin.

We managed to care about each other anyway.

She thought I killed Preacher because of what he did to her.

Because of the beatings.

Because of the club.

I suppose that was close enough to the truth.

I reached beneath my pillow and found a plastic gift-shop bag.

Probably where she bought the card.

Inside sat my wallet, my phone, my Zippo, the thumb drive, and two thick rolls of cash.

Ten thousand dollars each.

I started laughing before I could stop myself.

The effort turned into coughing halfway through.

There had been hundreds of those rolls inside Preacher's desk.

Sally took almost all of it.

And still left me twenty grand.

I smiled despite myself.

Then buried another laugh beneath another coughing fit.

Eventually, I stuffed everything back into the bag and listened carefully for sounds in the hallway.

Nothing.

I checked the clock above the door.

2:00 a.m.

Perfect.

I slowly sat upright and waited for the room to stop spinning.

Then I swung my legs over the side of the bed and tested the wounded one.

Tender.

Weak.

But functional.

Good enough.

I started pulling wires loose from my chest and arms.

The heart monitor behind me immediately flattened to a single, angry tone.

"Sorry," I muttered to nobody.

Then I yanked the IV free.

That one hurt.

I clenched my teeth and held pressure against the puncture site for a second before letting it go.

My clothes sat folded on a chair against the wall.

One pant leg had been cut all the way to the thigh, but everything else looked usable.

I dressed slowly, fighting dizziness the whole time.

Then I grabbed the plastic bag and stepped into the hallway.

The fluorescent lights felt blinding after the room's darkness.

The nurses' station sat at one end of the hall.

So I turned the other direction.

Fortunately, I found a stairwell.

This was the second time in recent memory I'd escaped from a hospital.

I had to admit... Night shift made it a lot easier.

The only person I passed was a janitor pushing a floor scrubber while wearing headphones.

I probably could've danced past him naked without getting noticed.

Instead, I quietly slipped down another hallway and followed the EXIT signs toward the front doors.

Outside, the cool night air hit me like medicine.

There was even a taxi number posted beside the entrance.

Like the hospital actually wanted people to escape.

Probably saved on paperwork.

I called for a cab.

Then asked the driver to take me to the airport.

I waited outside the terminal entrance and pulled out my phone.

My hands still shook a little as I typed out the message to Gunny.

'Mission accomplished. Contract completed. Flying out of Flagstaff. I'll see you tomorrow.'

I hit send and slipped the phone back into my pocket.

The airport was nearly empty at two in the morning.

A few exhausted travelers drifted through the terminal like ghosts.

Using my phone, I booked a ticket to Chicago.

There was a layover in Texas, but if everything went smoothly, I'd be back in Illinois by lunchtime.

Back home.

Whatever that meant now.

I limped up to the security counter and handed over my ID and boarding pass.

The man behind the counter glanced down at the bandage wrapped around my leg.

"Dog bite?" he asked.

I looked down at it.

"Snake," I answered. "Caught a rattler out in the desert."

The man clicked his tongue sympathetically.

"You got lucky," he said. "Could've killed you."

I gave a small nod.

"Yeah," I said quietly. "I know and happy that it didn't, but as you can see, I feel like hell."

He handed back my ID and waved me through.

I walked toward the gate without looking back.

- The End –

Get ready for Ben Shepard's next adventure – Deadhand's Vengeance (https://geni.us/BrokenBadge3).

Please leave a review on this book as well as the whole series, because all those stars look great and help others decide if they'll enjoy this book as much as you have. I appreciate the feedback and support. Reviews buoy my spirits and stoke the fires of creativity.

Don't stop now! Keep turning the pages as I talk about this book and the overall project that is Ian Bragg.

Author Notes – Larry Hoy

Written June 7th, 2026

Thank you for making it this far.

This book may be the most personal story I've ever written. Motorcycles have been a part of my life for more than thirty years. I've ridden across states, across borders, and through more adventures than I could ever fit into a single novel. Along the way, I taught both of my daughters to ride and bought them their first motorcycle—a Honda Rebel 250 that, as far as I can tell, is completely indestructible.

As I mentioned in the foreword, a few years ago my family took a motorcycle trip along the full length of Route 66. It was one of those rare adventures that stays with you forever. We learned that cities are often overrated, deserts are magical places, and there is absolutely nothing quite like riding through a monsoon-level storm in the middle of the desert.

My wife and daughters also possess what I call the Snow White Effect—the uncanny ability to attract stray animals wherever they go. This became a genuine challenge when we rode through a ghost town that happened to be overrun with feral donkeys.

For those who have never ridden a motorcycle in the rain, let me offer this observation: if you want to waterboard a biker, just wait for a thunderstorm. They'll do it to themselves.

Over the years I've ridden alongside a variety of motorcycle clubs, from social clubs to outlaw clubs. I've shared drinks and stories with men I was proud to call brothers, and I've spent time inside clubhouses that inspired portions of this novel. I was once a patched member of a club myself, and if you happen to visit my garage, you might even find an old three-piece patch hanging not too far from my motorcycle.

Beyoncé may be fictional, but she was heavily inspired by my own ride. My girl, Erinn, is a green-flamed 2003 Victory Vegas. I'm happy to report that she's still patiently waiting for me to finish writing so we can get back on the road together.

Most importantly, thank you for spending time with Shepard and his world. Writing his story has been an incredible journey, and I'm not finished with him yet.

Be sure to follow Craig and me, because Shepard will return in Deadhand's Vengeance.

In fact, I'm working on it right now.

Until then, keep the shiny side up.

Amazon—https://www.amazon.com/stores/Larry-Hoy/author/B01N8RLV9I

Facebook—https://www.facebook.com/LarryHoyAuthor

My web page—https://larryhoy.net

Author Notes - Craig Martelle

Written May 15th, 2026

I'm glad you're still reading. I hope you loved this book and want more of it. That is what keeps me telling stories. You keep reading. And I'll keep writing.

This story rolls fast and furious! A biker and a gang. All too real, like someone who's been there. Ben Shepard is only just starting, assuming he can get away without getting the snot kicked out of him each time. But we'll see. His luck is still holding out.

Winter is gone here in the sub-arctic. (It's the middle of May.) The last of the snow that had been plowed to the sides of the roads is holding on for a final few days, but it looks like spring is here. Green-up was declared yesterday. That's when all the birch leaves pop out of their buds. It happens within a day or two. The forests go from brown to green, just like that. We have twenty-four hours of daylight at present, so summer comes fast and furious.

We'll be working on the next book in the Ian Bragg Adventure Series while I'm working on the next medical thriller in the Surgeon's Series (look for ***Medical Thrillers*** by Craig Martelle and James Toouli).

That's it for now. Thanks for reading along. Best wishes for a great summer. I'll be here and fighting off mosquitoes who act like they own the place and every warm-blooded creature is a buffet.

If you liked this story, you might like some of my other books. You can join my mailing list by dropping by my website, or if you have any comments, shoot me a note at craig@craigmartelle.com. I am always happy to hear from people who've read my work. I try to answer every email I receive.

If you liked the story, please write a short review for me on Amazon. I greatly appreciate any kind words; even one or two sentences go a long way. The number of reviews an eBook receives greatly improves how well it does on Amazon.

Amazon— https://www.amazon.com/author/craigmartelle
Facebook— https://www.facebook.com/authorcraigmartelle
BookBub— https://www.bookbub.com/authors/craig-martelle
My web page— https://craigmartelle.com

Thank you for joining me on this incredible journey.

Other Series by Craig Martelle

#—available in audio, too

(#) (co-written with Michael Anderle)—a post-apocalyptic paranormal adventure

Gateway to the Universe (#) (co-written with Justin Sloan & Michael Anderle)—this book transitions the characters from the Terry Henry Walton Chronicles to the Bad Company

The Bad Company (#) (co-written with Michael Anderle)—a military science fiction space opera

Judge, Jury, & Executioner (#)—a space opera adventure legal thriller

Shadow Vanguard—a Tom Dublin space adventure series

Superdreadnought (#)—an AI military space opera

Metal Legion (#)—a military space opera

The Free Trader (#)—a young adult science fiction action-adventure

Cygnus Space Opera (#)—a young adult space opera (set in the Free Trader universe)

Darklanding (#) (co-written with Scott Moon)—a space Western

Mystically Engineered (co-written with Valerie Emerson)—mystics, dragons, & spaceships

Metamorphosis Alpha—stories from the world's first science fiction RPG

The Expanding Universe—science fiction anthologies

Zenophobia (#) (co-written with Brad Torgersen)—a space archaeological adventure

Battleship Leviathan (#)- a military sci-fi spectacle published by Aethon Books

Glory (co-written with Ira Heinichen)—hard-hitting military sci-fi

Black Heart of the Dragon God (co-written with Jean Rabe)—a sword & sorcery novel

Starship Lost – a hard-science, military sci-fi epic published by Aethon Books

Veracity of Failure – a hard-science technothriller, the race to Mars

I, Soldier (#)– military sci-fi

End Times Alaska (#)—a post-apocalyptic survivalist adventure published by Permuted Press

Nightwalker (a Frank Roderus series)—A post-apocalyptic Western adventure

End Days (#) (co-written with E.E. Isherwood)—a post-apocalyptic adventure

Successful Indie Author (#)—a nonfiction series to help self-published authors

Monster Case Files (co-written with Kathryn Hearst)—A Warner twins mystery adventure

Rick Banik (#)—Spy & terrorism action-adventure

Ian Bragg Action Adventure Series (#)—a hitman with a conscience

Broken Badge (an Ian Bragg Adventure Series, (co-written with Larry Hoy) —Memphis cop turned assassin

Published exclusively by Craig Martelle, Inc

The Gygax Odyssey – Luke Gygax and J. Clifton Slater – son of the legendary co-creator of Dungeons & Dragons™ retells the stories his father used to tell about the origin of the Gygax family

A Couples Travels—a nonfiction travel series

Love-Haight Case Files by Jean Rabe & Donald J. Bingle—the dead/undead have rights, too, a supernatural legal thriller

Mischief Maker by Bruce Nesmith—the creator of Elder Scrolls V: Skyrim brings you Loki in the modern day, staying true to Norse mythology (not a superhero version)

For a complete list of Craig's books, stop by his website—

Made in the USA
Coppell, TX
21 June 2026

82805497R00174